WORTH THE SEEING THROUGH

LISA M. OWENS

Dreamspinner Press

Published by
Dreamspinner Press
5032 Capital Circle SW
Suite 2, PMB# 279
Tallahassee, FL 32305-7886
USA
http://www.dreamspinnerpress.com/

Worth the Seeing Through
© 2014 Lisa M. Owens.

Cover Art
© 2014 Brooke Albrecht.
http://brookealbrechtstudio.blogspot.com
Cover content is for illustrative purposes only
and any person depicted on the cover is a model.

ISBN: 978-1-62798-881-0
Digital ISBN: 978-1-62798-882-7

Printed in the United States of America
First Edition
May 2014

Acknowledgments

THANKS FIRST of all, to the wonderful, adventurous readers who took a chance on a new author with *Worth the Coming Home*—you are my greatest encouragement. Extra thanks from the bottom of my heart to those who took time to leave reviews and ratings. I have learned so much from you.

Thank you again and again and again to the team that supports me: my husband, who does pretty much everything and anything so I can write; Eva, the greatest writing partner in the world; my beta readers Margo, Pam, Colleen, Mary Ann, and Marsha; and my chief encouragers, Connie and my Aunt Boots.

Also to Romance Writers of America for all it has done to champion the genre and protect writers, and to the officers and members of Rainbow Romance Writers, the LGBT chapter of RWA, for the hard work they have done to publicize LGBT romance. I am so very proud to be a member of both groups.

To Elizabeth North and the great and gracious team at Dreamspinner Press—endless gratitude to each of you for your marvelous help and continuing confidence in me. I am so grateful to be in your very capable hands.

And thanks so very much to the incomparable Joey W. Hill, who introduced me to Marcus and Thomas in *Rough Canvas*, showing me a whole new world of romance, and then suggested ever so gently when I was laid off that this might be what I needed to start writing my own stories. She was right, and I am forever grateful.

ONE

MY THIRD night patrolling downtown Bozeman on my own didn't start out as anything special.

I'd been on the job for nearly two months already, but I'd spent most of that time partnered with Nate Hamilton, a seven-year veteran of the police department. Not much had happened crimewise tonight. Well, nothing actually, when compared to a typical Friday night with the LAPD. But it sure was colder—about ten degrees above freezing in late April.

I was starving. I radioed Hamilton to tell him I was taking a quick break. But before heading for a fast-food place, I drove by the Gustavsson Gallery one more time. The building stood across the street from the hardware store, tucked into a block that included a pizza place, a yarn shop, a women's clothing store, and a fishing outfitter.

Like a lot of properties on this part of Main Street, the building was old, redbrick, and two stories high. The first-floor gallery space was clearly visible through two big bay windows and the glass entry door between them. Guy Gustavsson had taken full advantage of the glass too, displaying a combination of large freestanding metal sculptures and striking watercolor paintings in the windows. The second floor, I knew, was the multiroom apartment where the artist lived. I held out hope that I'd see the inside of it, especially the bedroom, one day.

I'd been watching the place off and on since my first day in town, and I'd caught a glimpse or two of Guy. Each time, he'd been laughing with someone. Make that giggling. Flirty, happy-go-lucky Guy was a giggler. He was also as good-looking as I remembered from that wild week in Los Angeles eight months before.

The gallery should have been dark at this hour. It had been the past seven Fridays. But tonight, at past ten thirty, the lights still blazed bright, though I saw no one inside and the Closed sign was out. I guessed Guy was working in a back office, or he'd forgotten to turn the lights off in his rush to get somewhere. Not a single light glowed upstairs. I made a mental note to check the place again when I got back from my fast-food run.

I swung through the drive-through, got a cheeseburger and a bottle of water, and parked on the street to eat. My mind wandered once more to the first time I met Guy.

CHARLES FORNEY, my sometime boyfriend, had nagged me for a week to go with him to the opening of a new art exhibit by some guy from Montana. I wanted to stay home with a good book, but he bothered me enough that I caved. Charles collected art and lots of other things, including me for a while. But we had an open relationship. He insisted on it.

Charles loved the gaggle of wine-guzzling wannabes—wanna be sophisticated, wanna be noticed, wanna be yours—who showed up at these second- and third-string art openings to impress each other. He enjoyed spotting his wannabe friends across the gallery of the moment, then watching them fly to his money and his side to demand he share his thoughts on the artist's efforts. A well-off investment banker, Charles moonlighted as a critic for one of the free weekly art-zines that littered the LA streets. When I was talked into attending these overwrought affairs, I spent a half hour looking at the art and the rest of the night wishing I'd stayed home.

That night was the same—right up until I saw the artist, Guy Gustavsson, an Asian with a Norwegian name. I heard his giggle first. When I saw him, I wanted to bend him over one of his erotic canvases and fuck him until he couldn't giggle anymore. He stood with his own gaggle of admirers under a ceiling spotlight that made his sandy-bronze skin glow like an angel's and his straight black hair, with purple highlights, glitter like he'd streaked diamonds through it. He was short, about five seven, but he had a hard, sculpted, man's body, and I wanted to bite, suck, lick, kiss, and nuzzle every inch of it. Then I wanted to ask him how he'd come by the misleading last name. Adoption was my guess.

Weaving my way through the room and groups of people, I studied each of his paintings. They were Western scenes—landscapes and depictions of ranch work and life—with a few giving prominence to shirtless cowboys dripping with seductive undertones. Three featured one lean, blond cowboy in particular. All were watercolors in a style that brought to mind Andrew Wyeth's Helga pictures but also used a technique that left something like little water droplets on the paper. It made the works appear lush and sensual and made you hungry for them—in the way the water they shower on grocery produce makes you suddenly desire parsley, peppers, and zucchini.

I wanted to get close enough to listen as folks talked to him, but stay removed too. A plant or a pillar would have been the perfect blind, but the room lacked both. I tried to stay inconspicuous and listen to one person after another say the obvious bit about him not looking like a Gustavsson. To his credit, he never rolled his eyes. I knew because I watched them.

I also knew the instant he noticed me. His eyes widened. And didn't that make my dick hard. But he continued to let me lurk until he was momentarily alone.

"So, do you like any of them?" he asked in a pleasing, musical voice. "I noticed that you've studied each one."

He'd been watching me? "I like *Cowboy and Cat* best, I think."

"Why?"

"The alliteration of the title, for starters."

He giggled at that, an encouragement for me to go on.

"I'm not an art person, so you know. I studied psychology and literature in college."

"I love Jane Austen."

"Very romantic." I nodded. "I read more Hemingway, I'm afraid."

"Ah, dark, manly men." He drew out the penultimate word so long that his tongue took up something approximating permanent residence near his lips—and didn't that turn me on. The thought of leaving, for my own good, occurred to me. But I forgot it when he spoke again.

"Plenty of artistic style in those books too, I think." He was mimicking me. Or mocking me. Glancing at his twinkling eyes, I suspected the latter. "So why do you like *Cowboy and Cat?*"

The painting was of the blond, from behind, his handsome face caught in profile. He wore tight jeans that hugged his ass, but no shirt, and a Stetson rode herd on his curls. Thick dark lines defined his work-sculpted muscles. The water droplet technique suggested dampness and sex, making him look sensual as hell. He'd perched one arm on a tall chest of drawers to look at a cat that sat atop it. The cat's orange-and-white tones echoed the color wash of the drawers' wood graining and the cowboy's tanned skin. For me, the whole thing was a cowboy-sized hard-on.

"The eyes." I looked deep into Guy's chocolate-brown ones as I answered. "The cat's are almond-shaped, like yours, and it looks like it would tell the man the meaning of life, if he would listen."

"Exactly right." Guy smiled broadly, revealing two deep dimples. He studied me for a moment before he continued, absolutely serious now. "Your eyes and face, on the other hand, suggest that you already know all about life, and it's difficult, and you can handle it."

I drew back. He couldn't be reading me that well. "What do you mean?"

He cocked his head, and his long bangs fell in his eyes. He blew them away with his next breath. "Your eyes are deep and blue as an ocean, and way too serious," he said. "And with that straight black hair—it's too short, by the way—you look…."

"Black Irish," I supplied. "The name's Connor. Maclean." I held out my hand.

"Exactly." He snapped his fingers and shook my hand. "Of course you are. That's what I was going to say." He held on to my hand a minute too long, grinned, and brushed his fingers across my palm as he pulled away.

All of my blood dropped south of my belt. I had to think hard to come up with another comment to keep the conversation going. "How did you make those water droplets on the paper? I haven't seen that before."

"That's top secret." He winked at me, and I swallowed a groan. Everything about him was a turn-on, and he knew it.

"Actually, it's called spattering." After a long, charged pause, he added, "You are an art person, I think."

"Absolutely not. Because my next question is, are the cats gay too?"

His eyes rounded and his lips crooked up until he exploded into a great giggle that drew looks from every corner of the room. Charles and five wannabes headed our way.

"My goodness, Connor," Charles said too loudly as he neared us, "what could you have managed to say to amuse our artist?"

"Not much." I took a step back and swallowed a gulp from my bottle of fancy water.

"I hope Connor wasn't too offensive," Charles said to Guy. "He's a Neanderthal cop, not an art patron."

"But I consider the Lascaux Cave paintings one of my prime inspirations," Guy replied. He batted his eyes—for my benefit—before adding, "Haven't you seen my website?"

Charles coughed and took a sip of his wine. "I'm afraid not. Sorry, no." He glared at me, nodded to Guy, and walked away. His sycophants frowned and followed.

Guy stifled his next giggle with a hand pressed firmly to his lips. I imagined kissing them hard enough to make his eyes pop. I had to blink to erase the picture. When it disappeared, I wanted it back.

"Sorry, I think his rudeness is my fault. We're together."

Guy tipped his head sideways and stared at me. "Why?"

"I'm wondering that myself."

"I'm going to Cuba when this is over," he said, naming a popular gay club. "Will I see you there?"

Charles's glare had already telegraphed that he'd be going home tonight with a wannabe or two, not me. "Quite possibly."

"I'd like that," Guy answered. "But I have to run now. The gallery owner is waving at me." He smiled and walked away, throwing an occasional broad hip swing in his step—I hoped for my benefit.

I looked for a place to put my bottle and left.

I couldn't arrive at Cuba too early, so I drove around, debating the whole time whether to go there at all.

Charles and I weren't a couple. We went out sometimes, and we had sex. The sex mattered most to him. I enjoyed our getaways. Looking back, I think I was making up for fun I didn't have as a teenager because my widowed mom couldn't afford much. I imagined repeating many of our trips with my own teenagers one day, but not with Charles. He didn't want a family.

Did Guy? I wondered.

Against my better judgment, I went to Cuba. He wasn't there yet, so I took a seat at the bar and ordered a Negra Modelo. The club was one of the more popular watering holes in a predominantly gay business district that was part of my beat. When I'd gotten the assignment, I was paranoid someone knew about me. Once I realized that wasn't true, I relaxed into the job. I brought more understanding to it, but I was vigilant not to out myself.

Cuba was upscale, with a clientele predominantly thirty and over. We didn't get calls to come here. The lovers' quarrels, fights, drug busts, and rapes were three blocks over, where the guys were younger, poorer, and lonelier.

I'd ordered my second beer when I spotted Guy in the middle of a crowd coming in the door. Disappointment flared, but I wiped it off my face. Of course he'd come with a crowd. I should have expected that.

As I continued to watch, though, people peeled off left and right until he was alone. When he spotted me, his dimples popped out. That's what I wanted to see.

I stood up and gave him my stool. He ordered a Grey Goose martini, very dry, with two olives, up.

"How did the opening go?"

"The gallery owner was thrilled with the crowd. Sold four paintings tonight, but not *Cowboy and Cat.* I think it's waiting for you." His giggle was mischievous. "And someone said there were two reviewers there, including one from *The Los Angeles Times*. I'll believe that when I see the review."

I didn't tell him one of them might have been Charles. "Are you hungry?"

"What did you have in mind?"

Suddenly, my pants were tight. Thank God I was still mainly turned toward the bar. I didn't want to let on yet the effect he had on me. I hadn't experienced such an instant attraction since high school, when I'd fallen for the football captain. A gigantic unrequited, that one.

I took a swallow from my bottle and noticed his eyes following my throat. That was not going to help me calm down. "I meant food. They're supposed to have good tapas here."

"Supposed to? You haven't been here before?"

"I've been in the neighborhood to make arrests."

"That's right. Thanks for reminding me not to give you any grounds to arrest me on lewd and lascivious." He giggled again, but he sounded nervous now.

"Relax. No arrests tonight. I'm just entertaining a new acquaintance from out of town. This is also supposed to be a good place for that."

"It's a good place for lots of things. My guidebook said to be sure to check out the men's room."

"Guidebook?"

"Being from Montana, I had to look up a few things before I came to LA."

"I thought everybody in Montana was into cowboy hats and spurs." Guy was wearing shiny loafers, tight black jeans, and a tighter white shirt that showed off his finely muscled back and chest. No hat.

He took a sip of his martini and licked his lips dramatically. "Don't knock what you haven't tried."

I nearly choked on my spit. He giggled long enough that I was able to recover, but my reply was lame. "If you want to try the men's room, you'll have to do it by yourself."

"Not-quite-out officer, is it? I'll just toast you instead of running my hands down your chest." He batted his eyelashes and raised his martini glass.

I clinked it with my bottle. "You are a bad boy."

"Guilty, Officer. Wanna cuff me?"

"Be happy to. But not here."

"My hotel is just a couple of miles away."

I waited for a giggle, but it didn't come. "Well, Giggles, drink up, and we'll go. I'll check out the door locks for you. Wouldn't want you to run afoul of any of the city's criminal element."

He arched an eyebrow. "Are you offering the opportunity to get to know you deeper?"

Even after I swallowed hard, I needed a moment before answering, "Definitely deeper."

He smiled and began to play with the spear that held his two olives, popping them in and out of rounded lips. I groaned. He giggled. I slapped three tens on the bar and turned toward the door. He was right behind me.

We had sex five times—imaginative and exhausting, simple and sweet—before I slipped out of his room thirty hours later, just in time for work. We saw each other every day for the next five, until he flew back to Montana. I never saw Charles again, but Guy and I texted and phoned each other twenty times a day for a month, with plenty of Skype sex besides. I began to believe he might be the one. I promised to visit Bozeman. I said I'd move there. He quit answering.

I moved anyway. I texted him when I did. He didn't reply. After that, I couldn't work up the nerve to do anything more than drive by his place. I didn't want to hear that he'd lost interest or, worse, found someone new. I probably shouldn't have come.

The crackle of the radio interrupted my thoughts. A robbery, two victims, one dead, one injured, suspect gone. At the Gustavsson Gallery.

"Nooooo!" My fingers shaking, I hit the lights and siren.

TWO

I ARRIVED before Hamilton and the EMTs. The gallery still glowed bright like every light was on, but I saw no one inside as I sprinted to the door. Guy could not be dead. He couldn't.

The front door opened when I turned the knob. Across the room, another door was ajar.

"Police! Anyone here?"

"Back here. God, hurry! I think he's dead," a weak voice called from the back room. It sounded like a kid's—definitely not Guy's. My heart sank.

I ran for the back and banged hard into the partly opened door when it didn't move.

"Back up!" I yelled at the person on the other side as I took a step back, then shoved hard. The door gave a bit, a terrible screeching and scraping from the other side indicating I was moving something heavy as I pushed.

When the opening was big enough, I squeezed inside the combination office and storage area and stepped around the upended desk. Papers, a couple of desk drawers, a smashed laptop, and several mangled canvasses littered the floor. In the middle of the mess, a skinny red-haired teenager with a bloody gash across his right temple squatted next to a man lying facedown and still. I could see blond streaks and blood in the shoulder-length, straight black hair that obscured his face. My stomach flipped.

"Guy?" I yelled. He didn't respond. I was already feeling for a pulse as my knees hit the floor.

"He's not dead, is he?" the kid asked, his voice jumping an octave midsentence. "He was already on the floor when I came in. This other guy was whaling away at him with that—" He pointed toward a brass obelisk-like thing lying near the exterior door.

"Shhh. I gotta concentrate on him for a minute."

The kid gulped back the rest of his words. My blood banged in my ears as I felt a weak, erratic pulse in Guy's neck. "Thank you," I whispered. I grabbed my shoulder mike and told the dispatcher we had two living and to steer the EMTs to the alley.

I brushed Guy's hair aside and groaned at what I saw. His face was bruised and cut. Blood ran down his forehead from his scalp. More of it pooled under his smashed nose. Near his right shoulder, his blue shirt was blood-soaked and torn, and sharp edges of bone stuck through the ripped material.

I bent over his face, trying to hear or feel his breath. The coppery smell of his blood clogged my nostrils. Bile rose in my throat. God, I had to keep it together. A puff of air tickled my ear. I froze and waited. It came again. Guy's breath—barely. The sound of sirens loud and close filled the air.

"Hang on, Guy. Hang on."

"He's alive?" the kid whispered.

"Yes." I sat back on my heels and looked at my other victim. His temple was bloody. I pulled a handkerchief out of my pants pocket and pressed it to the right side of his face. He winced.

"This guy hit you too?" I asked.

"Huh?" He took the cloth out of my hand, pressed it to his temple, then held it in front of his eyes and gagged like he might throw up.

"Hey." I grabbed his shoulder. "Look at me. Look at me." His blue eyes were clear and responsive as he focused on my face. Good, no concussion. Maybe he could tell me something. "You hurt anywhere else?"

"I don't think so." He looked at Guy again.

"No. You look at me," I said sharply. "What's your name?"

"Alex." He dragged his eyes back to my face. "Alex Whittaker."

"Are you hurt anywhere else, Alex?"

"No," he said slowly, like his mind was checking body parts.

"Tell me what happened."

He took a deep breath and started talking a mile a minute. "I just got off work—at Marconi's Pizza, I work at Marconi's—and I glanced this way 'cause the door was open and the lights were on and that wasn't usual. And I saw a guy in a leather jacket hitting him." He waved the handkerchief toward Guy, and his eyes followed his shaking hand. "Oh God." He saw his own blood again on the cloth and rocked back hard on his heels. I grabbed his shoulder to steady him.

"You're going to be okay."

"Me?" he shrieked. "What about him?" He waved both arms frantically. This time, despite the hold I had on him, his butt hit the floor. His feet flew up, and his left heel bumped into Guy, pushing him. Guy made no response.

"Oh God, Mister, I'm sorry," he wailed. "I'm so sorry. Oh God. Mom. I gotta call my mom—"

"Alex, take a few deep breaths now. We'll take care of that for you."

The squad pulled up, brakes screeching, followed by more flashing lights that had to be another patrol car. Hamilton, I hoped.

I rocked back on my heels and stood, lifting Alex with me. "Why don't you and I move over by the desk, so the EMTs can get to Mr. Gustavsson? Can you do that?"

"Yeah, okay."

I picked up and righted the desk chair and sat Alex in it as the first EMT came through the door. I recognized him—a guy named Wisniewski, who knew his stuff. He went right for Guy, while the second one, a woman, came toward Alex. Right behind them came Hamilton. He took in the scene, then waved me toward the gallery.

Wisniewski was already calling Guy's vitals in to the emergency room. They were bad, but I'd heard worse on victims who lived. I exhaled a breath I hadn't realized I'd been holding and followed Hamilton toward the gallery.

He stopped in the doorway, where we could watch the EMTs at work. "What you got?"

"The unconscious vic is the gallery owner, Guy Gustavsson. The teenager is Alex Whittaker. His only injury seems to be the cut to his temple. No concussion as far as I can tell. Whittaker says he was walking through the alley when he saw a man in a leather jacket hitting Gustavsson—likely with the metal sculpture near the door you came through. The kid came in to try to stop it. The robber hit him too, and fled into the alley. That's about it right now. The kid was starting to freak out."

Hamilton glanced back into the office, watching for a moment. The female EMT was cleaning Whittaker's wound, telling him he was going to be fine. He wouldn't even need stitches. Another EMT had come in, and he and Wisniewski were about to lift Guy to a gurney.

"Can't say I blame the kid for getting upset. It's pretty ugly in there." He sighed. "Damn. Gustavsson is a good guy. Always donating his time and art to kids' causes. I've worked a couple fundraisers with him." He shook his head. "Look around the gallery and see if you can find anything that might tell us what happened. I'll touch base with the EMTs and see about contacting the kid's parents."

I scrubbed my face with my hands. "I noticed all the lights on here as I headed for food. Damn, Nate, I should have stopped to check it out."

He shook his head. "Don't go there. Let's get some facts first." He moved into the office.

I started a slow circle around the gallery, looking for anything. The large room held a wide assortment of paintings and sculptures in multiple media, all carefully placed and arranged. Several of the paintings were Guy's. I recognized his style. In two of them, I also recognized a familiar blond cowboy.

A wooden bar-like structure took up lots of space along the gallery's west wall. Behind it, I found another desk. Unlike the one in the office, this one was still neat and orderly. Atop it lay a day planner open to today's date. In the nine o'clock time slot, in dark ink, were four words—*Jones. Cowboy and Cat*—and a Montana phone number.

Hamilton came back into the gallery. "Gustavsson is headed for the ER. He's touch and go right now."

I looked away, hoping to get my fear under control.

He noticed. "You okay?"

"Yeah." I clenched my fists and straightened my spine. I couldn't let him know how well I knew Guy.

"We should be able to talk to the kid in a few minutes," he continued. "They're almost done with him. His mom's on her way."

I nodded and pointed at the datebook. "It looks like whoever attacked the two of them had an appointment."

He came up behind me to read the notation. "I'm guessing Jones wasn't his real name."

"Probably not."

"It does suggest a perfectly normal reason for the lights to be on when you went by before, and no reason for you to stop. What's *Cowboy and Cat*, do you suppose?"

"The name of one of Gustavsson's paintings."

"And you know this…?"

I waved at the wall where two other cowboy paintings hung, each with a small white nameplate next to it. "One of those is called *Cowboy at Morning Light*." I hadn't read the nameplates, but I was pretty sure one said something close to that. I'd seen the painting on Guy's website plenty of times.

Nate nodded. "So Gustavsson was going to show a painting called *Cowboy and Cat*?"

"Something like that." I knew he couldn't possibly show it, but I couldn't reveal that yet either.

"I'm going to go sit with Whittaker. You wait here until his mom arrives. Then we can talk to him."

Five minutes later, a thin woman knocked at the gallery door. Like the kid, she had freckles and red hair. Hers was pulled back in a ponytail. Honestly, she didn't look much older than him. She frantically glanced around as I let her in. She wasn't going to be calm until she saw him.

"I'm Kellie Whittaker. My son—"

"Is going to be fine, Ms. Whittaker. This way." I led her into the office.

"Mom, I'm so sorry," the kid began.

Before he could finish, she was at his side hugging and shushing him. She pulled back to eye the bandage covering his temple. "You're okay?" She brushed it lightly with her fingers as he nodded.

"The EMT said he's going to be fine, Ms. Whittaker," Nate assured her. He flashed one of his trademark smiles, showing lots of perfect teeth and looking as trustworthy as the boy next door. "There was a lot of blood, but Alex didn't need stitches, and he doesn't have a concussion. Here." He handed her a folded piece of paper. "The EMT left instructions for you, advice on cleaning the wound, that kind of thing. They had another call."

He cleared his throat, giving her a minute to comprehend all that. "I'm Officer Hamilton, and that's Officer Maclean. We'd like to ask your son a few questions. Right now, he's our only witness to a pretty brutal robbery."

But she wasn't paying attention. She'd spotted the blood on the floor where Guy had lain. She paled considerably as she began to put together what her son had been through.

"Let's all move into the gallery, shall we?" Nate suggested.

We headed for the desk, which had two chairs by it, and Nate motioned the Whittakers into them. Once they were seated, he leaned against the desk so he didn't tower over them. I moved to flank the kid's chair but kept my distance. We didn't want to frighten them.

"So, Alex, Officer Maclean said he found you and Mr. Gustavsson in the office."

The kid turned wide blue eyes on me. "You're not in any trouble," I said quickly, reassuring him. "You're a victim too. We want to know what you saw. It may be a while before Mr. Gustavsson can tell us anything."

"Why don't you start by telling us why you were in the alley?" Nate asked.

Alex's mother looked Nate up and down, then me, assessing our intentions. She nodded to her son, giving him permission to talk, I guess.

"I'd finished work," he began.

"At Marconi's," she added.

With occasional prodding from Nate, the kid described how he noticed two men struggling, heard the robber yell something about money—"Give me the money. You promised me nine thousand dollars for the painting!"—while continuing to beat Guy with the sculpture. Guy fell to the floor as Alex entered the office, and the robber hit him too, and ran out the door. The kid provided a detailed description of the suspect. A cop couldn't have done a better job. I wrote it all down.

"This is great, Alex. How is it you're so thorough in your description?"

He looked at me like I'd asked the dumbest question in the world. "I'm an artist. I notice things."

At that, Hamilton grinned broadly. He snapped on a pair of protective gloves and began searching the desk drawers, taking care not to mess up any fingerprint evidence. "Do you think you could draw us a picture of the man?" Before he finished speaking, he'd pulled a pad of paper out of one of the drawers and given Alex a pencil from his pocket.

"No problem." The kid pulled his chair up to the desk, took the pencil and paper, and went to work. He soon crumpled up and tossed the first sheet he drew on, then the second, and I began to worry. But on the third, he hit a groove. He kept sketching and shading his drawing until, twenty minutes later, he put the pencil down and pointed a finger at the portrait. "That's him. That's him exactly."

Detailed as a photograph, the drawing showed a hefty white man, likely in his thirties, with high cheekbones, wide-set eyes, a crooked nose, and combed-back, wavy hair.

"Like I said, he was about five inches shorter than you"—Alex pointed at me—"with blue eyes and brown hair."

"So he was six feet tall?"

He nodded.

Nate pulled out his phone, snapped a picture of the drawing, and began pushing buttons to text it to the dispatcher.

"This is great work," Nate said. "This guy is distinctive looking. If he's still in town, we'll find him." He handed me the drawing. "Get this to the station and start writing up your report. I'll finish up here."

"Is my son going to be safe with this man loose?" Kellie Whittaker asked.

"Absolutely, ma'am," Nate said as I headed for the door. "But we'll have an officer follow you home and stay outside your house for a while, too, so you don't worry any."

By the time I headed home the next morning, we knew the phone number was a dead end, and we hadn't found "Mr. Jones." Doctors had removed Guy's spleen, eased pressure on his brain, and repaired his smashed right shoulder. He also had stitches across his face. He likely wouldn't wake up today. Maybe not for another day or more. Maybe not ever.

THREE

MY FIRST-FLOOR apartment was a furnished two-bedroom setup with one bathroom, a hall closet, and a living room/eating area with a galley kitchen. Beyond the door was a hallway that served three more apartments identical to mine and led to a security door and tiny entry lobby. At the other end of the hall, another exit opened on a stairway to four more apartments and another exterior door.

The place had three redeeming features: a large front window that, if I stood on my toes and craned my neck, included the barest glimpse of the distant Gallatin Mountains; a big-screen TV in the living room; and a painting in the bedroom. The painting was *Cowboy and Cat*, the most expensive thing I owned after a rusting Jeep Cherokee and my custom mountain bike.

Everything else in the apartment from the furniture to the carpet, floors, blinds, walls, kitchen appliances, tub, and john was beige.

I locked my gun in the gun safe in the entertainment center, changed into sweats, and flopped on the bed to stare at the painting. To buy it, I'd used all of the money my mom left me when she died. I paid cash and didn't give the gallery owner my name. Nobody knew I owned it.

So what kind of meeting had Guy had about it last night? Was he trying to get it back? Who knew he wanted it? And how did they know?

I jumped off the bed and made for my laptop, set up on my tiny dining table. I typed in Guy's name and *Cowboy and Cat*.

The first listing was from Guy's website. I clicked on the link and landed on a big picture of the painting on the front page of the site. Underneath it, in large type, a couple of sentences explained that Guy wanted it back. How long had that been up there? I'd never seen it. But I'd quit checking his site when I moved to Bozeman.

The second listing was a small story from *The Los Angeles Times,* dated in February—right after I moved—detailing how artist Guy Gustavsson, a rising star on the Western art scene, was trying to find the painting, which sold at the very end of the LA gallery show, that earned glowing reviews on both coasts and started his career on its sharp upward trajectory. A month later, a version of the story was in a national art magazine and a couple of East Coast art publications. Three weeks after that, *People Magazine* had a short write-up complete with a vague quote from Guy about how a major change in life circumstances had given the painting deep sentimental value, and he'd pay significantly more than the sale price to get it back.

Guess I should have been reading gossip magazines. Guy was actually looking for me. But what were the changed circumstances? Had the cowboy been one of his lovers and now he was dead? Had that been why Guy hadn't called me back? Had I left a promising career with LAPD to try to win back a man in mourning? Was the painting about to suck me into a crime investigation, not to mention out me, before I cleared probation?

My life could not be turning to crap again this fast. I'd already had my fair share of bad times, enough to protect me for another decade at least. But life was never fair. I knew that better than most, and after last night, I felt like I was on the fast track for a repeat visit to hell. The only thing worse than Guy being involved with someone else, or mourning someone else, would be losing him before I had a chance at… anything.

I called in what I'd discovered to the day sergeant, to share with the detectives continuing the investigation. Once he hung up, I stared at my phone. If Mom were still alive, she'd be sitting at her kitchen table, drinking her coffee and working her crossword puzzle. If she were still alive, she'd know what to say to calm me down.

I imagined the start of the call. We'd had pretty much the same beginning four or five times a week right up until she died of cancer five years ago. First, she'd ask how my shift went. She'd asked my dad that same question until the night he never came home again. He died in the line of duty, saving six kids on a school bus from a psycho kidnapper. She was terrified when I followed him into the department, but she supported me like she'd supported him. Even though her fear for him drove her to drink. She'd sobered up when I was eighteen, three years after he died.

After I told her I was fine, she'd ask what was wrong. She'd have heard something in my voice. I'd say what I always did before I answered—that if I could do that intuition thing like she did, I'd be chief of detectives already. She'd laugh and say, "You're going to get there. Take your time and enjoy where you are right now." She'd ask me again what was wrong.

I'd tell her about Guy and how scared I was that he might not make it. She'd wait a half minute and say the words I needed to hear: "Don't be playing what-ifs and if-onlys on yourself, baby. Promise me you won't. You think positive thoughts about Guy's recovery, and you wait and pray. It's the hardest part, I know. But anything else is wasted effort that drives you crazy. Let it go—"

"And let God. I know, Mom." She was an AA alum. I was so proud of her. God knew I wanted the chance to tell her that one more time. He knew I needed to hear her say those words one more time too. But she couldn't, so I imagined her saying them, and then I said them twice. It didn't feel the same.

WHEN I got to work that night, Guy's condition hadn't changed, and they still had no clue when he'd wake up. But we had a name and a rap sheet to go with Alex Whittaker's drawing: Jimmy Mitchell, thirty-two, a local who was jailed on burglary charges as a juvie, got out, and never went back in. Unfortunately, he hadn't been scared straight. He was the prime suspect in a series of thefts and burglaries involving lower-end luxury items, but there'd never been enough evidence to convict. He said there never would be—he wasn't going back to prison. He had an area address, but he wasn't there. He'd dropped out of sight.

My shift, 8:00 p.m. to 6:00 a.m., was routine. I asked about Guy's condition before I headed home. No change.

"Hey, Connor, wait up." Nate Hamilton headed across the parking lot. He was grinning, like always. "You want to go out for breakfast?"

"Sure."

"Let me call Jenna, and I'll meet you at the Leaf and Bean in about ten minutes."

He was nice to reach out to me. We'd talked a lot since I'd arrived, of course, since he trained me. But we'd also talked basic personal stuff. He was thirty-three, like me, married, and originally from Wisconsin. He liked patrolling, was senior guy on our shift, and didn't aspire to anything else. He was due to become a dad any day.

I moved my Jeep from the station to a parking lot on Mendenhall and walked the few blocks to the coffee shop, going out of my way so I didn't walk past Guy's gallery. Inside, the eatery was long and narrow, with a pair of high tables in the front window and a counter and stools along the east wall. The service area was opposite them, and beyond it the room opened up to include more tables, some easy chairs, and a couch. Watercolors of mountain scenes, birds, and animals, including one painting of a cougar and another of a pair of mountain goats, covered the brown brick walls. Bozeman was full of mini art exhibitions like that. After putting in an order for a breakfast sandwich, I took my plain black coffee to a table in the back. Nate came in right after I sat down.

"Thanks for coming here. I know it's out of your way, but it makes it easier for me to get my wife's breakfast."

"You get her breakfast here every day?"

"Nah. Normally she gets it herself. She works at the yarn shop a block down, on the same block as the Gustavsson Gallery actually. But the shop is closed on Sundays, so I'm getting it for her."

"That's sweet. All's good on the home front?"

"Oh, yeah. Jenna feels fatter every day, but she thinks she'll be able to work right up until the delivery. Things going okay for you?"

"Yeah. I've figured out the food co-op, explored the local hardware store you told me about, and pretty much got the street map down in my head."

"Has to be easier than LA." He grinned big. He liked needling me about LA.

"Nate and Connor," the college kid at the register called out, indicating our orders were up.

"I'll get them." I got up before he could. "You need to save your energy for the baby."

He made a rude gesture, and we both laughed.

When I got back with the food, he chowed down. My sandwich was great, but I had to force myself to eat it. Images of Guy lying on his office floor flickered through my brain like a short film stuck on repeat. He contentedly crunched his way through a bowl of granola.

"Man, that's noisy."

"Tastes great, more filling." He smiled big, showing his teeth and his granola.

"That is gross, Nate."

He gave an open-mouthed laugh—so I saw even more granola—and went back to chewing.

"Can I ask you a question?"

He nodded.

"What did the night sergeant mean when he told me I was hired to meet the Bozeangeles quota?"

He swallowed, thank God, before he started talking. "Some folks who've been here forever think Bozeman has too many transplants from Los Angeles. Hence, Bozeangeles. But there are folks from lots of other places too. Me, for instance. I'm a Wisconsin farm boy."

"I don't know anything about farms."

"Here's what you need to know: Milk comes from milk cows, which aren't at all like the cattle you see around here. Here, it's mainly Black Angus, which are beef cows, as in steak and hamburger. The best milk cows are black-and-white Holsteins. Don't let anyone tell you different. And chocolate milk does not come from brown cows."

"I know that."

"Just checking. Can't ever be sure what city boys know about farming and ranching. Especially those from Los Angeles." He grinned again. That was his way—lots of grins to keep things light. I appreciated it.

"What do you have planned for today?"

"Visit with Jenna. Find out what she wants me to do. Do it. Get some sleep before we start all over again. You?"

"Long bike ride. Then sleep." I left out the part about visiting the hospital to see how Guy was.

"You finding some good trails?"

"I'm doing Hyalite Canyon Road today."

"That's a great one. I'd go with you but…."

"You have a lot going with the baby coming. So, is it a boy or a girl?"

"Jenna won't let me tell anyone—"

"Forget I asked."

"The closer it gets, the more I feel like I have to tell somebody. Promise you won't tell a soul and never mention this to my wife? She'd shoot me."

I had to laugh. He was dead serious. "Promise," I said in the same tone.

"It's a boy." He sat up straight and grinned until his smile seemed wider than his face.

"Congratulations. I'm honored you confided in me."

He nodded. "You're a good guy, Connor. You're going to fit in fine here, despite being from LA."

He got an orange scone for his wife, and we both took off. I headed back to my apartment, changed, and grabbed my bike. I sprinted the miles to the trailhead, working to build my stamina. I'd done this trail before and liked it. I was eager to tackle the technical difficulty again and cut my time. And maybe quit thinking about Guy.

As if.

FOUR

EVEN AS I rode, my mind wandered back to that first night in Guy's hotel room. I'd replayed the scene so many times that, had it been a chapter in a book, the ink would have been worn off the pages.

He was on me as soon as I locked the door.

"You know," he whispered, pushing my chest against it, one hand grabbing my neck, the other groping my ass, "you look awfully good from the rear. Is this why cops always have the criminals turn around when they frisk them?"

I wasn't sure I liked being manhandled by a guy ten inches shorter than me—an artist at that. "What kind of game are you playing?"

"Hmm. A game. Cops and rubbers. What do you think?" He giggled, and that and the provocation in his words went straight to my dick.

I spun around easily—he hadn't been holding on hard—and grabbed him around the waist. "I think it's time you showed me what you've got. It had better be impressive."

He held both hands up. "You going to search me, Officer?" He batted his eyes.

"You like games, do you?"

"With the right partners."

He sprinted for the bed and vaulted into the center of it. He landed on his back, rolled to his side, and propped his head on his hand. "Come and get me," he purred, patting the comforter.

I kicked off my shoes and stripped off my shirt, pants, and briefs on the way to the bed. He eyed me hungrily and licked his lips with exaggerated effort. I fell on him, pushed him to his back again, pulled his hands above his head, and held them there while I licked and nibbled at his neck. He wiggled and let out a giggle that didn't seem like it would stop anytime soon.

"Be quiet."

"But… it… tickles."

"And stop squirming." I was going to shoot right away if he didn't quit rubbing our dicks together.

"Can't. Oh… can't." His giggle morphed into a squeal.

I rolled off him and huffed out a breath. "No one can be that ticklish."

He gulped down a laugh. "I am. Sorry." He smoothed his hand across my chest, fingered a nipple, and began to lick it. He had my complete attention again.

"I am," he whispered between licks. "I am."

"Be quiet and start sucking."

"Yes, Officer."

"You like this police thing entirely too much."

"Yes. I want to see your badge. Later."

"Enough!" I rolled off the bed.

Guy rose up in horror. "You're not leaving?"

"I'm getting a condom."

"What a relief." He flopped back dramatically, peering up at the ceiling like there should be a mirror there.

I laughed.

He turned his head to look at me, his eyes big and round. "What?"

"We sound like a bad porn novel."

"You read those? I'm shocked. I thought you said you studied literature."

I fished a pair of condoms from my wallet, returned to the bed, and crawled on top of him. "I did. Enough to know that you, Guy Gustavsson, are a drama queen."

"Only in bed, Officer. I swear." He smiled sweetly and closed his eyes.

I kissed him hard, until I had to stop to help him out of his clothes. Then I planted my face in his crotch and swallowed his cock, making him wiggle and giggle some more.

"Stop," he cried at last. "I don't want to come yet."

"On your knees, then."

"Yes, Officer."

The quiver in his voice rocked me. When he'd rolled over, I grabbed his hands, jerked them behind his back, and pressed him into the bed.

"You trying to be smart, boy?"

"No, sir."

I nipped hard at the soft spot where his neck joined his shoulder. "You're going to do exactly what I say."

"Yes, sir."

His voice was so breathy he had to be starved for oxygen. I liked that idea. I bit him.

"Oh God," he moaned.

"Quiet. Did I say you could talk?"

"No, sir."

I pulled him up onto his knees again. He groaned.

"Not a sound. Am I going to have to teach you what that means?" I grabbed his dick, sliding my fingers through his precum. He whimpered.

"You just cannot follow orders, can you?"

He squealed as I continued to pull on his cock. Mine began to ache, more so each time he made a new noise. He knew how to turn me on. I rolled him over and moved between his legs again, my eyes focused on his weeping dick, straight and hard and straining.

"Prep yourself for me."

He spit onto the fingers of his right hand and eased them between his legs.

"Can I put my finger in, sir?"

I wanted to growl. I licked my lips and nodded and watched him repeat my actions. He closed his eyes and sank two fingers in. I sucked in a breath that sounded like a whirlwind in the stillness.

"Look at me."

His eyelids fluttered open, revealing a need that burned me. Then they shut fast, like he was afraid he'd bared too much. I concentrated on his fingers, sliding in and out and around.

"You want to add another digit before I drill you?"

"No, sir." He pulled his knees toward his chest and spread them. "Please, sir."

I thrust into him, hearing his hiss and feeling his tight heat in the same instant. I licked one of his nipples. He giggled again, and I felt the wonderful side effect, his inner muscles grabbing me hard. I thrust deep and slow. His giggles slid into a higher register.

"Gonna come," he whined, rocking and thrashing and massaging every inch of me. "More." His tongue flicked in and out of his mouth. "More, please."

I grabbed his hips, driving into him, and he tugged fiercely at his dick, like he was trying to separate it from his body. I matched my thrusts to his chants of "Yes, yes, yes," then whispered, "Come for me."

He wailed and shot a long white stream across both our chests. I exploded as soon as it hit me, shuddering, and biting my lip to stay silent.

My bike tires hit gravel on the side of the road, startling me back to the present. Guy had to recover now. And I had to see him.

MONDAY MORNING, as I was going off shift, word came that he was awake, talking, and making sense. He was going to be moved out of ICU. I couldn't believe how relieved I was.

A detective was interviewing him at ten. I should be safe showing up around one. Now I needed to kill a few hours. I went home, hopped on my bike, and rode eighty miles. Didn't remember a thing I saw, except the hospital. As I was riding past it for the third time, I realized I'd stand a better chance getting into Guy's room if I was in uniform. I rode home to shower and change.

The receptionist at the hospital information desk gave me Guy's room number right away. I walked to the elevators, even though my pulse raced like it wanted me to run. Eight long months I'd wanted to see him again. Even the elevator chime that announced the passing floors seemed to say, "Faster, faster."

When I turned onto the hallway where Guy's room was, I spotted a dayside officer I didn't know sitting in a chair outside the room. He saw me too. *It's okay*, I told myself. *You can come up with a valid professional reason for being here.*

"Connor Maclean," I said as we shook hands. "Part of the nightside team that handled the call. How's Mr. Gustavsson? Has he had any visitors?"

"Just Detective Haney," he answered. "Now the guy's sleeping again. It's been quiet."

"That's what we want."

"Mind if I take off for five minutes while you're in there?"

"No problem."

"Thanks."

He left, and I slipped into the sterile white room. No flowers broke the monotonous color scheme. Wasn't there anyone in his life to send them? He looked so tiny in the big white bed, propped up on a couple of pillows, a thin white blanket tucked around his waist. An IV pumped a clear liquid into his left arm, and additional tubes and cords connected him to a couple of monitors. His face was as white as the bandage across his nose, except where he had bruises and scattered stitches. He had lots of bruises, and a couple of bare spots where they'd shaved his head now bore stitches too. His right shoulder was bandaged, the arm in a sling strapped tight across his bare torso. Stitches from the surgery to remove his spleen were visible under the arm; they continued across his midsection until they disappeared beneath the blanket.

I wanted to yell or punch the wall. I had to swallow hard against the nausea. "Oh, Guy." I brushed my fingertips across his left arm above the IV.

"Josh?" he whispered.

My stomach dropped like a roller coaster hurtling down a record incline. I couldn't come up with an intelligent rejoinder. Did he have a new life with someone else?

He turned to me and opened his eyes.

"Surprise," I said, trying to give him my best smile. I didn't succeed. He gazed at me in confusion. "Connor. From LA, remember?"

"Connor." His voice was a hoarse rasp. His face scrunched up like he'd felt a sharp pain, and his eyes snapped shut again. Not a great beginning for anything. I held my breath.

When he opened his eyes again, he looked a little more with it. "Water?"

"Sure."

A plastic pitcher and a matching cup with a bent straw sat on the table next to the bed. I poured water in the glass and held it as he took a slow drink.

"Thanks." His voice sounded the slightest bit stronger. "What are you doing in Bozeman?"

"I work here now. I sent you a text, remember?"

He cringed.

This was going south so fast. I didn't want him to be thinking about how we'd lost touch and he'd found someone else. I didn't want him to be thinking about anything except how I was here and Josh Whoever wasn't. "I got a job with Bozeman PD.... I was the one who answered the robbery call at your gallery."

"A detective already interviewed me. I don't remember anything." His voice was fading.

I had to say something to get this conversation on the right track. "That's okay. I wanted to see you, to see how you were. I've wanted to see you since you left LA." Talk about putting pressure on a guy when he was down. I was an idiot.

He winced.

"Are you in pain? Do you want me to call a nurse?"

He shook his head and groaned. "Head hurts…. Stomach…." He closed his eyes. "Tired now." He turned his head away from me.

My hopes evaporated with my exhale. "Sure. I'll come back tomorrow."

He didn't say anything. He didn't turn back toward me. He kept his eyes shut like he was sleeping. I slipped out of the room, nodded at the dayside officer, and left the hospital.

Now I knew why he hadn't returned my calls and texts. He had Josh Whoever.

FIVE

I RETURNED to the hospital late the next afternoon. I couldn't get him out of my mind. He was an itch that wouldn't stop until he dumped me with real words. I was an addict and he was my drug.

This time, I came bearing gifts. "How's the patient?" I asked as I entered, hoping he'd forgotten my first visit. He hadn't.

"I thought I dreamed you." He was sitting up today and looked fifty times better. Plus he had some color, other than purple and green, back in his face.

"So you dream about me?" I smiled.

He didn't. "Why are you here?"

"I wanted to see you."

He swallowed. "I didn't return your messages."

"I didn't take it personally." Overnight, I'd brainstormed responses for nearly anything he might say.

"I was mean."

"No," I lied. "You must have had a reason." I smiled again. I was going to give him every out until he explained why he'd stopped communicating with me.

He sighed, giving up the topic for now. He raised his left arm slightly, barely waving at the bag I'd brought before settling his hand back in his lap. The effort must have been overwhelming. He winced, then closed his eyes for a few minutes. But when he opened them again, they held a spark of interest. "What's in there?"

"Presents. I got you an art magazine. I don't know which ones you read, but I thought it might help you pass some time for a while at least. And some puzzle books to keep your mind sharp." I arched an eyebrow as I said that last bit, hoping it came across as a tease. I thought I saw the corner of his mouth edge up slightly.

"Plus an assortment of Lindt truffles. I remember how much you like chocolate."

Now he nearly did smile. He reached out his left hand, closing and opening it several times. "Give."

"Say, 'Please, Officer'?" I'd crossed the line into cheesy.

He groaned and cleared his throat. He was trying not to grin. I put the bag in his lap, and he put his left hand in it and felt around until he found what he wanted. He pulled out the bag of chocolates first. But he frowned as he stared at it, trying to figure how to open it one-handed.

"Let me help you with that." I ripped open the package and held it out for him to grab the chocolate of his choice. He did, but then he stopped again, holding it in midair. He couldn't unwrap it either.

"Aww, shit." Without looking at him, I took the chocolate, undid the twisted ends, and held it out to him, the chocolate sphere resting atop the paper in my palm. "I'm sorry, Guy."

He took the chocolate and carefully popped it in his mouth so he didn't have to answer. A second later, he really smiled, his dimples showing for the first time. "Mmm, good."

Maybe I hadn't been so stupid.

His eyes warmed, nearly shining as he looked at me. "Thank you for being so thoughtful, Connor."

I was pretty sure he meant it. "Want another?"

"Gotta wait and see," he said slowly. He wasn't doing anything fast. "The pain meds make me nauseous."

"I'm sorry. Do you feel any better today?"

"Maybe." He cleared his throat and shifted, trying to sit up a bit more. "How do you like Bozeman?" He seemed genuinely interested in my answer.

I put the chocolates, magazine, and puzzle books on the movable table next to his bed. "The city is as great as you said, and my job is going well. It's a good department. I love the mountains, and I've found some great bike trails." I paused, wondering how long to talk before handing the conversation back to him. "Your gallery is amazing, and I see where your painting career has taken off since LA."

Wrong thing to say. His face fell and he turned his head away. "That's all over now," he breathed. His chin trembled. He shrank away from me like he was trying to disappear.

I reached out and lightly touched his good shoulder. "Don't think that way, okay? Give yourself time." With my thumb, I rubbed small, gentle circles against his skin.

"Right." He didn't move closer, but he didn't pull away either.

Encouraged, I spoke again. "You look a lot better."

He glared. "Don't lie, Connor. It's not your style. I've seen a mirror. I look awful." He stuck out his chin, daring me to dispute him.

Feeling like I'd been too forward, I dropped my hand from his shoulder. "You're going to get better. Everything's going to get better."

He huffed out a frustrated breath, but his lower lip trembled too. I looked for a way to change the subject. "Was I surprised to read in the paper how well-known you are. The mayor and even the police chief had comments about you. My boss called you a great philanthropist."

He shrugged, and that made him wince and reach for his right arm. *What wrong thing could I say next?*

"I won't be a philanthropist or anything else for a while." He looked at his right arm like it had betrayed him. "I'm not going to be able to do anything."

"Want to try another chocolate? I'll keep feeding you chocolates until you're better."

He gave me a sardonic look but nodded, too, and I unwrapped another one. He put it in his mouth, swirling it around with his tongue, and eventually, though he tried to stop it, a sigh escaped him. He loved chocolate.

"Do you think I can paint left-handed?" he asked softly. He couldn't look at me.

"You can, but you'll be back to painting with your right arm in three months tops, believe me. It's amazing what they can do with shoulders."

"How do you know?"

On firmer ground now, I answered enthusiastically. "A guy I used to play basketball with smashed his up in a game. Fourteen weeks later, he was playing again, good as new."

"Really?"

"It'll be the same with you."

He nodded like he might believe me, and my heart lifted. I kept talking. "When are they thinking you can go home?"

Before he could answer, two men walked into the room. The leaner, younger one wore a Stetson atop curly blond hair—the cowboy in my painting come to life. I froze.

Cowboy didn't notice. He'd gotten his first look at Guy. He blanched and stopped moving. The taller, grimmer man behind him showed no response. With a military haircut and a Rangers tat on his forearm, he exhaled testosterone.

I could match that. I was taller than either of them. By simply standing straighter, I took up considerably more space in the room. I moved closer to Guy.

"Josh!" The patient attracting all the attention grinned as best he could, his dimples making a shallow appearance on both cheeks. They vanished as Ranger moved farther into the room.

Josh, the person Guy had wanted to see yesterday, was the cowboy from *Cowboy and Cat?* My gut seized up. I had to be looking at the living, breathing reason he had quit answering my calls and texts. But who was Ranger? A bodyguard? His escort?

Guy looked like a kid whose Christmas presents had been stolen. I felt sorry for him. Cowboy seemed uncomfortable, especially once he looked at me. And didn't that make Ranger mimic my movements and step closer to him. I had a vision of two cartoon roosters squaring off, displaying their feathers, and scratching in the dirt.

"You know," I began, hoping to inject some levity into the tension, "if we have any musical talent at all between us, we could give the Village People a run for their money."

Cowboy drew his eyebrows together, clearly puzzled. Guy gave a tiny giggle. I winked at him. Ranger frowned. He had no sense of humor, or I needed to explain.

I pointed at each of us, starting with him. "Soldier. Cowboy. Artist. Cop. Get it?"

Ranger shrugged. Cowboy finally got it and laughed, and didn't the bastard look too damn handsome doing it.

Guy made introductions. "Connor, this is my college roommate, Josh Brooks, and his friend. Dane, isn't it?"

Brooks nodded. "Dane Keller," he said to me. Ranger didn't move a muscle. Guy continued, "Connor is a friend from LA."

Cowboy turned all of his attention on Guy. "I didn't learn about the attack until today, or we'd have been here sooner."

So these two were a pair. I saw Guy sink into the pillows like he'd run out of gas, or reasons to live. Brooks's "we" hung in the air a few minutes, looking for a landing it never found.

"It's okay, Josh," Guy said at last. "I only woke up today."

Ranger turned to me. "I didn't catch who you were."

"Connor Maclean. I'm with Bozeman PD."

"You're investigating what happened?" he asked pointedly.

"No. But I am the one who found Guy."

"What happened, Guy?" Josh asked.

He hesitated, almost like he was too embarrassed to say. Keeping his eyes on his right arm, he began to tell the story. "This man called me about one of my paintings." He paused again, like he couldn't figure what to say next. I noticed he wasn't naming the painting. I glanced at Cowboy. He was oblivious. Like his partner, he merely waited for Guy to continue.

Guy cleared his throat. "I guess I should have suspected something when he told me his name was Jones. But I didn't. He came into the gallery just before nine Friday night—the time he'd set up. He got me into the back office by asking to see additional paintings, I remember that, and he demanded money and beat me up. The police tell me a teenager walking through the alley came in and tried to stop him…."

He looked up at me. I nodded, and he continued. "I was already unconscious, but the police say he hit the kid, too, and took off."

Both Brooks and Keller looked angry. "Are the police close to finding him?" Cowboy's question was aimed at me.

"Not yet, but the kid, who's also an artist, was able to draw us a great picture, so we've got an ID. We'll find him soon."

Guy looked at me in surprise. "He's an artist?"

"A good one. His drawing looked like a photograph."

"Good. I don't remember a thing about what the man looked like. I don't remember anything." He stared at his useless arm again. Then he focused on me, as if he couldn't bear to look at Brooks. "What's the kid's name?"

"Alex."

"I need to thank him."

I nodded. "I can arrange that."

Cowboy took over the conversation, stepping up to Guy on the opposite side of the bed as he asked his next question. "So, what do the doctors say about you?"

Guy turned toward him but didn't quite look at him. His gaze returned to his damaged arm. "I'm doing great after surgery to remove my spleen and ease pressure in my head. I have a concussion." Guy didn't look up at all, like he was bothered about something. But what? That he'd been beaten up? Or that Brooks was seeing him at his worst?

He continued his answer to Cowboy's question. "My face is healing nicely, whatever that means. Between it and my scalp, I have a bunch of stitches in my head, and more in my stomach. My right arm will stay bound up like this for weeks, until my broken shoulder heals. I may need more surgery on it. Meanwhile, I can't do anything, and there's no telling if I'll be able to paint again. But I may be able to go home in a few days."

He turned to look at me again, like I was his lifeline, or a security blanket. "What about my gallery, Connor? Is it okay?"

"The office is a mess, and a few canvasses are damaged, but nothing was stolen, and he didn't touch your apartment. We're checking the building a couple of times a night now. Some of your neighbors are keeping an extra eye on things too. I told them you'd appreciate that."

I put my hand on Guy's blanket-covered thigh as I said that, and he laid his left hand on it. We were putting on a nice act for somebody, but I didn't know who. And I wasn't sure of our motives, especially mine.

"Are you going to be able to stay at your place when you get out of the hospital?" Brooks was nothing but questions. That one, though, had Ranger paying close attention.

"Not right away. The doctor says I can't do the stairs. And I won't be able to do anything to take care of myself until I figure out how to do things left-handed."

"What are you going to do?"

"I don't know, Josh." Guy began to chew on his lower lip.

Silence followed his statement. Cowboy appeared supremely uncomfortable, like he should offer something but knew he needed to talk with Ranger first. Guy looked not just beaten up but beaten down—like every stray dog I'd never been allowed to keep after I brought them home.

The protector side of me jumped forward. "You can stay with me, Guy. No stairs. It's small, so you can get around without much effort. And we can figure out the rest."

"You're serious, Connor?" He brightened up again, almost as much as he had when he'd seen Brooks. This time, I was the reason.

"Absolutely."

"I won't be a bother."

"I know." The hell I did. Guy was high maintenance. Who would take care of him while I was at work? It didn't matter. I would make good on my offer.

"That's great, Guy. I'm glad," Brooks said.

I didn't believe him.

"We're going to go so we don't tire you out," he added. "But I'll call you, if you don't mind, and come see you again."

Guy nodded.

"Do what the doctors tell you and get well soon, Guy," Ranger said sincerely.

They left, and Guy and I didn't talk for a good five minutes. He looked out the window. I stared at the sparkling clean floor.

I had no idea what he was thinking. I was fighting second thoughts. If anybody in the department found out, I would be questioned about hooking up with the victim in an ongoing investigation. I pushed the worries out of my mind. I *would* be there for Guy.

"Is there anything you need?"

"You're sure about me staying with you, Connor?"

"Is there someone you'd rather stay with? Is there someone I can contact for you?"

His face fell. He turned to the window again. "The person I'd have felt comfortable asking…." The sentence died right there. I knew the ending: The person was Brooks. But he had Ranger now.

"Then you're staying with me."

He tried to smile, but the grim line his lips made was full of pain. Was it from his injuries? From realizing he didn't have many close friends? Or was it the pain that squeezes your heart dry as you watch your dream walk away with someone else?

I had no idea how to comfort him, and I was due in to work. "I'm sorry, Guy. I have to head to the station now. But I'll see you tomorrow morning, okay? We'll make plans."

He nodded. I patted his thigh again, but he didn't touch me this time. He didn't move. Still, I decided to look on the bright side. I'd come to Bozeman hoping I could start something with him. Here was my opportunity.

SIX

WHEN I got to work that night, Alex Whittaker sat at a desk waiting for me. The night sergeant waved me toward him with a cock of his head and a raised eyebrow.

"Alex, what can I do for you?" I pulled up the chair from the next desk and sat down so I wouldn't tower over him. I had him by a good six inches now, though he might be close to my height when he quit growing.

"I hope it's okay that I'm here," he began.

"Absolutely. Did you remember something new or want to know more about your case? You'll want to talk to the detective in charge, Detective Haney, for that. He's the one with the wavy white hair, bushy eyebrows, and gray mustache."

"I know," he answered. "Looks like that cop on *Law and Order.* He's talked with me twice already. I wanted to talk to you."

"Sure. You want something to drink? We've got bad coffee, better water, and there's a soda machine in the break room."

"No, I'm good." He looked around nervously, turning his eyes quickly back to me when a couple of the other officers met his gaze.

"Come on." I stood up. "We'll move to the break room. It'll be more comfortable for you, and more private."

Once there, I steered him toward an isolated corner table, headed for the soda machine, and slipped a dollar in the slot. "What kind would you like?"

"Diet Coke would be good. Thanks."

I got his selection, put another buck in the next machine and got a bottle of water, and sat down across from him.

I opened my bottle and took a drink. He followed suit with his. "So, are you doing okay? Have bad dreams or anything?"

"I'm good," he insisted. I wasn't convinced. He leaned toward me and lowered his voice. "Maybe I have some trouble sleeping. Is that normal?"

"It is. Sometimes, after a rough night at work, I have bad dreams."

"You do?"

"How bad are yours?"

"Maybe not so bad." If he noticed how I'd coaxed the answer out of him, he didn't let on. "I wake up as he's starting to hit me."

"Good. That's good that they're not worse. Have you talked to your mom about them?"

He nodded and gripped his bottle with both hands. "She... hears me, you know?"

"She helps you get over them, right?" I thought back to the short time I'd seen Kellie Whittaker. She was young, but she was an involved mom.

"She sits with me until I fall asleep again."

"My mom used to do that for me." I smiled at the memory. "Not recently," I added, in case he misunderstood.

I took another drink of water while I tried to figure whether he needed to see a professional. If he could afford one. I had no idea what his mother did for a living. "Have you had the dream every night?"

"Yeah, but it's shorter every night. I can make myself wake up."

"That's great. Next time you have it, try to change the outcome. See if you can punch the guy back."

"What?" He looked at me like I'd sprouted a third eye.

"It works. It's a great coping skill. Sign of advanced intelligence too."

"You're making that up."

"No, really." I grinned.

"Does it work for you?"

"Sometimes." I held up my right hand like I was promising to tell the whole truth in court. "Honest."

Now he gave me a half smile. "Maybe I'll try it. How's Mr. Gustavsson? Is he going to be okay?"

"Yeah, he is. It's going to take a while, and he'll need therapy and maybe a follow-up operation on his shoulder, but he's going to be okay. Didn't Haney tell you?"

"Some. But I figured you'd know more."

"How so?"

"You called him by his first name as soon as you saw him that night."

The kid noticed everything. I shifted in my seat, my mind running through the possible scenarios that might follow this revelation.

"Don't worry," he added quickly. "I didn't say anything about it to anybody. Not to Haney for sure. I'm not going to."

The kid was too smart for my good. Probably his own too. I shrugged. "You don't have to keep that a secret. You can tell anyone you need to." But, God, I hoped he wouldn't.

"No one's asked. No one needs to know. I'd like to meet Mr. Gustavsson, when you think he's up to it. I admire his work. It's different than what I do, but I want to know more about what he does, and his gallery."

Maybe this was all he wanted. I relaxed. "When I told him you were an artist, he said he wanted to meet you too."

The kid's eyes shone with excitement. "Because you told him I'm an artist?"

"That, and the fact that you saved his life."

Alex shook his head. "I didn't. I should have gotten there sooner."

I touched his shoulder. "You couldn't have. You were working. What you did was more than enough. You're very brave." I didn't insult him by adding "for a kid." Most adults wouldn't have done what he did. "You saved Guy's life. That man would have killed him. Guy is grateful." I paused, debating with myself, then decided to trust the kid. "I am too. Thank you."

Embarrassed, he stood up to go. "Thanks for the Coke, and the advice about the dream."

I got up too. "Guy will call you when he feels better, and I'll get you two together. Do you need a ride home?"

He shook his head. "I rode my bike."

"You ride a lot? Distances?"

"Yeah. Trails too."

"Do you know some good ones?"

His face brightened. "You ride?"

"Yeah. I've found a few. I'm going through a local trail book."

"Forget that. I can tell you about some—when you introduce me to Mr. Gustavsson."

"It's a deal."

I walked him out to his bike, which was cheap and old and banged up in spots. Clearly, he'd tried to maintain it, but not always with the right parts and never with the best ones. I glanced at him and this time noticed his well-worn clothes. His mom wouldn't be able to afford a psychologist. I hoped my advice would help.

THE NEXT day when I visited, Guy was still in bed, pillows propped all around him, the white blanket pulled up to his chin, and his face turned toward the window. His concentration on whatever was out there was so intense, he didn't seem to be in the room.

When he turned toward me, recognition flickered, but nothing else. He looked like he'd received the worst news in the world.

"What's the matter?"

He moved to pull his knees up to his chest, like he wanted to curl up and hug himself, but he froze and gasped in pain. Defeated, he slowly stretched his legs out again and turned back toward the window.

"Nothing," he said at last.

"Have the doctors been in today?"

He nodded and winced, like his head still hurt. "They said I'll be able to leave in two days. Then the social worker came in to discuss moving to a nursing home for rehab. She said lots of people in my situation do that."

"But you're coming home with me. Didn't you tell them that?"

He sank back into the pillows. "You made that offer out of pity. I know that. You don't have to worry about me, Connor, or feel obligated to take me in, or even visit me anymore. I'll be fine. I've always been alone."

What about his parents? Wasn't that a whole book of information to chew on? Later. I returned to the issue at hand. "Guy, I said you could stay at my place because I want you to."

Before he could answer, Brooks and Ranger blew in. Guy perked up.

"I brought you your favorite magazines," Brooks announced, putting the latest issues of *People* and *Vanity Fair* in Guy's lap.

"Oooh, Angelina's on the cover. You know how much I love her."

And I didn't. Was that the message?

"How are you feeling today?" Cowboy asked.

"Not so great."

He grabbed the chair, straddled it, and sat down. "Tell me." He laid his hand on Guy's arm, and Guy melted into his caring attention. The quiet in the room swelled until we were all uncomfortable.

Ranger caught my eye. "Why don't you and I go find some coffee and let the old roommates talk for a bit?"

"Sure." I was surprised by his suggestion. I wasn't sure I'd let someone who so obviously wanted my guy be alone with him. But Ranger didn't seem worried. Without a word, he led me out of the room and down the hallway.

I broke the silence after he'd punched the button for the elevator. "You think that was a good idea? Dane?"

"Or Keller. Or Master Sergeant. Take your pick."

The doors opened on an empty car. He stepped aside so I would get on first. He hit the button for the cafeteria, turned toward me, and leaned his back against the wall—the picture of perfectly relaxed, not a bit bothered that I was slightly taller.

"Yeah, I think it was fine," he answered. "I know all about the two of them. I also know it's over. And I think Guy needs some time alone to talk with someone who's known him longer and better than you or me, don't you?"

"Yeah," I said reluctantly.

We didn't say anything more until we'd each bought a cup of coffee and sat down at a cafeteria table. The lunch crowd was gone. The place was nearly empty.

He took a long drink from his cup. "So what brought you to Bozeman?"

Why not tell the truth? It might keep him pleasantly disposed toward Guy a while longer, and Guy needed every one of the few friends he had, even Cowboy. More likely, especially him. "The police department had an opening. I applied and got the job. I wanted to see Guy again. We spent a week together in LA last fall."

He nodded. "I came to Montana straight from Afghanistan and the Rangers. I came because I couldn't do it for another minute, and Josh's brother is my best friend. I was a mess, and Josh saved me. He loved me into the man I could be. I know that. I make sure he knows every day how grateful I am."

I swallowed a big gulp of coffee, digesting his words. His honesty surprised me. When I responded, I surprised myself. "We had one great week together, and a month of near-constant communication. Then he quit answering my texts and calls. I don't know why, but I'm not ready to give up."

He nodded. "It'll be a while before Guy is in good shape."

"I know."

"Can you handle that?" He was asking for information, not challenging me. It was a fair question.

"I want to try…. But I don't know for sure that I can give him everything he needs." What had me in such a confessing mood all of a sudden? Keller was a soldier, not a priest. Still, I continued. "We don't know each other well, not like you and Josh. But I want to see if we can get closer to what you have." I shrugged, embarrassed by all I'd revealed.

Keller let out a half laugh, half sigh and smiled. Had I relieved his worries? "That's not a bad start."

"I hope you're right."

"You give him time and be there for him, and I will be." He nodded encouragingly and drained his cup. "Come on. Let's get up there while Josh has still left something for you to do. Sometimes he tries to fix everything at once."

"Right." I followed him back upstairs, marveling at how well he knew his guy and how secure he was.

I couldn't say the same for me, for so many reasons. The more I thought about taking care of Guy once he got out of the hospital—and I'd thought of little else—the more I realized it could easily sink our relationship. I was going to have to be patient and calm all the time. I would need everything my education, police training, and experience with Mom had taught me. I could do it. I wanted to. But failure was a real possibility.

I was afraid, too, that Guy might find *Cowboy and Cat* one night while I was at work. How would I explain I'd had it all along? The truth might not be enough for a man who'd been physically wrecked over it. I'd already taken the painting off the wall in anticipation of hiding it. But where? The apartment was so small it wouldn't take much for a bored man to find it. Even one hampered by a bad shoulder, pain, and nausea from pain meds.

Every time I walked into my bedroom, it mocked me from atop the dresser, daring me to try to hide it from Guy. Even after I turned it facedown—because I couldn't stand to see the half-naked cowboy now that I knew him and what he meant to Guy—the thing taunted me.

I thought about stashing it behind the couch or entertainment center, but that seemed like asking Guy to find it. The closets were bad for the same reason. I even thought about renting a storage unit, but I couldn't spare the money. In the end, I taped it to the bottom of the box spring, Brooks's image facing the ceiling.

And if Guy and I ever managed to make love on my bed? I hoped I would be so involved I wouldn't remember who was under it.

SEVEN

TWO DAYS later, I took Guy home. He wore a black sweat suit I picked up for him at Walmart. He stiffened as soon as I pulled in to the alley behind his gallery, folded his good arm across his bad one, and hugged his sides. He wouldn't look at his own back door.

"Are you okay?" He remained silent, and I put my hand on his shoulder. "Guy?"

He jerked away from me, paled in pain, and flushed with embarrassment. "I'm sorry, Connor. I didn't mean to do that."

"It's okay. I'll hurry up getting your stuff, and we'll get out of here."

He closed his eyes and nodded.

I didn't want to leave him alone in the Jeep, but I didn't have a choice. He couldn't go with me, and he had few other friends. Brooks, Ranger, and I—and Detective Haney—had been his only hospital visitors.

"As soon as I get upstairs, I'll call you, okay? You can tell me where things are."

"Yeah, that's good," he said weakly. He was tired after all the hassle of getting out of the hospital.

Inside his apartment, I needed more than thirty minutes to gather his stuff. The problem wasn't finding things. Everything was neat and organized. He kept changing his mind about what clothes to take.

Getting the right notebooks, paints, and pencils was easier. He knew exactly which of those he wanted, and the paints and pencils were in one cabinet, the notebooks in another. As instructed, I picked up the two big notebooks on the top shelf, his working notebooks, he called them. The two bottom shelves were filled with many more, with identifying names or letters and dates on the spines. They were arranged alphabetically, and the dates went back nearly ten years.

"Got all the art stuff," I told him in my next call. "I'll be down with this load in a few minutes."

"Would it be too much trouble to bring my easel too?"

"No problem. I'll make another trip."

"Never mind. I'm sorry. Leave it." He fretted. "Leave all of my art stuff. It's not like I can do anything with it."

"No. You want it, you got it. I won't need a bike ride today now."

My comment was met with silence.

"Guy, I'm teasing."

"Oh, okay."

"I'm hanging up. I'll be down in a few."

But I didn't leave right away. His neatly arranged notebooks fascinated me. I wanted to see what was in them. On a whim, I pulled out the one labeled JB 2011 and flipped through it.

The entire notebook was male nudes, all of the same headless body as near as I could tell, because the musculature was the same. So was the cock, which was always erect. Guy had drawn the same man over and over from different angles, in different poses, sometimes quickly, sometimes with deliberation. Some of the illustrations were in black pencil, in fine or thick lines. In others, he'd added shadings of colored pencils or smears of watercolors. The work was good. Erotic as hell. I was stiff. Guy had poured a lot into these images. But was the person real or imaginary?

I flipped through to the end and found my answer. In the last drawing, the body had a head and a face—Josh Brooks's, wearing a cowboy hat and nothing else. I should have known. They must have had fine times in 2011. Did Keller's "knowing all about them" include this? Hell, did Brooks know about these? Did he pose for them? Or did Guy draw them from memory? Either way, what chance did I have against such graphic visualizations?

I closed the notebook and put it back on the shelf. I didn't see one labeled CM, and I looked.

I grabbed the two bags I'd packed, one with clothes, one with art supplies, and headed down the stairs and out the door.

"Connor, I don't need the easel," Guy said as soon as I opened the back of the Jeep to load the bags.

"Huh?"

He turned around to look at me and winced in pain.

"You've gone to enough trouble. Let's just head to your house."

"Guy, it's no trouble. I'll be right back with it."

Instantly, he was overjoyed. "Thank you so much."

I had to smile. A joyous Guy was something to behold.

"I'll be right back."

I returned with the easel, and Guy again thanked me repeatedly. He hardly said anything during the ride to my place. Maybe he was enjoying the sunshine of this great day in early May. Trees were in leaf, and flowers bloomed everywhere—from the ground and all manner of containers. People seemed anxious to hurry along the flowers, and spring in general, because winter lasted so long. That's what I'd been told.

At my place, I helped Guy inside and got him settled on the couch with a pillow and blanket. When I came back in with his clothes, he was staring at the wall across from him. I looked around and realized my place was going to drive him crazy. His apartment was a riot of color. The kitchen was blue, with lots of yellow accents and shiny appliances. In the large living room, the walls and the rugs atop the plank floor were shades of green. The L-shaped brown leather couch and matching chairs bore yellow pillows. Paintings and photographs of all kinds of scenes and people covered the walls. His bedroom looked like something out of a magazine, with red fabric walls, a black bedspread, and red-and-black striped curtains. Huge male nudes, all Guy's work, hung there. The bathroom was shiny gold and white, with mirrors everywhere. The effect was dazzling and overwhelming both.

Nothing dazzled in my beige apartment.

"I guess you're going to have to turn on the TV to get some color in here. It's not like your place. Sorry."

Guy gave me a half smile. "It has possibilities. It does."

"It was already furnished. It was easier. I didn't have to move as much."

"I understand."

"I'll put your clothes duffel in the bedroom and your meds and toiletries in the bathroom. I can set up your easel and your work stuff here in the living room or in the spare room. But the light is better in here."

"Whatever is easiest for you."

"Living room is best. Are you hungry?"

"Not now. Maybe later."

"About that. I'll be sleeping later, to get ready for work. I thought I'd do the grocery shopping now. There's not much here to eat. What would you like me to get?"

"I'm not fussy." He returned to staring at the beige wall. In that instant, I realized he was going to be here alone a lot, and he was going to have a rough time.

"Like hell you're not fussy. I've eaten with you before." I laughed, so he'd know I was kidding. He wrinkled his nose and stuck his tongue out. I was glad to see it.

"I'll get you some paper and a pen, and while I bring in the easel, you make a grocery list of what you usually eat. Anything at all. Well, except for filet mignon and lobster, okay? I hate cooking them."

He giggled, and I felt better about everything. I could make this work.

A half hour later, I was in the grocery store buying a lot of yogurt, fruit, and frozen dinners, a box of artificial sweetener, a box of green tea, and another of chamomile tea, whatever that was. Like me, Guy didn't cook much. But where I favored deli chicken and salads, he seemed partial to Lean Cuisine. That got me a few weird looks from women shoppers.

When I returned, he was asleep in a corner of the couch, sitting up, folded in a fetal position over the arm, two blankets half-tucked all around him, three pillows cushioning his right arm and shoulder. It seemed a weird way for a grown man to doze, and I didn't remember him sleeping anything like that way in LA. Was it because of the attack? I wondered what a shrink would say.

I put the groceries away as quietly as I could, hoping the whole time that Guy would wake up. I wanted to be sure he'd taken his pain meds. And I couldn't figure out what to do now that he was sleeping on the couch. I'd told him to take the bed, that I'd nap in the living room before work. So where was I going to sleep? I didn't want to use the bed. I'd put clean sheets on it. And I didn't want to wake him. Finally, I grabbed an extra blanket from the bedroom closet and fell asleep atop the bedspread.

When I woke up, Guy was watching TV.

"You doing okay? Do you want me to make you anything to eat? Have you taken your pain meds?"

"Connor, you don't have to be my nurse."

"Sorry." I was quiet a minute, trying to figure out the weird vibe I was getting. When I couldn't, I busied myself putting his things for tea out on a counter within easy reach.

"I need to take off for work. I'm going to open up one of each of the frozen dinners but leave them in the freezer, so you can eat any one of them you like. Or more than one, if you like. I've made you a peanut butter and jelly sandwich and left it in the fridge. And I've opened a couple of the yogurts too. I think you'll be able to manage everything one-handed."

"Connor, I'll be fine."

"I know." Why was he being so cranky? "I want to make sure everything's easy for you. Is there anything else you can think of? Are things set up okay in the bathroom?"

"Everything is fine."

"Okay. I gotta go. Make sure you take the bed when you go to sleep, and call me if you need anything. Anything. You understand?"

"Anything. Got it." He didn't bother to hide the irritability in his voice. "Go."

I was glad to, and I felt bad about that.

THE CALL came through about 2:00 a.m., a neighbor reporting muffled screams at 222 Maple Street, Apartment 2. My place.

I called dispatch, told a story about having a houseguest who was probably having a nightmare, and got the okay to answer the call.

When I pulled up out front, not a single light was on in my apartment, but the one above it glowed bright as a lighthouse. The caller, I presumed.

I slipped through my door and waited for my eyes to adjust to the dark. I couldn't see a thing. "Guy?"

Sniffles came from the couch, followed by a mumble. "It's not time for you to be home yet." Tears clogged his voice.

"I'm on my break. We got a call that someone heard screams in my apartment." I said it as gently as I could.

"Oh God." His voice cracked. "I'm so sorry, Connor." He barely got the words out for the sobs.

I wanted to put my arms around him, but I still couldn't see enough to make it to the couch. "It's okay. Please don't be upset about it. Can I turn on a light?"

"I'd rather you didn't see me like this," he pleaded.

"Sure." I stepped carefully toward the couch, not wanting to trip and startle him, and sat down. "What happened, baby?" I marveled at how easily the word came to my lips, how good it felt.

Like a child in need of comforting, he crawled into my arms, dragging his covers with him, moving as fast as his bound arm and pain allowed. I wrapped my arms gently around everything. He was shaking.

"This reporter called me." He gestured at his cell phone, which was on the floor near the window, like he'd thrown it there. "He's called twice already. He wants to interview me about the attack. Says it might help catch the guy. But I don't want to, you know? I don't want to think about it. I told him that, but he pressed.... I finally hung up. Then I couldn't stop thinking about the attack. I had this dream of someone without a face beating me. It scared me. I must have screamed. I'm sorry. I was so scared." His voice trembled. He sniffed hard.

"Shhh." I tucked his head under my chin and rubbed my hands up and down his back. "I think it's pretty common after what you've been through. You're probably going to experience things like this for a while. I'm sorry I wasn't here for you."

"Don't," he ordered. "You're doing too much already. And now I've caused trouble for you." He stopped, embarrassed. "How are you going to explain this?"

"I already have."

"What? You told them you have a screamer houseguest who has nightmares?"

"Something like that." I rubbed his back some more. "But I gotta tell you. When we start having hot sex, you positively can't scream. Whoever called this in will call about that, too, and I don't know what I'll say."

He pushed against my chest and glared at me. "What makes you think you're getting hot sex?"

"It's the only kind you have."

He smacked my chest halfheartedly and giggled the tiniest bit. At least he'd stopped sniffling. "You're awful. You know that?"

"I think I told you that once. Do you want me to make you some of that tea?"

"That would be nice."

"How do I do it?"

"You are a Neanderthal."

"No. Manly men don't drink tea."

He rolled his eyes. "Put some water in a coffee mug and stick it in the microwave for two minutes. Then bring me a teabag and a packet of sweetener."

"I can do that." I went into the kitchen to follow his instructions. "I told you to sleep on the bed," I called back. "That couch isn't that comfortable, especially with your right arm tied to you."

"This is fine. I've kind of made a nest. I'm good."

I brought out the mug of hot water, with the teabag and sweetener already in it, and handed it to him. "I hope it's to your liking."

The mug was nearly to his mouth when he froze, glared at me, and stuck out his tongue.

I frowned back at him. "Not nice, Giggles."

"I am so glad you didn't call me that in front of Josh and Dane."

"You're welcome." I sat down next to him, then said as casually as I could, "So what's the story with you and Josh?"

"Is this Cop Connor asking?"

"Just curious."

"We met in college, shared an apartment with some other guys, and were friends with benefits. He met Dane. End of story."

His tone didn't sound like anything was over. And that notebook I'd seen didn't suggest it either.

I changed the subject by pushing and pulling on a few of his pillows and rearranging him on them. He still had some trouble moving. "How's your tea?"

"You can boil water with the best of them. Do you need to go back on patrol now?"

"Soon. You know I'd take off work and stay with you if I had any personal time yet."

"Don't even say that," he fumed. "You are doing more for me than anyone has a right to expect, especially considering how little we know each other." His dismissive description of our time together made me flinch, but he didn't notice. "I feel bad about imposing on you. Please don't make it worse by worrying about me too."

Did he think so little of himself? Did he not realize I cared about him? I didn't have enough time to get into that conversation. With the pain meds he was taking and his resulting mood shifts, we'd have likely ended up in an argument.

"Okay," I agreed. "No worrying. Other than the nightmare, are you doing okay by yourself? Can you reach everything you need? Did you manage to eat something?"

He put on a brave face and nodded. "I'm fine. Your peanut butter and jelly sandwich was first-rate. Better than my mom used to make."

"Now you're making fun of me."

"I wouldn't make fun of you, Officer." He drew out the last word, leaving his lips slightly parted, expectant. I leaned in and kissed them softly, then nibbled on his lower lip. I had to make myself end it.

"You are the best kisser." He kissed me briefly back and pulled away. "Now, get out there and serve and protect. I'll be fine."

I gave him a slow once-over. "You already are, baby. You already are."

EIGHT

I FINALLY got two days off to stay home with Guy. He slept a lot, which was good. I made sure he ate even though he still had little appetite because of the nausea. The home health nurse who visited every couple of days had stressed that. When he was awake, we watched movies together, alternating between the action flicks I loved and his favorite romantic comedies, mainly starring Cary Grant or Julia Roberts. I offered to take him by his gallery so he could check on it, but the idea scared him. I backed off that fast.

The second day, I got takeout from his favorite Asian restaurant, and he finally enjoyed something. He ate a little bit of every dish. I drove us to a city park, and we took a short walk on one of the paths. We moved slowly, but the sun was warm and bright.

"I haven't done anything like this since I got here," I told him. "It's nice having you around."

"Yeah, because every cop needs a screaming house guest who causes the police to be called to his home," he said dismissively. "How are you going to explain it if it happens again?"

"It won't. I talked with the neighbor. She knows what's going on and won't call again."

"How embarrassing." He stopped and stared past me, not looking at my face. He was ashamed.

"It's not at all." I touched his arm, and he began walking again. "She understood. She was glad to learn a police officer had moved into the building."

"I'll bet. Especially a good-looking one."

"She's at least in her seventies," I countered. I needed to switch topics, and maybe his mercurial mood. "So, there's something I've wanted to ask you forever."

"How come there's no one else I could ask to take me in? Pathetic, isn't it?"

This time I stopped. His self-contempt was heartbreaking. He kept walking, though, and I moved to catch up. "No. What I wanted to know was, how did you end up with a Norwegian last name, and what nationality are you?"

He puffed out an exaggerated breath and arched his eyebrows. "Very bad attempt at changing the topic, Connor."

I smiled back and raised my eyebrows as much. "Well?"

He rolled his eyes. "Obviously, I was adopted. While my dad taught engineering in Japan. I'm half-Japanese, half-Korean. My parents brought me to Bozeman when he got a job at Montana State, and I had every advantage a kid could want. When they died, they left me set for life financially. They just never loved me."

He said it like he was sure of it, almost like it didn't matter to him. I was stunned. Both of my parents loved me. They told me so all the time. While my dad was alive, the three of us did every fun thing functional families do together. My mom's drinking wasn't so bad in those days. After Dad was killed, she drowned herself in a bottle, constantly apologizing to me for it. Then she found AA and stopped cold, and we both found our way back to normal. Through it all, I knew she loved me.

"I'm sorry, Guy."

"We all have our baggage." He sighed and wrapped his good arm around his sling, like he was hugging himself. "But I shouldn't dump mine on you. You're doing so much for me, and being so kind to me, even when I'm not kind back. I don't understand why. That week we had in LA was good, but…."

I wanted to take him in my arms, but I couldn't. Not out in public. I touched his left arm briefly. "That week was better than good," I assured him. "I'm hoping that when you feel better, we can pick up where we left off and build on it."

"That would be nice," he sighed. Then he yawned.

"Come on." I turned him around toward the Jeep. "Time for you to rest a little."

Once we returned to the apartment, I brought him his pain meds and water, along with some crackers, tucked him in on the couch, and kissed his forehead. He was asleep in minutes.

I retreated into the bedroom. No matter how I tried, I couldn't get him to sleep anywhere but the couch, so I'd taken my bed back. That was likely for the best, with *Cowboy and Cat* still tightly taped to the box spring. I'd double-checked that plenty to make sure.

I stretched out to take a nap, but drawings from the JB notebook bothered my thoughts: Josh, nude and erect, from the front, from the back, in profile, with a cowboy hat, and without.

The images changed. I was the naked model, posed on a pedestal. Guy stood at an easel, drawing my picture in that dazzling gold bathroom of his where, if you stood right in front of the mirrors, you could see yourself in an unending reflection.

"Come on, Connor," he said. "I need you hard."

I looked down and wanted to die. I was shriveled up like a cheerleader's pom-pom in a soaking rain.

"Please, Guy, make me hard," I whispered. I tried to move my arms to pull him to me, but they were as limp as my dick.

He walked out of the room, sneering back at me, "Josh is so much better at this. I'm going back to Josh."

My dream went dark. The rest of my sleep was fitful.

I AWOKE to the sound of animated conversation in the living room. At first, I thought Guy had the television on too loud. Then I realized one of the voices was his, he was giggling a lot, and he had a male visitor.

The clock said 6:00 p.m. I got up, pulled on some sweats, and walked into the living room.

Above the back of my couch, I spied Josh Brooks's head in profile, cowboy hat and all.

I blinked. He was still there, leaning forward, both arms extended, eyes closed in concentration. A pleasurable moan came from the vicinity of where his hands should be. My dream flashed in my mind and my anger flared.

"What the fuck?"

Brooks jumped off the couch so fast he lost his balance and tumbled to the floor. Guy's head came up slowly, then swiveled in my direction. His mouth opened in a big O, but he didn't say anything.

"You've got a lot of nerve, making out in my living room, Brooks." I stormed toward the couch. "And is this how you show your gra—"

They were both fully clothed. I stopped talking but too late not to sound like an idiot.

Brooks scrambled up off the floor. "This isn't how it looks, Connor. I was—"

"He was rubbing my back." Guy had found his voice, and he was indignant and loud. He rose up off the couch, winced in pain, and faced me. "We weren't making out. I hardly have the energy for that," he snapped. He turned to Josh. "Can you give me a ride to my place?"

"No, he can't," I growled. "You know that's a dumb idea."

Guy glared at me. Cowboy took a step back, out of the line of fire, and waited. Why hadn't I waited a minute more?

"The dumb idea was coming here," Guy replied. "I will be fine at my house."

"Be reasonable," I implored. "You can't climb the stairs."

To prove otherwise, he took quick steps toward his easel and the bag that held his art supplies. But when he bent over to pick it up, he fell against the window. "Owww," he cried, grabbing at his right arm.

I rushed to his side. "Are you all right?"

"Get away from me." He pushed at me, but his shove had no force to it. "I can do this on my own. I don't need your help." He straightened up, but he had to lean against the wall again.

"Guy, don't do this."

"Leave me alone."

Brooks came up beside me. "I'll take over for a minute, Connor. Give him some space, okay?"

I bit my lip and took a step back, my hands up in the air.

"Did you hurt yourself?" Josh asked.

Guy shook his head.

"Good. Why don't we make you comfortable on the couch again, and I'll make you some tea?"

Guy nodded and let Brooks lead him to the couch. I watched in frustration, mentally kicking myself for my stupidity. Guy wouldn't look at me, even after Brooks headed into the kitchen. I knelt down next to him, but he crossed his arms and turned away from me.

"Guy, please." I brushed my hand across his shoulder. He flinched—even though it had to hurt him to do it—and I pulled back like I'd been burned.

"I'm sorry, baby. I had this dream—" No. I was not going to tell him about that. "I woke up, came out here, and drew the wrong conclusion. I'm sorry."

He turned to look at me. My gut flipped when I saw the pain in his face. I was never this out of control on the job. What was the matter with me?

"Connor, this isn't going to work. I need to leave."

"Please, Giggles. This won't happen again."

"Here's your tea," Cowboy said, handing him a mug. "Just the way you like it."

"How does Guy like his tea, Josh?" I worked hard to make sure I didn't sound sarcastic.

"Two sugars."

"I'll remember that."

"I know you will," he said evenly. "Why don't you get ready for work, Connor, and I'll talk some with Guy before I make supper for us."

"You don't have to do that. I can make spaghetti fine."

"Why don't you let me?"

"Yes, Connor," Guy agreed. "Josh is a fabulous cook, and I'll tell him where things are."

"You're not getting off this couch," Cowboy and I said in unison.

I felt ridiculous, but it made Guy giggle.

"Sounds like a plan," I said and retreated toward the bedroom.

"He calls you Giggles?" Brooks whispered to Guy. "It totally fits. I wish I'd thought of it. Giggles." He drew out the last word.

Guy groaned. I almost smiled.

Thirty minutes later, the three of us sat at the dining table eating really good spaghetti. I had no idea what happened while I showered— other than Brooks did the cooking. But Guy smiled at me again when I came back in the living room. He didn't say another word about leaving, and I was grateful for that.

I swirled a few strands of pasta onto my fork. "This is good, Josh. How'd you make something so fantastic in my kitchen?"

"Josh cooks for guests at his family's dude ranch," Guy said.

"You two will have to come out when Guy feels better," he said. "The four of us can go horseback riding."

"Never been," I admitted.

Brooks turned to me with a look full of pity. "Now that is just sad." He turned to Guy next, waving his fork at him. "We'll have to fix that as soon as you're able, Guy."

Guy nodded. "I say we put Connor on Hurricane." He smiled as he said it, but I was suspicious.

"You trying to get your guy killed?"

"Guy?" I arched an eyebrow. He giggled.

"Okay. Okay," he said. "Sugarpie for Connor."

"That's probably a better choice," Cowboy agreed.

"Sugarpie," I repeated, my voice rising slightly on the last syllable.

He laughed. "That's the way Dane said her name when he rode her the first time. But, Connor, she's a good horse for a beginner."

"Sugarpie," Guy repeated in a singsong voice.

"You." I pointed at Guy. "Enough making fun of the greenhorn. That's not nice."

"You're right. I'm so sorry, Connor." But he was teasing me and giggling again.

I smiled. "I forgive you, Giggles."

"I love that nickname. If you're not careful, Guy, I'm going to start calling you that."

"Yes, Guy, be very careful," I echoed.

His eyes grew round in mock alarm, but he couldn't hold the look. He started laughing. "Remember, both of you, I'm sick. Laughing hurts. Quit picking on the invalid."

"Poor baby."

"How long are you going to milk this?" Cowboy asked.

"As long as I can," Guy replied. "You know I'll do anything to get my way."

Brooks rolled his eyes. Guy grinned in triumph.

I was jealous of the easy manner between them. They would have been a good couple. But it didn't happen because of Ranger, and he was sure they wouldn't hook up again. I wasn't.

"Connor," Guy interrupted my thoughts. "You've got to get going, or you'll be late." I glanced at the kitchen clock. He was right. I had to leave right now. Just what I didn't want to do.

"You go on, Connor. I'll clean up. I've got to be heading home."

He'd better. But I couldn't say that. Not after the idiot way I'd behaved earlier. I plastered a smile on my face. "Thanks, Josh, for making dinner and for visiting."

I turned to Guy. I wanted to touch him, but I was afraid he might pull away. I kept my hands to myself. "You've got your phone handy, right? Call me if you need anything. I can swing by during my dinner break. And call me before you fall asleep, okay?"

Guy nodded.

"Thanks," I whispered. I turned to Brooks. "And thanks again, Josh. Be careful driving home."

On my way to work, I remembered Brooks's comment about me being Guy's guy. Was he trying to make a point to Guy about him and Keller? Did he think Guy and I could be a couple? Or were they going at it like rabbits now that I was gone? No, that was impossible. Brooks was not going to cheat on Keller. He didn't even want to. He was Guy's friend, and a good one. He'd been a friend to me, too, letting me off the hook tonight.

I owed him.

NINE

ONCE MY night started, nothing was easy. A DUI and an assault, and that was before Nate's wife called him to take her to the hospital. He assured me it would be a false alarm, but he never came back. Next came an accident that took forever to clear, followed by another DUI that kept me on the clock past the end of my shift. To top it off, I had to wipe vomit out of my patrol car. Long before I finished, the smell scorched my nostrils.

When I got home, the odor hit me in the face again.

"You've got to be kidding."

No one answered me. The blinds were drawn. The apartment was too quiet.

"Guy?"

The coffee table was askew. An open, near-empty bottle of No.3 London Dry Gin lay on its side atop the table, its journey to the floor stopped by a stack of magazines. The gin pooled beneath its mouth flowed to the table's edge and dripped into the carpet.

Guy's pile of blankets likewise spilled onto the carpet. A still hand stuck out underneath it, the fingers reaching for the overturned glass inches away.

"Guy!"

The fingers didn't move. Neither did the blankets. My stomach seized up. I rushed across the room and ripped the blankets back. He lay on his side, his visible eye closed as if in sleep. A crust of vomit rimmed his lips. More stained the blanket under him.

With a horrible feeling of déjà vu, I found his pulse. I shook him. "Guy, wake up."

As I pulled him back onto the couch, his eyes fluttered but didn't open. "No, Josh, let me sleep."

"It's Connor. And you're getting up."

His reply was to vomit again, though he hardly seemed aware he was doing it.

I lifted him into my arms, blankets and all, and dashed for the bathroom. He vomited once more inside the door, splattering the blankets and my chest.

"Sorry," he mumbled between heaves, conscious at last. "Sorry."

I sank to the floor and held his head up as he continued to retch, nothing coming up now. When he finished, I pulled out my phone and punched 9-1-1.

"I've got a male, Asian, about twenty-five. Ten days ago, he had his spleen removed and was treated for a concussion after a beating. He's been home four days. He's drunk nearly a bottle of gin and he's vomiting—"

"Hang up," Guy shrieked. He tried to grab for my phone, but I pushed his hand away.

"And he's conscious now, but he wasn't when I found him," I finished.

"Stop. Stop." He was crying now. He crawled away from me and curled into a fetal position against the wall. "Please, Connor, stop."

I continued answering the dispatcher's questions. He fell silent.

"Yeah, come in the street entrance. I'll open the security door when I hear the siren."

I hung up and turned to Guy. "I have to change, then I'll get you as cleaned up as I can. Stay still, okay?"

"Call back," he whispered. "Tell them not to come."

"I can't. You might need your stomach pumped."

I removed my soiled uniform in the bathroom, swiped a dry towel across my torso, then headed to the gun safe with my weapon. In the bedroom, I pulled on clean jeans and a shirt and grabbed a clean sweat suit from Guy's clothes bag.

He was still curled up on the bathroom floor, shaking all over now. I knelt beside him and ran hot water in the tub. I put in the plug and tossed in a hand towel.

"Let's see if some warm water won't stop your shakes, okay?" He wore only briefs and socks. He had to be freezing. Blobs of vomit spotted his chest. Tears streaked his face. I wrung out the towel and swiped it down his goose bumps-covered left arm and his chest.

"What happened here last night?" I kept my voice as low and gentle as I could. I didn't think I wanted to hear the answer.

"Nothing," he mumbled. A sob escaped when he opened his mouth. "Please, Connor, take me home."

"You're going to the hospital."

I continued wiping his chest, and it heaved the whole time with silent sobs.

"Please," he pleaded. "Home now."

"We have to make sure you're okay. You're going to the hospital."

He closed his eyes in resignation. I sat him up. Like a doll, he moved however I made him as I swiped the towel across his back and down the front of his thighs. I tossed it back in the tub and concentrated on getting the sweats on him. I wanted to yell at him, ask questions. But I didn't. He wasn't up to it. So I kept tending him like I was on the job in action mode, a zone where I was a lot more comfortable and competent.

When I heard the siren, I squeezed his shoulder. "Don't move. I'll be right back."

The EMTs hit the building's front entrance as I reached the security door. I led them into the apartment, told them what I could, and let them take over. Guy had stopped crying. He responded when questioned, but his voice was barely audible. He didn't move unless he was moved. The one thing he managed on his own was to keep repeating that he wanted to go home.

"Okay, Mr. Gustavsson, we're going to transport you to the hospital now," one of the EMTs said at last. He and his partner gently lifted Guy onto the stretcher.

He began to shake again with silent sobs. I followed the three of them into the living room. They headed straight out the door.

"I'll be right behind you, Guy," I called.

I grabbed my wallet and keys off the dining table and looked around the mess that was my living room one more time. Guy's phone was under the coffee table. I picked it up, too, and slipped it in my jacket pocket. I righted the gin bottle and took off.

At the emergency room, the staffer manning the desk wouldn't give me any information. I wasn't family. I gave him my name and said I'd wait anyway. I started pacing the room, fifteen medium strides in each direction. After I'd lapped the room a couple of times, I became aware that the other people in it—women mostly—were staring at me. I sat down and hunched inside my jacket, trying to keep the room's stale smell and angst-filled air at a distance.

The women were better at waiting. Each sat quiet and still, tucked into her own chair, her own untouchable space, communing with her thoughts. I didn't want to spend that much time with mine. They flew through my mind like the wailing banshees of Irish lore.

What had Guy been thinking, mixing alcohol with the painkillers he was on? He'd had to search to find that bottle, a gift from a friend when I left LA. I'd stashed it in the back of a high cupboard. And why had he drunk himself into oblivion? Did he and Brooks fight? Had they fucked? Had they not? What was taking the doctors so long?

Two hours later, a nurse a few inches shorter than me came into the room and called my name, thankfully without the "Officer." I got up and headed toward her.

"Mr. Gustavsson is being admitted and suggests you go home. He wants you to get some sleep before you have to go to work." She gave me an efficient nod of dismissal.

"I'll stay until I can see him."

"He doesn't want you to." She stared at the wall across the room for a minute, clearly uncomfortable. "He's recovering. That's all I'm allowed to say." She pressed her thin lips together, a clear sign that her need to talk to the loser waiting for word about an overdose patient was over. To be sure I got the message, she glanced at the security guard who'd entered the waiting room.

"Fine." What? Did she think I'd poured the alcohol down his throat? And didn't Guy have some nerve treating me like a nobody now? He wouldn't even let me know how he was?

I turned around and made for the exit, my mind swirling with hot, wordless anger. I didn't realize how hard I hit the door until it flew wide and stayed that way. I left it and crossed the parking lot to my Jeep.

I got in and slammed the door with such force my seat shook. I took a deep breath, then another, to calm down. I needed to get home and get some sleep so I could go back to work. But first I needed to clean up the mess so I could sleep. Fuck. And fuck Guy too.

My internal rant was interrupted by the ring of Guy's phone. I fished it out of my jacket and flipped it open.

"Guy?" The voice on the other end belonged to Brooks.

"It's Maclean. Guy's in the hospital. What the hell did you do after I left yesterday, asshole?"

"He's back in the hospital? What didn't *you* do?" he shot back.

"Wasn't me. I can't be the one who drove him to drink nearly a whole bottle of gin." I hung up.

The phone rang again. Brooks again.

"Is Guy okay?"

"How the hell should I know? He told the emergency room staff to tell me to go home, so they're not saying anything." I ran my fingers through my hair in frustration, deciding as I did to tell Brooks what I did know in clear, precise prose. "All I know is I came home from work to find him passed out on the floor, covered in vomit."

"After you went to work, I cleaned up your kitchen and left. Guy was fine *and* sober," Brooks said slowly, like he was speaking to an uncomprehending child.

He was telling the truth. He wouldn't let Guy drink like that. No way Guy would have drunk that much around him. That was something a person did alone. Shit, I'd embarrassed myself in front of Brooks again.

He didn't belabor that point. "Can I see Guy? Where are you?"

I swallowed my apology and answered his question. "I don't know if you can see him. I'm leaving the hospital because he won't see me, and they're not telling me anything. Maybe you'll have better luck." He probably would, and that made me angry all over again.

"Look," I continued, as politely as I could, "it's been nice talking with you, but I have to get home and clean my apartment so I can get some sleep and go back to work. Call the hospital yourself."

I hung up, turned the phone off, and threw it in the backseat. I peeled out of the parking lot and headed back to my place.

I STUFFED the two soiled blankets and the towels I'd used to clean the carpet into trash bags and hauled them out to the dumpster. My place still stank. I opened every window. I was debating whether to scrub the couch and carpet or go to the grocery for air freshener when the door buzzer rang. Had to be Brooks.

Wrong. When I opened the security door to the lobby, Keller stood there like an immovable force. He could look awfully big and intimidating when he wanted to. And he wanted to.

"If you want to punch me out because I insulted your boy, do it and get it over with. I've got a lot to do yet before I can get some sleep."

"So you admit you acted like an asshole on the phone?"

"Yeah, I did." I turned around and headed back into my apartment. He followed.

"Whew, that's some smell," he announced as soon as he came through the door.

I sat down at the dining table. I was getting tired. "I was debating whether to keep cleaning or go to the store for air freshener."

"You go to the store. I'll clean. Is there more besides the carpet and couch?"

"The bathroom floor. It's a lot worse."

"I'm sure I've seen worse—while being shot at, too, cop."

I couldn't believe him. Or Brooks for that matter. I'd treated the cowboy badly, and now he'd sent Keller to help me clean my place? "Why don't you want to kick my ass for being mean to your boy?"

Keller actually smiled. "Oh, I want to. But he won't let me. He's grateful for all you're doing for Guy. He insists I help you while he finds out what's up with *your* boy." He didn't even sneer as he said it.

"How'd you get here so fast?"

"I was already in Bozeman when Josh called. Lucky for you, he could understand why you were upset." Ranger's finger punched the air in my direction for emphasis.

"He's too damn good."

Keller nodded. "For me most of all. Now tell me where to find what I need."

"Cleaning supplies are in the hall closet. I'll be back as fast as I can to help you."

I was fast, but Ranger was faster. He was finishing in the bathroom when I got back. He sprayed air freshener in there while I soaked the couch and carpet with more stuff to remove bad smells.

"Come on," he said when we'd finished. "Let's go get you something to eat."

"What?"

"I'm starving. And you can't sleep in here right now. It smells like someone dumped gallons of perfume in a flower shop. You'd be asphyxiated. I'll drive. You look like you're late for bed."

"Yeah."

"We'll leave all the windows open until we get back. That should help."

He didn't say anything the whole time we were in his truck. I leaned back and closed my eyes. Maybe I fell asleep. I wasn't aware of anything again until he turned off the engine in the parking lot of a fast-food restaurant.

We went inside and ordered. He insisted on paying, and I let him. I followed him to a table once we'd loaded our trays with drinks and condiments.

He took a couple of bites of his burger. "Josh called while we were driving over here. Guy is okay, but they want him to stay in the hospital for a day or two."

"I so don't want to deal with this again." I put my burger down.

"What?" Keller stared at me.

I sighed. "I've done this before. Nothing helps if the person doesn't want to stop drinking." I stuck a french fry in my white paper ketchup cup but tossed it aside without eating it.

"What do you mean you've done this before?" Keller had quit eating, and he was looking at me like he wasn't going to let me do anything else until I explained.

"My mom. She began drinking heavily after my dad was killed on duty. He was a cop too. She eventually got sober for several years, then died of cancer."

"I'm sorry." Keller picked up his soda and took a long drink. "You're sure Guy has an alcohol problem?"

"Who else drains a bottle of gin days after getting a concussion and having surgery to remove their spleen?"

Keller considered that a moment. "Josh says he never saw evidence of a problem before."

Suddenly, I knew I was looking at the reason we had a problem now. Likely the same reason Guy had quit calling me in LA. The attack had brought Josh back into Guy's life, but the lovers weren't going to get a happily ever after, no matter how much Guy wanted it. He probably believed he had plenty of reasons to drink.

I didn't want to think about it. I'd get annoyed again. And Keller and Brooks were being too nice for me to get angry with them. "What else did Josh say?"

Keller smiled, like he couldn't ever think about his cowboy without grinning. "That Guy is convinced you won't want him back at your place, but he wants to return there."

"Guy said that?" I felt lots better.

"He did." He stood up and picked up his plastic tray. "So why don't I get you home so you can sleep on it, cop? I think you get cranky when you get behind on your sleep."

Back in the truck, he changed the subject, and he was enlightening.

"Look, I don't know Guy," he said as he pulled out onto Main Street. "Josh says Guy always felt like his parents didn't want him, like they adopted him and regretted it."

He shrugged. "It might be true. Josh says Guy stayed on or near campus the whole time he was in college, even though his parents lived ten miles away. Even in summer. They paid for it. Guy thought he was always in their way somehow. Now that he can't do much of anything, he must feel that way again."

He checked his rearview mirror and switched lanes to turn onto Nineteenth. "Josh wants to help you. Guy took it hard when Josh and I got together. He loved Josh, while Josh thought they were best friends with benefits. He feels bad about that. So he'll be there for Guy. But Guy wants you there too."

"Josh is sure about that?"

Keller cocked his head at me. "Guy told Josh he hoped you'd visit him tomorrow. But now he wants you to sleep. He's worried about you, that he's set you up to get hurt at work."

Keller stopped in front of my apartment. I opened the truck door, stepped out, then leaned back in. "Thanks for your help today. I owe you."

He shook his head. "Stay alert tonight, hey?"

"Yeah."

That night, I didn't let myself think about Guy except on my dinner break. A memory of my dad came back to me too.

I was thirteen. Mom already drank too much some weekends, though things wouldn't get awful until Dad died two years later. They'd been out with friends and come back late, and she was drunk and argumentative. She yelled heavily slurred words I couldn't make out in my bedroom upstairs. Dad could vent an Irish temper when he wanted to, but he kept it in check with her. That night, he raised his voice twice, each time to say, "That's enough, Jean."

The second time, a hard slap followed. I thought he'd hit her, and I ran down the stairs, determined to protect her no matter what he did to me. When I entered the living room, he was seated on the couch, holding her in his arms, his cheek a fiery red.

"Shh," he whispered to her, rocking her as she cried halting, ugly sobs against his chest. "It's going to be okay, Jeannie. We'll be okay, love. This is worth the seeing through."

I turned and fled the room. If he saw me, he never spoke of it. Neither did I. And I never mentioned it to Mom. I was ashamed for them. I stuffed the image down deep in my memory.

I played it through a couple of times, watching his gentleness with her. Now, I saw his love for her, and his devotion, strong as the commitment he showed her until the day he died. I thought about the great mom she became again when she quit drinking when I was eighteen. I remembered the good times she and I had after that, how much she loved me, how much I missed her.

And I knew what I was going to do for Guy.

TEN

BY THE end of the shift, I'd heard from Nate. Baby Andrew Nathan Hamilton weighed in at seven pounds and was twenty inches long. He was born grinning and bald. I was invited to see him at the hospital around noon. I told Nate I'd be there.

I went home, took a nap, and got up around eleven to head to the hospital again.

I stopped in first at Jenna Hamilton's room. Nate sat on the edge of the bed, grinning like a crazy man and whispering to a little blue bundle cradled in his arms. He introduced us right away.

"Andy, this is Daddy's good buddy Connor. He's a cop, just like Daddy." He raised his arms so I could see the sleeping face beneath the blue knitted hat. "Connor, this is my son, Andy."

"He must take after your wife. He's pretty good-looking for a baby."

"Like you've seen lots of babies."

"Hey, I delivered one."

"Haven't we all." He shook his head. "I gotta tell you, it's a lot different when you're watching and it's your own coming."

"I imagine. How's the wife?"

"She's good. She's taking a shower right now, isn't she, Little Man?" he cooed to his son. Then, like he realized he looked silly, he asked, "You want to hold him?"

"Heck, no. I might drop him."

"You didn't drop the one you delivered, did you?"

"Of course not."

"I trust you."

Nate's words struck deep, warming my chest. We were on our way to being friends, and I needed one about now.

"I appreciate that, but I think I'll wait until he's bigger."

He laughed. "They get lots squirmier as they get bigger. Right now, they lie in your arms pretty still, unless they're hungry or want their diapers changed." He looked back at his son and said, "We all get to go home soon. Little Man's going to love it."

"There goes your sleep schedule."

"Speaking of that, you don't look like you're getting much. What's up?"

His question was friendly. I couldn't figure out how much to tell him. "A friend is in the hospital. As a matter of fact, I'm going to visit him next."

"Who?"

I swallowed hard and said it. "Guy Gustavsson."

"The artist you saved from being beaten to death?" Nate wrinkled his nose. "Tell me you know better than to get involved with the vics."

I'd figured that was coming. "I do. I knew him before." I brushed my forefinger tentatively along Andy's cheek. "I met him during one of his art shows in LA."

"You met him once in LA., and you saved him, and now you're visiting him in the hospital?" His voice pitched louder near the end. "Please tell me you don't have some savior complex."

"It's not like that, Nate."

The bathroom door flew open. A bright, happy voice entered the room seconds before a small brunette in yoga pants and a Bozeman PD T-shirt did.

"Boy, do I feel a thousand times better." She stopped short when she saw me. She must have felt the tension. She cast a wary look at her husband. "Sorry, I didn't realize we had visitors."

He beamed at her. "Babe, this is Connor Maclean. Connor, this is Jenna."

I nodded. "Nice to meet you."

She looked at her husband and arched one brow. "You said I was going to like your partner, Nate. What's up? Why are you two fighting when all he should be doing is admiring our son?"

Boy, she got right to the point. "Nate and I are just having a difference of opinion about whether it's wise for me to visit a man I saved from a beating, even though I knew him before I arrived in Bozeman."

She looked at her husband and a slow, easy grin spread across her face. "You asked me out after you gave me a speeding ticket," she reminded him. "What's the difference?"

How did she know Guy and I were romantically involved? Had she outed me? Shit, could I save this? I glanced at Nate, but he was smiling at his wife, remembering that traffic stop. She was watching him, too, a flirty look in her eyes. Neither of them seemed the least concerned that this might be a gay relationship. "Yeah, Nate, like she said." I gestured lamely at his wife.

He shook his head and cooed at his son, "Andy, what is Daddy supposed to do with these two?"

Andy was one smart baby. He didn't answer.

I stuck my hand out toward his mom. "I'm going to like you, Jenna." She shook my hand with both of hers, squeezing warmly. Her gesture said she knew, and she was fine with it. I felt the tension melt out of my shoulders. These two were going to be good friends.

"Nice to meet you, Connor."

"Andy is one cute baby, Jenna. Clearly, he takes after you."

She laughed, and it sounded like bells jingling. "Of course he does."

"Enough." Nate stood up and carefully positioned his son on his shoulder, then pecked his wife on the cheek. "You ready to take Little Man home, babe?"

"Yesterday," she replied, reaching to take the baby from him.

She'd barely finished speaking when a nurse appeared with a wheelchair.

"I won't keep you two. Andy"—I looked once more at the baby, now settled in his mom's arms—"go easy on your old man, okay?"

Nate smiled at his son and gave me a meaningful look. "Be careful, Connor."

"I promise. But don't worry about me." I grinned at his wife. "Be seeing you, Jenna."

"Visit us anytime, Connor."

I left them with the nurse and headed for the elevator, wondering what landmines I was headed for next. I wanted to be like my dad in my relationship with Guy. Could I?

As I neared his room, I hit a spot where I could see in without his seeing me unless he turned around. He still looked like a little kid in the hospital bed, but at least he wasn't as white as the sheets anymore. He wore a light blue gown and a heavy dark blue sling on his right arm.

He was awake, and he and Brooks were watching a game show. Josh sat in a chair on the far side of the bed. I sucked in a breath. Guy heard it, turned around, and saw me. His eyes widened in something like fear. I was surprised when my reaction was grief.

Josh turned next. He was glad to see me. "Hey, Connor. How was your night?"

"Long but uneventful, thanks. Where's Ranger?"

"You didn't call him that to his face, did you?" Josh asked anxiously. A funny look crossed his face, like he was imagining the possibility and wanted to see it.

"No. Is he around?"

"He's at the ranch, working on a dining room set for some music star who's bought a big home in Paradise Valley."

"Huh?"

"He crafts custom furniture. He's filling three rooms for this guy. He's been busy nearly full time since he started his business," he said proudly.

"I'm even more grateful for his help yesterday. Tell him I said thanks again."

He nodded. He looked from me to Guy, and my eyes followed his. Guy studied his sling like he meant to paint a masterpiece on it, or he was afraid to look at me. I wanted to give him a hug and smooth away his mixed-up feelings, and his pain, and all that had happened to him. I wanted to persuade him to adore *me,* and that's what I went with. I walked over to the bed and put my arm around him.

"You look a lot better today. How are you feeling?"

His lower lip quivered, but he didn't answer. Like I had with Nate's baby, I brushed my finger across his cheek.

"It's okay, Guy. Everything's going to be okay."

"I'm so sorry, Connor."

I rested my hand on the side of his face. "I know you are."

"Later," Brooks said. He got up in one smooth movement and slipped from the room.

"Thanks, Josh," I called after him.

I sat on the bed. Mindful of Guy's right arm, I pulled him gently to my chest. "Why, baby?"

"Too much," he whispered.

I couldn't figure if he meant he was in too much physical pain, or he cared too much for Josh, or he couldn't tell me yet what made him drink the gin. It didn't matter, I guess. I'd decided to see things through.

"Everything's going to be okay," I said again. "I'll help you, if you let me."

He put his good arm around me, grabbed me hard, and held on.

ELEVEN

THE NEXT morning, Guy called to say the doctors were ready to discharge him.

"They'll release you this afternoon?"

"No, now."

"Right now?"

His response was tentative. "Yes, if you want me."

"Of course I want you. I wouldn't have gotten you this great welcome home present if I didn't, Giggles."

"You got me a present?" He was as excited as a little kid. "What is it?"

"That would wreck the surprise, wouldn't it? Let me take a quick shower, and I'll be there in half an hour to bring you home." I liked saying that word to him.

"I'll be waiting. And, Connor, thanks."

GUY WAS dressed and sitting in a chair when I walked into his room. He wasn't alone.

Leaning against the bed was a thin man, about five ten, maybe forty years old, with straight dark brown hair liberally salted with gray at the temples. The natural accent was a handsome addition to his prominent, tanned cheekbones and statuesque nose topped by silver-framed glasses. They were engaged in a serious conversation that stopped the second I walked into the room. The stranger wore jeans and a shirt instead of a white coat, so he wasn't a doctor. I was immediately on guard.

He sensed it, but he was friendly as he held out his hand. He had a firm grip when he shook. "I'm Walker Stevens. You must be Connor."

"I am. Are you on the hospital staff?"

"No, I'm a pastor. I've visited Guy a couple of times now, when I've been here to see parishioners."

I was hearing this for the first time? But what I said was, "Guy hasn't had a lot of visitors. That's nice of you. I'm sure he's appreciated it."

"It has been nice," he said. He flashed me a grin that said he was glad to see me, and I relaxed.

"We've been talking about some programs that might help Guy as he recovers."

"Physical therapy programs?"

"Something like that." He smiled warmly to cover what he wasn't saying.

I let it go. "Are you a free man now, Guy? Can you leave?"

"As soon as the nurse with the wheelchair shows up." He looked at his bag of stuff atop the wheeled table at the foot of the bed.

I walked over and picked it up.

"I'll let you two take off," the pastor said. "I know he's eager to get home." He stepped toward the door, then turned to Guy. "I'll call you in a day or two."

"Thanks, Walker. I'd like that."

"Good to meet you, Connor." He disappeared out the door.

I gave Guy a quizzical look.

"He visited me once the last time I was here and twice this time. He's easy to talk to," he offered.

The nurse arrived with the wheelchair, Guy sat in it, and we were on our way home.

"I can't wait for you to see your present," I said as we walked toward my front door.

"I hope it tastes good."

"Are you going to be surprised."

He shrieked as soon as he entered the apartment. The cushy forest-green easy chair that could flip into a near bed at the touch of a button occupied the prime spot in the living room. That it wasn't beige and I'd put a big red bow on it made it hard to miss.

"You got this for me?"

"So you'll be more comfortable when you're watching TV and resting. But when you want to sleep, take the bed. We can both sleep there." I casually slipped in the last bit. "Want some tea?"

"Connor, this is too much. The couch is fine, and I don't deserve this, and—"

I took him in my arms. I meant to hug him lots more from now on. It seemed to calm him down and lift him up. It clearly showed him my intentions for us. I was ready to give up being subtle about that.

"Shh. I want you to be comfortable as long as you're here. And you can stay here as long as you like. Got that?"

He shook his head but didn't say any more, and I led him to the chair and sat him down in it. "You enjoy your present, and I'll make you some tea and a sandwich."

He'd pushed the chair into full recline by the time I came back with the food, and his eyes were closed. I put his plate and cup on the table beside the chair, leaned over, and kissed his forehead as I moved it back into the upright position. His eyes flew open.

"Fun ride, right? You're going to like this chair, I know it."

"It's wonderful." He smiled mischievously. "And it's big enough that we can sit in it together."

"You weren't supposed to notice that so fast. Eat up." I pushed the plate closer to him.

"If I do, will you sit here with me for a bit?"

"Sure. I can do that before I need to get some sleep. Meanwhile, I'll put your bag in the bedroom and arrange your meds in the bathroom."

"Maybe you should have been a nurse instead of a cop," he said through a mouthful of ham, cheddar cheese, and bread.

"No talking with your mouth full," I called from the bedroom.

"You missed your calling," he yelled back. I was happy to hear it. I liked the teasing Guy so much better.

He'd eaten half the sandwich when I returned to the living room. "Come on." He patted his chair. "Let's try sitting here together."

I helped him stand and flopped down in the chair. "Hey, this is pretty comfy. I may have to fight you for it once you're healthy."

"You won't win," he insisted, his eyes flashing brightly. "I fight dirty."

"I do recall." I held out my arms. He sat down slowly, carefully protecting his right arm, and laid his head on my chest.

"That was some week in LA." He sighed. Like the sex fiend he'd been then, he ground his ass into my lap.

"Hey!"

"Just trying to get comfortable." He let go one of his high-pitched squeals, and my prick hardened so fast his squirmy little ass had to feel it.

"Poor Connor. I can't do anything."

I rested my head on his. "One of these days soon. You'll be able to do anything you want."

I should have waited a few more weeks to say that.

TWELVE

WHEN ALEX Whittaker called to ask again about meeting Guy, I decided an outing was what Guy needed. True to his promise when we met at the station, the kid had taken me on a couple of mountain bike rides on intermediate trails that showed his toughness. He was easygoing and enthusiastic about keeping a conversation going, too, not moody and sullen like so many teens I met on the job. I gave up wondering why I was also involved with the other victim in Guy's case and accepted that it worked for everyone. I liked Alex more each time I saw him.

Still, it took some doing to talk Guy into meeting the Whittakers for dinner. He was nervous. "I owe my life to a fifteen-year-old kid, and I don't know what to say to him."

"Thank you is enough. Ask him about his art. He admires yours. He's told me so several times."

Guy looked at me like I was a simpleton and my suggestion too dumb for words.

"Relax. It's going to be easy. You're *his* hero. He wants to know all about your art and the gallery. He's thrilled that a real artist wants to meet him. He'll be the nervous one."

"He'll be terrified once he gets a look at me. I look awful." He was standing in front of the bathroom mirror in nothing but sweatpants and his sling, studying his appearance.

"You look great." I walked up behind him, wrapped my arms around him, and spoke to his reflection. "Your stitches are long gone."

He grimaced. "I still have scabs on my face and bald spots on my head."

"The scabs are tiny, and we'll comb your hair to cover the spots." I kissed each one of them.

He didn't giggle. He didn't even smile.

"The kid is in awe of your talent. He's not going to notice how you look."

"He's an artist. He'll notice."

"I think you look great. Sexy, even." I kissed his earlobe.

"Do not make fun of the sick boy." He tried to wiggle away from me, but I wouldn't let him.

"You're not sick. You're healing nicely. *Very* nicely."

"Humph!" He blew out a breath that made his bangs fly up.

I pinched his waist the tiniest bit, goosing him. He squirmed and yelped. "Careful!"

"I'm being careful. Come on. Let's give you a bath."

"See how sexy I am? You're going to bathe me like an invalid."

"Stop." I spun him around gently. Trailing my lips along his jaw, I felt the pleasant scrape of his whiskers, then kissed him hard. "Nothing like an invalid," I promised.

I sat him down on the edge of the tub and started the water running, then moved in front of him and gently tugged at his sweatpants. "Up you go." I removed them and his sling, and reseated him. He squealed at the coldness.

"Shh. I'll warm you up in a second." I leaned in close and teased his lips, not quite kissing them.

"What are you doing?" His voice quivered.

I knelt in front of him. "Getting you ready for your bath."

Spreading his legs, I slipped between them and ran my fingers up the insides of his legs to his crotch. He sucked in a breath. I blew on his dick and dipped my head low, inhaling his salty musk. When I licked him, I tasted the ocean. He thickened, and I swallowed him down, not pulling back until his whole body vibrated.

"Careful. The bathroom is the most dangerous room in the home," I teased.

I reached a hand into the water to test the temperature, then mouthed him again. He moaned, slapped his left hand on my shoulder, and held on tight as I worked him hard, once more stopping before he could shoot.

"For example," I whispered, sliding my tongue up his flat stomach and circling his belly button, "some people get scalded in the bath." I turned the water off. "But not you. The water's perfect."

"Connor," he whimpered.

"You're going to love this bath, I promise. Nobody's ever given you a bath like this. Hold on, now."

I stood up and stripped off my clothes. Mindful of his right arm, I lifted him, stepped into the tub, and lowered us both into the water. It sloshed around in gentle waves as I sat, settled him on my lap, and kissed him again.

"There. Safe as can be." I nibbled at his neck and ran the washcloth down his side. He began to giggle.

"There's a sexy sound. No invalid in this tub."

He kissed back ferociously, chewing at my lower lip, thrusting his tongue deep, stoking my need. Keeping my right arm firmly around him, I smoothed my left hand up and down his thighs and grabbed him for a quick pull. He shrieked.

"Too soon?" I chuckled into his open mouth. "Okay." I set my hand to roaming down one of his thighs and up the other, then up his belly until I tweaked a nipple. He inhaled sharply and breathed out a long sigh that sounded like "Please."

"The noises you make. I can hardly stand it." I lifted him slightly and thrust my needy prick between his thighs. "There. Better."

"Poor Connor."

"No longer."

"You're much longer," he quipped, then began a fit of giggling that left him shaking in my arms.

"Definitely longer," I agreed, and he shook still more. "Enough with the giggles," I scolded in mock frustration. Taking up the washcloth, I wrapped it around his length and tugged. He moaned.

"Yes, baby?" I kissed him again, all the while moving my hand around him.

He clasped his thighs around my prick, rocking back and forth, a slick friction of water and his hard muscles against my harder flesh. All the while, he kept his eyes shut tight. His face was taut with his need, and with concentration, too, as he rubbed against me.

"Beautiful baby, come for me," I whispered, pumping him hard.

He yelled, and I captured the sound with my mouth. I felt his release, and mine followed, cum jetting like a geyser, water sloshing over the tub and onto the floor until we both stilled. He sighed and kissed me hard and long, before pulling his lips away at last and giggling again.

"What?" I searched his face, trying to figure out what he was thinking.

"Now I need a bath," he exclaimed. "So do you."

"I think you're right."

The water was cold by the time we got out, but Guy had finally relaxed.

ALEX AND Kellie were seated at a table when we arrived at the Mexican restaurant he'd chosen. We were right on time, but they already had their drinks, and Alex's soda was half gone.

"See," I whispered to Guy as we moved through the dining room. "He's the nervous one."

Guy took one look at the kid, who was moving awkwardly to stand up as we approached, and a change came over him. He squared his shoulders, and he was once again the charming, affable artist I'd met in LA, eager to put everyone at ease.

"Alex, I'm so honored to meet you," he said sincerely, putting his left hand on the kid's shoulder and looking up into his face. "Thank you hardly seems enough to say for all I owe you. You saved my life. Lots of men wouldn't have been brave enough to come through that door."

The teen blushed deep enough that his face nearly matched the color of his tousled hair. His mother, whose own red hair fell neatly around her shoulders, sat back and beamed.

"How are you feeling, Mr. Gustavsson?" Alex asked like he'd been rehearsed. When he added, "You're looking better," and glanced at his mom, I knew he had. He shook my hand, then seemed at a loss for words. He'd forgotten the script.

I reached out to shake hands with his mom. "Good to see you again, Kellie." I hadn't seen her since that night at the gallery, but Alex had talked enough about her that I felt I knew her a bit. I figured he'd talked about me to her too.

"Thanks for the dinner invitation, and for your interest in Alex."

"He's doing more for me than vice versa."

She shook her head. "It's always good for a teenage boy to have positive male role models." She turned to Guy, now seated in the chair opposite her. "Alex is happy to meet you, Mr. Gustavsson."

"Let's skip right to first names, all of us, okay?" he said, smiling broadly and casting his spell over both of them. "Alex, I want to hear all about your art. Connor told me what a fabulous portrait artist you are. What else do you do?"

The kid leaned forward, putting his elbows on the table. "I do manga, in color mainly," he said shyly.

Guy nodded enthusiastically, captivating me with his magic too. I sat back to watch him. "Individual drawings or books?" he asked.

"Alex does both, but his books are fantastic," his mom interjected, pulling a large purse up off the floor. "Would you like to see?"

"Mom!" The artist looked horror-struck, but Guy was already reaching for the notebook she held out.

In seconds, Guy and Alex had their heads together like two kids, the younger of them flipping through the notebook excitedly, pausing now and again to point things out. Guy was right there with him, asking questions and saying complimentary things. From the little I could see of the notebook, the praise was warranted. Alex's notebook contained page after page of colorful, detailed fantasy landscapes, creatures, and people. I was impressed.

Kellie and I worked around them to order more soda and an assortment of nachos, burritos, and fajitas. We continued a side conversation about Alex and school—he liked art and band and little else—and how she'd always been a single mom. I put her at ease when I skipped to the part of my life where my mom was one too. She opened up a bit about how she'd moved to Bozeman to go to college, met a guy who disappeared as soon as Alex was on the way, been abandoned by an aunt, her only family, and started her own cleaning business to support herself and Alex. She was tough and protective, like the first time I met her, but she was proud of her son too. She had every reason to be. She should have been equally proud of herself, but she was modest instead.

I asked how Alex's pizza job was going.

"He's quit. I'd always worried about him working late, and what happened that night cinched it."

I nodded, hoping that would make her worried look disappear. But it didn't. She lowered her voice so Guy and Alex couldn't hear and asked me what was on her mind. "Do you think we need to be worried about Jimmy Mitchell coming after Alex? Detective Haney says no, that it's his pattern to commit a crime and move on. But I'm afraid."

"Haney is pretty familiar with Mitchell. He's followed him for a long time," I answered slowly. What should I tell her? Guy was still afraid, too, and a voice in the back of my mind occasionally reminded me that maybe he should be because Mitchell had deviated from his pattern by moving from burglary to robbery. "Mitchell's past MO has been to hit empty businesses or homes. He'll probably go back to that. And it's likely he's moved on. We haven't found him."

I leaned back in my chair, hoping a more relaxed position might put her at ease. "Remember, he doesn't know Alex's name. We've kept that out of the papers. But Guy has taken precautions at the gallery. There's a security system now, with video. And he's been avoiding returning to his apartment. Is Alex still afraid?"

"You mean his bad dreams? They've stopped. He's quit talking about the attack altogether." Kellie sighed. "I don't know whether that's good or bad."

"That's pretty normal, and good," I encouraged. "But if you're worried, there are a few things you might consider at your house—simple things. Buy cheap alarms for the windows. You need to tell Alex about them so he doesn't set them off. And I can come by and look over your door locks and make recommendations. I'd be happy to. Another good trick is to put filled dog food and water bowls near a window so they can be seen from outside. That's a known deterrent."

"I can do that. And maybe I will take you up on the home visit— if you're sure you don't mind?"

"Not at all. I'm off again in a couple of days. We'll set something up."

Our food came, served family style, and we all quieted down to pass plates and eat. I enjoyed watching Alex take big servings of everything, pile sour cream and salsa atop that, and dig in. I glanced at Guy to see his reaction, but he was pushing his fork and his small helpings around his plate. His mind was on something else.

"What kind of job are you looking for now, Alex?" he asked once the kid had taken a break from eating.

"Anything," he admitted with a sigh. "It's a bad time to look because most of the summer jobs are already promised to college kids. I'm going to have to take anything I can get."

"What would you like to do, though?" Guy prodded.

Alex cocked his head and studied his inquisitor, like he was having some kind of internal debate. "Honestly?"

When Guy nodded, he went for it, a self-conscious blush spreading across his face as he talked. "I'd love to work in an art gallery. I want to learn everything I can about art and the business of art."

Guy grinned. "How would you like to work for me? I need to open the gallery again, and I'm going to need help because of my shoulder."

The kid's mouth dropped open. Kellie's almost did, too, but she immediately moved to lower Guy's sense of obligation and her son's excited expectations. "You do not owe my son a job, Mr. Gustavsson. He did what anyone would do."

"It's Guy, Kellie. And Alex did far more for me than he had to, or the law required. Don't ever kid yourself about that." He folded his napkin and placed it alongside his plate. "Furthermore, I do need help, and I'd love to help Alex after what he's done for me." He turned to her son, whose face was nearly as red as his hair once again. "When can you start, Alex, and when can you work?"

He answered quickly and a little too loudly, partly from excitement, partly to ward off more objections from his mom. "School ends in two weeks. Until then, I can be there every afternoon around two thirty on school days, anytime on weekends. And I can work as late as you need. Once school ends, I can work every day, whenever. Will that work?"

Guy laughed in delight, like I hadn't heard him laugh since LA. "That's great. I want to open for half days, from two thirty to eight, the Wednesday after Memorial Day. Is a quitting time of eight o'clock okay with you, Kellie?"

She wasn't ready to back down yet. "You're sure about this? It isn't a charity job?"

"I'm sure, and it isn't a charity job. I needed help before the attack, because the gallery was doing quite well. I need help for sure now, because I can't use my right shoulder. But I also intend to teach Alex all I know about sales and the art business, as much as he's interested in. I'll pay thirteen dollars an hour to start, and employ him thirty hours a week in summer, less during the school year. He'll always be done by eight o'clock, and I'll make sure he gets home safely once I can drive again. How does that sound?"

"It's a deal," Alex said firmly.

"That's very kind, Guy," Kellie added. "Alex won't let you down."

Guy grinned broadly. "I know he won't."

"So when do you get your arm back, Guy?" Alex continued.

Guy's grin vanished, but he kept his tone upbeat so neither Whittaker noticed. "I start physical therapy soon, and the doctors say I should be good as new in two to three months."

"When will you start painting again?" Alex's question was full of enthusiasm, like he couldn't wait to watch Guy at work. I winced inwardly as soon as I heard it.

But Guy was not going to let Alex be embarrassed. "Very soon, I hope."

"Do you need help with anything?" Kellie asked.

"No. Everything's good. Connor is taking great care of me. I'm fortunate."

"How about when your physical therapy begins?" she persisted. "Are you going to be able to manage that? Because I had a friend go through PT last year, and a bunch of us had to help her manage the crazy time schedule she had."

Surprise crossed his face, and I paid close attention. He hadn't said anything yet about his therapy schedule.

"They want to schedule me so early in the morning that Connor won't even be off work some days," he admitted.

Kellie nodded knowingly. "You tell me when you need to be there. I can take you if Connor can't. I work late afternoons and evenings mainly."

"You're serious?" Guy asked. "I hadn't even mentioned this to Connor yet because I didn't know what we were going to do."

"When do you start?"

"The Tuesday after Memorial Day."

"You call me. End of story."

ON THE ride home, Guy was nearly bouncing, he was so happy.

"Alex is going to work out fine, don't you think? I can't wait to get back into the gallery now that I know what he's like and he'll be helping me. Weren't his drawings great?"

"I was impressed."

"He's gifted. I want to help him all I can, and not just because I owe him. I'm going to have to do some research into manga."

"You'll figure it out. Heck, you probably know somebody who knows somebody."

"Wouldn't it be great if it worked out that way?" He skipped on to his next subject. "Kellie is incredible, isn't she? She's a great mom with a fabulous kid, she's got her own business, and she's done it all herself."

"She's impressive. She's going to be pretty helpful with physical therapy too."

"You're not upset about that, are you? I was going to tell you eventually, but I didn't want to burden you with more."

"It's fine. I'm glad you got it all figured out. I'm sorry I can't help much with that."

"You're doing all the important things, Connor, honestly." He took my hand and squeezed it. "I don't know where I'd be without you."

I squeezed back. "I'd be awfully alone in a new town without you, Giggles."

THIRTEEN

A FEW mornings later, I was sleeping in after a night off work. I'd gotten over to Kellie's and installed new door locks for her. Beyond that, all my time was filled with taking care of Guy. It had taken some patience too.

He'd had two doctors' appointments the day before and was moody after, even though they'd said he was coming along fine. They were easing off his pain meds, and he hurt, and he was tired of all of it. On top of that, he didn't want any help, but he didn't want me out of his sight. When we couldn't agree on anything to watch on TV that night, I headed off to the bedroom to read and eventually fell asleep. He stayed alone in the living room all night.

His loud cursing jerked me awake, and I dashed into the other room. He was silhouetted against the window and the midmorning sun, madly stomping on a flipped-over artist's palette, paintbrush, and piece of paper. Already large splotches of blue and green paint stained the beige carpet. The easel lay on its side next to the mess. Dollar signs blinked in my mind as I focused on him, trying to figure what had happened, what to do about it, and whether my security deposit was going to cover the carpet damage.

"Guy?"

He wheeled around to face me, clutching at his right arm as he did. He was wearing a sweat suit but no sling. Clearly, he'd been trying to paint, but with which hand? Had he reinjured himself?

"Leave me alone," he cried. "Get out!"

"And go where?" I yelled back. He went still. I took a step toward him and lowered my voice. "Tell me what happened."

"I dropped the palette and brush," he spit out, "and the paper fell on the carpet." He moved to his easy chair, leaving a trail of colored footprints behind, and slumped into it. "I can't paint anymore."

"You can't paint *right now*."

He ignored that. He turned toward the wall and stared at it, picturing the end of his career, I guess. I was too concerned about the carpet damage to think up anything consoling to say. I took the palette, paintbrush, and paper into the kitchen and put the first two in the sink. The crumpled, painted paper went into the trash. It bore a few blue smears and a glob of green, nothing resembling a shape or an image. I returned to the living room with a sopping dishcloth and went to work on the mess.

"Do you want to talk about it?"

"No," he snapped. "My life is over."

"It's not," I said gently.

"What do you know?" He rose up, walked into the bedroom, and slammed the door behind him.

I was nearly finished cleaning up—a few faint smudges remained on the carpet—when the bedroom door opened and Guy emerged, his clothes duffel in his left hand, his cellphone in his right.

"I'll pay for the damage," he said without looking at me. He headed for the window, stepped around the easel, dropped the duffel, and stared outside. I stopped between the kitchen and the living room, waiting for him to tell me what was going on. But he stayed quiet.

"Let me get dressed, and we'll go out for breakfast, okay?"

"The cab's here," he replied, turning from the window. He winced as he lifted the bag again and headed for the door.

"Where are you going?"

"Home."

"What?"

"I'll pay you, like I said. Throw all of my painting stuff away. Thank you again for all of your help. I appreciate it, but I need to go home now." He dropped the duffel to open the door. When he picked it up, he flinched again.

"Guy, this is not a good idea. You still need help with things. You're in pain right now. Let me get dressed and take care of the cab, but you stay here. Please."

"It's time I figured out how to take care of myself."

He opened the door and turned toward me. He even managed to look at me. His face was a mask of anger and pain. "I need to be in my own space. I have things to figure out. I'll call you in a few days." He disappeared, leaving the door open. He couldn't close it.

"Don't do this. You're not even cleared to drive yet." I yelled after him. "Send the cab away, and let's talk about this."

But he was gone. I went to the window and watched him hand the bag to the driver. He let the man open the back door for him and climbed in. In another minute, the cab pulled away, its brake lights blinking twice at the corner before it turned out of sight.

What the hell did he think he was doing?

I stomped to the kitchen to make coffee, but I spilled grounds all over the counter and water all over my gym shorts before I succeeded. While it brewed, I took a shower. I dropped the soap three times and slipped and bumped my head on the soap dish when I tried to pick it up.

I toweled off, pulled on sweats, and headed back to the coffeepot. But when I tried to pour some into a cup, it hit my hand instead, and I dropped the cup and it broke. Hot liquid splattered my bare feet.

"Son of a bitch!" I yelled, and the old lady in the upstairs apartment dropped something. Or maybe she threw it. It clunked right above my head. At least it didn't break. "Sorry," I yelled again.

I wasn't, but I felt like I had to apologize to her. I felt like I wanted to break something else too, but I didn't. I put the coffeepot down on the counter, abandoned the kitchen, and tromped into the spare room. For an hour, I pumped iron like a maniac, banging weights together when I changed them and grunting with every lift. But I had no one there to hear even that. I was alone. I hated it. It hurt like hell. And I couldn't do anything about it. I couldn't believe it.

Eventually, I sent Guy a text asking if he was okay. I got one back.

"*Please leave me alone*" was all it said.

I was mad enough to do that.

AT MIDAFTERNOON I called him. He didn't answer. A half hour later, I was on the sidewalk in front of the gallery. The front door was locked up tight, the "Reopening Soon; Thank You for Your Concern" sign untouched in the front window. The back door was locked too.

I let myself in with my key, calling Guy's name as I did. He wasn't anywhere downstairs. I climbed up the steep stairs to his apartment, being sure to make lots of noise, and knocked on the door. No answer.

"Guy. Are you in there?"

When I got no response, I banged louder. "Guy! Are you okay? I'm coming in."

I tried the doorknob. It turned right away, but the chain guard abruptly stopped my entry. So he was in there. But in what kind of shape? I pictured him passed out in the bathroom. "Guy! Let me in! I'm worried about you."

"Go home, Connor." His voice, faint and strained, came from far inside the apartment.

"Not unless you come with me." To make my point, I pushed the door open as far as I could, then sat down on the top step and leaned back against it. No way was he going to shut me out.

"Come on, Guy. Come back to my place. Let me make you something to eat and we'll talk about this. Open the door."

"I don't want to talk, Connor." His voice sounded closer now, but he wasn't going to cooperate. "Go home. Thanks for putting up with me so long. I'm grateful, but I need to start taking care of myself now, and figuring things out."

"Guy, please. I miss you…. This is a temporary setback. We can—"

A hard shove on the door startled me off my perch. I had to move fast to stop from falling down the stairs as he pushed the door shut. The deadbolt clicking into place was the loud period at the end of his nonverbal statement.

I rested my forehead on the closed door. "Please don't do this, Guy." No sound came from the other side. "At least set the damned alarm, would you?" I yelled.

I stomped down the stairs and drove home. Walking into the living room, I spotted Guy's pile of blankets on the couch and something close to pain hit me in the chest. I was furious with him. I grabbed the blankets, took them into the bedroom, and tossed them in the closet. There, I spotted some of his clothes. I backed away from them and headed for the bathroom. Some of his meds were on the counter.

His stuff was everywhere in the apartment. He'd all but moved in. I should have enjoyed being alone again. I'd been alone for years by choice. But I didn't like it now, and I didn't want it. I missed a damaged, depressed artist who likely wouldn't cheer up anytime soon. Who sometimes drank too much. Who'd kicked me down the stairs, for crying out loud.

I missed him badly. That was the truth of it. I'd moved to Bozeman for him. Living with him had grown on me fast. I liked having him to come home to, to take care of, to hold close. He made me laugh. He made me mad. He made me hot as hell. He made me feel something I didn't want to examine too closely. I wanted him back, baggage and all.

TWO HOURS into my shift that night, I'd buzzed Main Street more than usual. All the lights in Guy's apartment were on. At midnight, as I was taking a break to eat, they were still on. I parked the patrol car in the alley and dialed his phone. It went straight to voice mail.

"It's me. I'm on my lunch break. I'm in the alley, and I'm coming up there. I don't want you to be scared." He didn't pick up. I hung up, unlocked the door, and started up the stairs, calling out as I climbed.

"Guy? It's Connor. Let me in, okay?"

I didn't hear a sound. When I rapped on the door, he didn't answer.

"Guy, come on. I'm worried here. Answer the door." I tried the doorknob, not expecting any luck after his actions in the afternoon. But it turned, and the door swung open. My heartbeat accelerated. I had no idea what I'd find, or say.

"Guy?" I stepped quickly through the kitchen and peered into the living room.

He sat on the couch, an empty glass in his hand. On the coffee table were a half-empty vodka bottle and an open bottle of tonic. He turned toward me slowly, squinting like he was trying to focus. His eyes were red and swollen and drunk.

"Has the door been unlocked all night?"

"No," he mumbled. "I opened it and disconnected the alarm, too, when you called."

"Good." I nodded. "How are you feeling?"

"Great. I feel great. How 'bout you? Hey"—he pointed to my uniform—"are you working?"

"I'm on lunch break."

"That's right. You said that. There's nothing here to eat. I looked." He leaned unsteadily toward the coffee table and clunked his glass on top of it.

"When's the last time you ate?"

He paused a moment, thinking. "Your place."

"You left my place fourteen hours ago. Have you had any pain meds since?"

"No." He put his head in his hands. "I hurt. I thought the vodka might help, but it didn't. And I... feel kind of sick."

I sat down next to him. He didn't protest. I took that as a good sign. "Have you had a lot to drink?" I kept my tone nonjudgmental.

He raised his head to look at me. "Huh?" He looked at the bottle. "Oh, no. The bottle was already open. I've had a few, a few glasses. And I drank it with the tonic. See?" He gestured wildly toward the bottle, nearly knocking it over. I reached out and steadied it. He didn't seem to notice. He slurred a few of his words, too, but he was making sense at least.

"Good. That's good. Why don't you let me take you back to my place now? We'll stop on the way and get something to eat. Then you can take your meds and go to sleep. That sound good?"

"You'd let me come back to your place?" His voice was eager, but his brows knitted together like he was worried.

"Of course." I smiled at him.

"But I left your place."

"You were upset is all. You had every reason to be."

"What am I going to do if I can't paint again?" His lip trembled. He swiped a shaky hand at his eyes, and I realized he'd cried a lot.

"You're going to paint again. You tried too soon." I put my arm around his shoulder, and he leaned into me.

"You think so?"

"I do. Everything's going to be okay. You need to give it some time."

"Time...," he repeated, his voice fading to a whisper. "I don't like to wait."

"I'm learning that." I smiled at him, and he gave me a lopsided grin back. So cute. My heart melted. "Maybe don't look at it as waiting," I suggested, scrambling for the next positive thing to say. He was hearing me, and he wasn't arguing. Could I come up with anything to lift his spirits? "Look at it as us getting to spend good time together. We've had a good time, haven't we?"

He nodded, his face a picture of serious. "A good time."

"I'm glad you agree." I got up and helped him to his feet. "Let me take you back to my place, okay?"

"Okay. Have to get the lights." He took a wobbly step toward the wall switch. I put my arm around his waist, steadying him. "How about you let me do that?"

"Thanks, Connor. I'm tired."

"We'll get you in bed soon."

He leaned his head on my shoulder, and we made our way through the apartment, turning out lights and locking the door behind us.

"Be careful on the… on the stairs," he warned.

"I will. You, too, okay? How 'bout I hold on to you as we go down?"

"Good idea."

We made it down the stairs, and I set the alarm and locked the building. We got into the car with no problems. He didn't even protest when I had to put him in the backseat. I shut the door, and he rested his head on the window. He didn't say a word until we were leaving the drive-through, where I ordered two cheeseburgers and fries.

"Smells good. I'm hungry," he said once I'd pulled the bag into the car.

"Good. We'll be at the apartment in a few minutes. We can eat together before I go back on duty. How does that sound?"

"Good. That sounds good. I can sleep there. I was afraid to sleep at my place."

At my apartment, we ate in comfortable silence. I helped him settle on the couch with his blankets and a pillow, and brought him his pills and a glass of water.

He took them and looked up at me. "Why are you so nice to me after what I did today?"

I sat down next to him. "It's easy to be nice to you, Giggles."

"I was awful to you."

"You were hurting and upset. Things are going to get better, Guy. They already are."

He put his left arm around my neck and pulled me close. "I've decided to start believing you about that," he whispered in my ear.

NEAR THE end of my shift, I had a chance to catch up with Nate. We parked side by side in a parking lot for a few minutes and got out to stretch our legs.

"What did you do for dinner your first night back on the job?"

"I went home to check on things with Jenna and Little Man. You?"

"I went home too. Guy had a rough day."

"How's that going for you?"

I thought back on Guy's parting words. "He's getting better every day. But tell me about Jenna and the baby."

Nate's smile lit up his face. Heck, it seemed to light up half the parking lot. "Man, watching that baby is the most amazing thing. When he opens his eyes and looks at you, you think you've seen the face of God. I can't believe he's mine. I can't believe Jenna and I made him. I can't believe I'm responsible for them both."

I laughed. "Yeah, I think that would be a serious adult moment."

"You ever going to have kids, Connor?"

My brain froze. How honest should I be? "I've dreamed about it…. But probably not."

Nate nodded. He seemed sad for a moment. For me? Then he offered a comment that left me speechless. "Plenty of gay men have kids nowadays, you know. Not just famous ones like that actor from *How I Met Your Mother*."

"What?" He grinned a big-watt, deep-dimple grin. "All right. Jenna figured it out. Relax. We don't care. Your secret's safe. But what I haven't figured out is, are you and Guy a couple? Or are you just the caretaker? You don't have to tell me," he hurried to add, "but it would keep me from sticking my foot in my mouth."

I blew out a breath that morphed into a laugh. This was going to be okay. And I did want to talk about this with him. "We were together for a week in LA. I came here hoping we could get something serious going. It's all up in the air since he was attacked. He's not himself, you know? But yeah, I'd like us to be together."

"You going to be okay, with all you're doing for him, if things don't work out?"

That was the question, wasn't it? I wanted to have some pride left if he said good-bye once he could be on his own. "I have to be, don't I?

I like being with him, but he might not feel the same about me when he's fully functioning again."

Nate nodded. "He seemed like a good man the couple times I met him. But he's having more problems than just his injuries, isn't he?"

"Yeah. Nightmares, the usual stuff after an attack like that." I wanted to tell him about the drinking, but I couldn't. That was secret, a secret you didn't share unless other people discovered it, like Ranger and Brooks had. "Can I ask you something?" I said instead.

"You bet."

"How are you managing it all? Juggling Jenna and the baby and the job, I mean?"

"Honestly? I'm not managing at all. I don't know how Jenna does it. She is with him all the time, and so tired, but she's happy about it no matter what's going on." He shook his head in wonder. "Me? I do what she says and whatever I can think of. When I'm not doing things, I'm trying to catch up on my sleep. Little Man has his all turned around. And I try to remember to be grateful, because any minute it could all change."

He grinned. "You'll figure it out, Connor. Your head's in the right place. You let me know if Jenna and I can help you. I mean it."

He did. "Thanks."

When I got home, Guy was asleep, curled up in the fetal position he seemed to favor these days. But his face was relaxed and peaceful. Beautiful, even. The bruises had faded, and the scabs were less noticeable. No pain or worry lines circled his mouth or marched across his forehead, like when he was awake. They'd been there since that first day in the hospital. With physical therapy ramping up and bills coming in, they'd probably be around for some time to come.

For a good five minutes, I watched him. He smiled for a second, and my heart warmed. I hoped I was the reason, that he felt safe and cared for at my place.

FOURTEEN

WE WERE invited to Nate and Jenna's for Memorial Day, and Guy spent a good part of the morning fretting about what to wear. He settled on black jeans and a red polo shirt. The combo set off his black hair, and I couldn't stop touching it, especially the red diagonal streak he'd had his hairstylist put in above his left ear when he'd gotten his hair cut on Saturday.

"You going to keep doing that at the Hamiltons'?"

"No. I promise. You know, I haven't visited another cop at home since I was in the academy."

"You're kidding? And who was your date for that momentous occasion?"

"No date. How do I look?"

"You're wearing old blue jeans, an older blue T-shirt, and sandals." He wrinkled his nose in disgust. "You've got nothing to worry about."

Guy made sure we stopped at the grocery and picked up flowers on the way—a bright big multicolored bouquet he had the clerk make up special. He laid them on the backseat next to the plush blue baby toy he'd purchased on Saturday after visiting three different stores. He was going to make sure we made a good impression.

Jenna met us at the front door of the two-story townhouse. She was wearing a striped knit sweater that clashed a little with the flowers, and she looked tired. But she beamed like parenthood agreed with her. She gave Guy a big hug, even before he handed over the presents.

"Aren't you the sweetest!" she said. "You know, I walk by your gallery a couple of times a week. I love the pieces you show and especially the colors you use in your paintings."

Guy giggled and blushed and asked her if she'd knit her sweater. I'd never have thought of that. She had, and that earned him another hug that had him blushing more. He was a looker when he turned on the charm.

Nate came out of the kitchen with Andy on his shoulder. Like me, he wore jeans and an old T-shirt, plus a giant cloth that covered his entire shoulder and chest underneath the baby.

"You expecting an accident there, Nate?"

"You aren't the only one with your own artist, Connor. My son is a spit-up artist like you wouldn't believe."

"Nate!" Jenna slugged the shoulder the baby wasn't on.

"What? You said yourself we'd be lucky if he doesn't do it while we're eating." His wife tried to scowl but broke up laughing. She scooped her son off Nate's shoulder like a pro and led us through the living room and kitchen, out onto the deck. Even as he followed, Guy turned around to glare at me.

"You could have warned me about the spit-up," he mouthed.

"Honestly, I didn't know. Don't worry. The baby wouldn't dream of spitting up on you."

Guy rolled his eyes, then took a seat at the umbrella-shaded table. Jenna and I joined him, and Nate headed for the grill. Jenna turned to Guy. "Would you like to hold him? I know you can't, with your sling, but I could lay him on his back in your lap."

"I don't know anything about babies," he replied.

"Don't worry," Nate said. "You hold him and wave the toy you brought in front of him, and he'll love it. What would you like to drink? We've got iced tea, water, or lemonade."

Guy chose lemonade and sat statue still as Jenna draped a brightly colored baby blanket across his lap and put Andy on top of it. He looked so petrified that I moved my chair alongside his to provide moral support. Thank goodness, Andy stayed still, staring up at Guy like he'd never seen anything like him. Funny. That was pretty much my reaction when I looked at him too.

I took up the toy and waved it in front of the baby while Guy held his legs stiff and gripped the little one's arm with his left hand.

"You're sure he can't get away from me?" he asked Nate.

"Naw, man, you're good. The book says we have another month at least before he can roll over. He's not going anywhere."

"The book says?"

"Yeah, you have a baby, you read a book. That's all there is to it."

Guy's eyebrows shot up in alarm, and Nate broke up laughing. In another couple of seconds, Guy couldn't help giggling too.

Jenna came back with our drinks and eyed her husband suspiciously. "What did I miss?"

"Nothing," Guy said, giggling again. "Just something about how everything he knows about babies he read in a book."

"Don't you believe him," she deadpanned. "He can't read at all. I tell him what he needs to know."

Guy erupted in another giggle that had everyone laughing and made Andy coo, wave his arms, and kick his legs in disjointed jerks. Guy stilled and looked at him in wonder, transfixed.

"See, man, he likes you," Nate said.

"He does?" But Guy didn't look up for confirmation. He kept his gaze on the baby and lightly ran his fingertips up the baby's round tummy and down his cheek. A smile, punctuated with a tiny bubble, lit up the little face.

"Of course he does," I assured him, not taking my eyes off the appealing picture of my Guy with Nate's Little Man, who was now trying unsuccessfully to grab at the fingers on his face.

Guy bent his face closer, and his hair fell down like a curtain, narrowing his vision to Andy. To everyone's surprise, mine most of all, he began to sing softly. The words weren't English or anything resembling an Asian language, either, but the tune was sweet, and Guy's tenor tone was lovely. The baby lay still until Guy finished. Then he kicked his legs, waved his arms, and cooed.

"That means he wants to hear more," Nate volunteered.

"That was beautiful, Guy. What was it?" Jenna asked.

He looked up, and his face colored in embarrassment, like he'd forgotten we were there. "It's a Norwegian lullaby. My mother used to sing it to me. I didn't even realize I remembered it."

"How cool that you have memories like that."

Guy frowned at me like I was stupid. "Yeah, right."

Andy cooed again, changing the subject before he could elaborate.

"That's Little Man's way of saying you did fine," Nate assured him, raising his glass of iced tea to Guy in a toast.

"More than fine," I whispered. Guy looked so appealing I wanted to scoop him up and kiss him. I stayed rooted in my chair.

Jenna covered everything over with a jab at Nate. "Andy loves being sung to. Guy, I swear, if my husband ever asks me out on a date again, I'm going to call you to babysit."

"If I ask?" Nate was incredulous. "I've asked. You said Little Man was too little to be babysat."

"That's because I couldn't imagine who we'd find to watch him. Now I'm not worried." She smiled broadly at Guy.

"Hey, I was a baby when I learned that song," Guy sputtered. Then he pitched his voice high. "I don't know nuthin' about babies, Miss Jenna."

Nate laughed wildly, and Guy grinned, pleased with himself. "Don't worry," Nate said. "I'll loan you the book. We've never gone this long without a date, and it's killing me."

"What do you think, Connor?" Guy asked.

"Seriously? I know less about babysitting than you do. I can't sing."

"If we timed it right—between feedings—and I wrote detailed instructions, I'm sure you two could do it," Jenna encouraged.

"I'd maybe do it for you, Jenna, and Andy here," I offered, "but not so much for that guy." I pointed a teasing finger at her husband.

Nate ignored my dig. "I knew there was a reason I invited you two over."

We continued the banter, and Guy kept Andy entertained on his lap, talking to him in Norwegian and making goo-goo eyes until he fell asleep. Jenna expertly transferred her son to some kind of hooded baby carrier, and Nate served dinner—a feast of grilled vegetables and burgers and potato salad Jenna made from scratch. Brownies topped everything off, accompanied by more iced tea and lemonade.

Watching Nate and Jenna interact left me with a sense of something like homesickness. My folks had been like them. I wanted what they had.

After dinner, Jenna disappeared to feed Andy. Guy listened to Nate and me talk shop. When Jenna and Andy returned, the conversation turned to sports, with Jenna fully participating. Guy totally tuned out to concentrate on the baby, who was again cradled in his lap and reaching for his face. He let Andy grab his nose and pull his hair, giggling all the while. That set the baby to cooing, and I found my attention wandering time and again to watch them, Guy especially. He looked so relaxed, like he had no worries or pain, like his future was secure. I wanted that. I wanted him. Jenna caught me and gave me a smile that practically hugged me. I looked at Nate to see if he was bothered. He wasn't. He gazed at his wife like I was looking at Guy.

I'd never imagined Guy would be so great with kids.

"You know, you're going to be great with Alex on Wednesday," I whispered to him.

He looked up at me. "You think so?"

"Who's Alex?" Jenna asked.

"The kid who saved me when I was attacked," Guy answered with no problem. He was totally comfortable with her. "He's going to start working in the gallery with me this week. I want him to have a safer job with better hours and better pay."

Jenna raised her eyebrows in delight. "Guy, that's a wonderful thing you're doing."

He blushed, but he grinned too. "Thanks. But he's helping me a lot more than I'm helping him."

A fuzzy, warm feeling sprang up in my chest as I watched him. He glanced up from the baby to find all three of us peering at him.

"What?" he asked.

"Nothing," I said quickly.

Jenna leaned over and gave him a big hug. "Guy Gustavsson, you are an absolutely wonderful human being." She kissed his cheek.

Guy giggled in embarrassment, and I fell in love.

FIFTEEN

TUESDAY MORNING, I came home from work to an empty apartment. Guy was at his physical therapy appointment, and the place was too quiet. I couldn't figure out what to do as I awaited his return. I changed my clothes, made some coffee, and picked up my book. I put it down and picked it up again at least three times.

Guy would probably be moving back to his place soon, I realized. He could get dressed, take a shower, and wash his hair without help. He had no problem climbing stairs, as he'd demonstrated the day he went back to his apartment.

He had to be looking forward to returning to it too. Unlike mine, his was beautifully decorated. With all of his shiny kitchen appliances, he'd be totally self-sufficient. And with his gallery reopening, he'd likely want to stay put after work. Heck, he'd probably want to move back by the weekend, maybe even tomorrow. I was going to be pathetically lonely, especially after my realization at Nate and Jenna's. I couldn't control my feelings, and I couldn't do anything about them— except wait. Didn't that suck.

A knock interrupted my miserable ruminations. I opened the door to find Guy slumped against the jamb. His face was sweaty and pale. He looked exhausted.

"That bad?" I put my arm around him, pulled him into the apartment, and steered him toward the dining table.

"What makes you say that?" he snapped. He groaned as I eased him into a chair.

"Maybe it was," Kellie offered, following us in. "Guy needs some tea and something to eat. After that, he needs his pain meds and a nap." She didn't hesitate about taking charge—she was in the kitchen opening cupboards already. Heck, I almost felt like a teenager again.

"It's a plan, Kellie. I'll make some eggs. You want some?" I followed her into the tiny space and began removing pans, plates, and silverware from cupboards and drawers. She'd moved on to heating a mug of water in the microwave.

"I don't want to impose," she insisted as she took the mug and a box of teabags to Guy and sat down next to him at the table.

"You can't possibly. We couldn't manage this PT schedule without you."

"Guy did well, Connor. Even the therapist said so. She's a lovely young wo—"

"She's a sadist," Guy exclaimed, all the air rushing out of him as he did. A moment later, he mumbled, "I'm not hungry," and plunked his head down on the table like a little kid ready for a nap, or a good cry.

"You have to eat. You haven't eaten anything today. That was part of the problem," Kellie scolded. "On Friday, I'm coming over here early to make sure you eat and take pain medication before we leave."

"I'm not going Friday."

"Oh yes you are," we said together, surprising ourselves. She caught my eye, and we laughed.

"Leave me alone," Guy muttered into the table. "I want to die for a little while."

But he raised his head a few minutes later when I put a steaming plate of eggs and bacon in front of Kellie. I put another in front of him and returned to the kitchen to get my own. "Did the therapist say anything about when you can start painting, Guy?"

"She told him to give it a try by the weekend," Kellie answered. "She said it would be good exercise for him as long as he didn't overdo or stress out by judging his efforts." She looked his way as she said it, like she was reminding him of a homework assignment.

Guy ignored her and picked up his tea mug. He dropped it immediately. "Ouch!" he yelped.

"Are you okay? Do you want an ice cube?" I moved toward the fridge to get him one.

"No. I'll be fine…. Shit, Connor," he moaned. "I hurt."

"I know. Let me get your pills."

I was back with the bottle in seconds. "Here you go. Take two, and eat your breakfast." I slid into my seat.

"Yes, Mom," he muttered. He picked up his fork with his left hand and went to work on his eggs.

"By this time next week, you'll be eating with your right hand again," Kellie encouraged him.

"Sure," he replied without energy.

"How was therapy really, Guy? There had to be something positive about it."

"It ended."

I laughed, too long probably, until he finally gave me a short, sardonic smile, enough that one of his dimples made a quick appearance, then fizzled like a shooting star.

He waved his fork in my direction. "I know what you're trying to do, and it won't work."

"Yes, it will."

He stuck out his tongue.

"See?" I teased.

Kellie huffed out a bothered breath. "Thank goodness I only had one son."

Guy and I grinned like kids.

THE NEXT afternoon around two, I loaded the easel and the bag of paints, paper, and brushes into the Jeep and drove Guy to the gallery. Following his detailed instructions, I set everything up in his office.

"You sure you don't want this in a front window, where there's some sunlight?" I was worried about him spending too much time in the room where Mitchell had attacked him.

"Definitely not," he snapped. He'd been edgy all day.

"Do you want me to get you some tea from the Leaf and Bean?"

"No, thanks." We stood about five feet apart, staring at each other across the tiny space. He looked at me expectantly.

"Would you like me to stick around until Alex arrives?"

"No, thanks, but you can turn the Closed sign to Open and leave the front door unlocked as you go."

"So you want me to leave?"

"Yes, please." He could have sounded less eager.

"You sure you're okay alone?"

"Don't you think it's about time I should be?"

"Guy, you can stay at my place forever if you like. It'd be fine with me."

His eyes widened in alarm, then slammed shut. When he opened them again, his face was scrubbed of emotion. "That's… kind of you to say," he offered. He paused for long moments before adding, "I guess I'm a little nervous today. Thanks so much for helping me, Connor, and for… everything. I'll be fine, and I'll see you around six, okay?"

"Sure." I made my face as blank as his. I was being dismissed. I crossed the space between us, kissed his forehead, and headed out. "I'll see you at six. Have a good first day."

He didn't reply.

I should have headed straight home, but the Jeep detoured to Nate and Jenna's. She answered when I knocked.

"Connor! Come on in." She was glad to see me, and I relaxed a bit.

As she closed the front door behind me, Andy started to cry in a distant bedroom, the noise quickly escalating to squalling.

"Bad time?" I followed her toward the noise.

"Not at all," she replied, her tone giving the lie to her words. "Nate's not here, but he'll be back soon. He's at the gym."

"I didn't realize. I should have called first. Maybe I should go." I stopped in the hallway.

She spun around and grabbed my arm. "Please don't." Her weary stare made clear she'd been dealing with the fussy baby for too long. "Nate's been gone awhile, and I'd love to talk with an adult right now—about anything."

I laughed. "You're desperate, and I'm your guy."

She gave a faint smile. "Maybe he'll quit crying for you."

"Let's give it a shot."

When we entered the bedroom, Andy's cries escalated again.

"I've fed and changed him. I don't know what this is all about."

"What do you want me to do?"

"Pick him up and walk him around? Maybe if it's not me doing it, he'll stop crying."

"You bet."

She tossed the towel she'd been carrying over my shoulder and stepped aside. I leaned over the crib rail to find Andy on his back, kicking and screaming, his little eyes shut tight, a single tear on each cheek.

"Hey, Little Man, what is up with you?" I lifted him to my shoulder and followed Jenna from the room. By the time we reached the doorway, he was silent.

"I knew it," she muttered. "He hates me."

"Yeah, right up until the moment he needs to eat again," I consoled her. "I think it's that he hasn't realized my hair is nearly black, not blond like his dad's."

"Whatever. Just so he's quiet. Would you mind entertaining him while I clean up the kitchen a little?"

That's what we did, me walking around or standing by the back door window bouncing Andy while Jenna started in on the dishes in the sink.

"Sorry the place is a wreck."

"It's not. Nate couldn't stand the heat, huh?"

She laughed. "No. I encouraged him to go to the gym and work out so he could sleep some before work. Andy has kept him up all day already. What's got you out and about this afternoon?"

"I took Guy to work at the art gallery today."

"Was he excited about going back?"

"More like anxious. He seemed glad to see me go, actually."

She tossed me an understanding smile and went back to scrubbing a pan. "I can't imagine going back to your office and home after being attacked in it. I'd be terrified."

"I think he was, a little bit anyway. But Alex Whittaker should be with him by now."

"It's nice what he's doing for that kid. Even more amazing is how much you've helped Guy. Nate told me you two didn't know each other that long before you came to Bozeman."

"True." I lifted Andy above my head and blew a breath into his face. He batted his eyes and cooed at me. If only things with Guy could be so easy. Actually, some things were. "I liked Guy a lot as soon as I met him."

"Things are working out for you?"

I knew Jenna's interest was friendly, not prying. I wanted to open up with her. "I'd like them to. I'm not sure the feeling is totally mutual."

She stopped with the dishes and turned to look at me. "You two seemed to be getting along great this weekend."

"We did. And we can be real good together, unless he's distressed or in pain." I focused on flying Andy over my head, but not too actively. I didn't want to find out how good a spit-up artist he was. "We'll have to see what happens."

Jenna picked up a ring of heavy plastic measuring spoons from the kitchen counter and waved them in front of Andy like a rattle. He made a series of uncoordinated, unsuccessful grabs for them, earning a big smile from his momma. I righted him in my arms and took the spoons so he could continue to play with them, and she started wiping down the stove.

"You know, after I met Guy the other day, I realized I knew him from high school."

"You're kidding."

"He didn't know me," she added quickly, pushing a thick lock of hair behind her ear. "He wouldn't remember me. He was a senior my freshman year. We weren't ever in a class together or anything. I saw him in the halls. He had only a few friends—girls mainly. And he was always quiet."

"That doesn't sound like him."

"I know." She turned around to look at me. "He was involved in a few things—the high school magazine. Art exhibits, of course. But he rarely looked happy. The first time I ever heard him laugh was when you two were here on Monday."

Now she looked at me—maybe because my mouth had fallen open. "Seriously, Connor. He didn't laugh in high school. I had no idea his giggle was so high-pitched. It's cute." She smiled at the recollection.

"He was all fun and giggles when I met him in LA."

"Then something happened to change him after high school."

"I think I know what—or who—it was."

She quirked an eyebrow.

"He fell hard for a guy he met in college, a cowboy from Paradise Valley. I'm pretty sure he still loves him, even though the cowboy is in a permanent relationship."

"How sad for him." Jenna sighed. She was quiet, and I concentrated on Andy. He'd lost interest in his spoons and gone still and sleepy in my arms. I settled him on my shoulder again and headed for the back door window, so Jenna couldn't see my face.

"You think Guy's the one for you?"

I didn't answer right away, and she waited. Finally, I told her the truth. "Yeah, I do."

She nodded, like she'd expected that answer. "Then don't give up easily. Guy's a good man, and a smart one." She pointed her dishrag at me. "You make sure you tell him how you feel soon."

"Yes, ma'am."

She blushed and laughed at herself. I smiled, and we were pleasantly quiet in each other's company. A few moments later, Nate's car pulled in to the driveway.

"Little Man," I said to the sleeping bundle on my shoulder, "I think Daddy is home." I stepped back from the door so Nate could enter.

"Hey, partner," he offered, not at all surprised to find me at his house. He smiled at his son, scooped him off my shoulder and put him on his own, and moved to greet his wife.

She returned his easy kiss. "How was the workout?"

"Great. Thanks for suggesting I go. How's Little Man been?"

"He quit crying as soon as Connor picked him up. Thank God he came over."

Nate grinned at me. "Thanks, man, for saving my wife's sanity."

"Anytime. I guess I sensed her distress from afar and headed over."

"That's how it was?"

"No. Guy was a nervous wreck and didn't want me around when he went back to the gallery today."

"Things must be going okay now. I saw two shoppers heading inside when I drove by."

"That's good news."

"Let me take a quick shower, and I can make us something to eat," Nate offered.

"No, thanks. Jenna's already told me you haven't gotten any sleep yet, and I need to go home and catch a nap." I headed for the front door. "See you later. Thanks, Jenna, for the baby time." I let myself out.

"Hang in there, Connor," she called.

MY PHONE rang about five thirty, waking me up. It was Guy.

"How are things going? Did you have any customers today?"

"I did," he answered giddily. "They didn't buy anything, but I enjoyed talking to people about art again. One of them was Walker Stevens."

I couldn't place the name.

"The priest from the hospital," Guy said. "Hey, I'm taking Alex to the pizza place down the street. Then I'm going to crash here for the night, okay? That'll save you a bunch of driving before you have to go to work."

He was going to leave faster than I imagined. "Sure. You guys have fun. How about I stop by around midnight on my lunch break? I'll bring Chinese."

I counted to three before he came back with an answer. "Okay." Another pause. "Thanks, Connor, for everything."

Would he say no the next time I asked? I ended the call, reset the alarm, and lay back on the bed, but I didn't fall asleep before it went off again.

AT MIDNIGHT, when I drove past the gallery, all the lights in the apartment were on, like Guy was trying to drive away the dark and maybe would-be robbers and memories. I parked in the back alley and called to let him know I was on my way up. He picked up on the first ring. I wasn't halfway up the stairs when the door at the top flew open.

"Hi there!" His greeting was enthusiastic.

"Hi, yourself. I brought Chinese." I held up the bag.

"How did you know I'd be starving?"

"I seem to recall cleaning your fridge a month ago and tossing everything out."

We were eye to eye as I reached the second to last step, and I stopped. He wrapped his left arm around my neck, pulled me close, and kissed me hard. I returned as good as I got until he slipped away from me with a breathless laugh.

"If we don't stop, you won't have time to eat." He grabbed my arm, tugged me inside, and closed the door.

The kitchen table was set for two, with a glass of ice water at each place. Three tall candles flickered between them, long wax drippings indicating they'd been burning for some time. Like he'd been waiting for me? Guy took the takeout bag from me, set it on the table, and began to place the white containers in front of the candles.

"Sit." He gestured carefully with his right arm. "What did you bring?"

"Sweet and sour medley, kung pao chicken, and pad thai noodles. All of your favorites. But didn't you eat dinner with Alex?"

"Do you have any idea how much a teenage boy eats? I think I had all of two pieces of pizza, and they were the tiny triangular ones at the curves."

"But you had a good time?" I sat down and watched him slide into his seat.

He appeared tired but pleased with his day too. "I had a great afternoon. Alex did so much around the gallery. After we ate, he came back here and helped me clean up the apartment, too, before Kellie picked him up. Wasn't that great of him?"

He took big helpings of the pad thai and chicken and pushed the containers toward me. Once he was sure I was going to eat something, he dug into his food with an eagerness he hadn't displayed at my place. Being home agreed with him.

After a couple of bites, he paused. "How's your shift so far?"

"Routine."

"Good."

We ate in silence. I wasn't pleased that he wouldn't be coming back to my apartment. But he was happy I was with him now. I went with that.

"So what's your plan for tomorrow?"

He put down his fork. "I'm free until I open the gallery around two. I thought I might drive to your place in the morning, if you don't mind?"

I couldn't stop the big smile that took over my face. "Sounds great."

He smiled shyly. "I thought we could nap together for a while before I meet Alex for work."

"Absolutely."

SIXTEEN

GUY LOOKED spent when he came into my apartment after his second therapy appointment, but he was more upbeat. Maybe that was because I'd made sure to fill the kitchen with good smells, and the teakettle was whistling when he walked in.

"What's this?" he asked in surprise.

"French toast and bacon. I thought you might be hungry after your big workout. Where's Kellie?"

"She had to take off right away. Too bad. She's going to miss a great breakfast."

"Did you have a better time today?"

He didn't answer. He popped a piece of French toast into his mouth, sighed, and gave me a slow thumbs-up—with his right hand.

"Look at you. You're definitely making progress."

He grinned and waved his fork at me and over his plate. "This is fabulous. Why haven't you made it before?" He gobbled up another bite.

"I didn't think it would complement all the Lean Cuisines you eat," I teased. "It's my dad's recipe, and there's nothing low calorie about it."

"I love it."

"I can make it again whenever you like."

"You going for a bike ride today?"

"I was thinking about one—later, when I drop you off at the gallery. You got a bike? You can start going with me soon."

"I don't think I could keep up with you."

"I'd slow down if you wanted to go riding with me, Guy. It'd be fun if we could bike together."

"I don't own a bike."

"That's easy to fix."

"I'll think about it."

"I'd be willing to go out painting with you, too, if you do that."

"You'd paint?"

"No. But I could take along a book, and carry your stuff for you."

"You'd be my porter?"

"Yes, sahib." I got up to get more coffee but gave him a little bow first.

He groaned. "I usually paint indoors and have people pose for me."

My nightmare of me on the pedestal flashed through my mind. "With or without clothes?"

"Either way." He stayed quiet, pushing his food around his plate, until he finally said, "I may not be able to paint."

I moved behind his chair, put my cup on the table, and wrapped my arms around him. "You're going to paint again, and soon. You had a great therapy session today. Give yourself a little more time. It's only been five weeks."

He settled back into my arms. "It feels like it's been forever."

"I know. But you'll do it again, even better than before." I kissed his cheek. "How about a nap now?"

We woke up a couple of hours later and went out to lunch. Halfway through the meal, I realized we were on a comfortable date, and I wanted lots more days like this. I dropped him at the gallery and headed out on my ride.

The day was sunny, warm, and breezy. I passed plenty of bicyclists out on the country roads south of town having a good time. Many waved at me. Pretty soon, I was waving without prompting. Maybe I should surrender and buy one of those grinny "Life is Good" T-shirts some of the downtown shops sold.

In LA, most rides involved battles against traffic, smog, and jerks, both the driving and bicycling kind. Bozeman had clean air, open spaces, and stunning mountain scenery. I had close friends in Nate and Jenna, and the beginnings of a relationship with Guy, a good man who tried to do right by people, enjoyed babies, and went out of his way to help Alex. My life had leaped way beyond good.

MY SHIFT was a long one, full of way too many drunk and disorderlies. I got home two hours late to find a bundle of white blankets mounded in the easy chair, Guy's black hair sticking out from an opening at the top. I hadn't expected him to be here, and the sight made me smile—until I noticed the glass and half-empty vodka bottle on the coffee table. My chest constricted like it had so often with my mom.

Guy's face appeared among the blankets, and he opened his eyes and smiled at me. "You're home."

"And you're here."

"I hope that's okay?"

"It's always okay. How was your day at the gallery?" I sat down next to him, and he crawled into my lap and put his head on my shoulder.

"Good. Long and tiring after therapy. But good. How was your night?"

"Full of drunks," I said, without thinking.

"Oh." He glanced at the vodka. "I only had two drinks, Connor, to relax."

Instantly, I was sorry I'd said it. I didn't want to start a conversation about his alcohol consumption. He wasn't hung over. People who drink don't get drunk every time. "Are you still having trouble sleeping?"

"Only in my apartment, I guess. When I fall asleep here, I don't wake up until you get home."

"That's great. Stay here. How'd you get here?"

"Kelly brought me. She said she didn't mind at all, even though it's out of her way. Wasn't that kind of her?"

I hugged him close. "We have a couple of people helping us pretty regularly, don't we?"

"I don't understand why."

"A lot of good people here, I think."

"What if I can't repay them all? I don't like owing so much to so many people."

Including me, I thought. I framed my answer as a "we" statement. "I don't think anyone expects us to repay them exactly. It's enough that we're grateful, and we try to help the next guy. And you are helping. Look what you're doing for Alex."

"I'm paying Alex."

"You're helping him with a better-paying, safer job, and with his art career. He and his mom are grateful, and they should be." I kissed his forehead. "What's on the agenda today?"

He sat up straight, excited about something. "Josh and Dane are in town tonight. They'd like us to meet them at Ted's for dinner. You're not working, right?"

"We can do that." Guy would be upbeat while Josh was around, and I'd be able to thank Keller again for helping me clean my apartment the day Guy had gone back into the hospital. Which happened right after the last time he spent time with Josh. I pushed that thought out of my head.

"So dinner's taken care of. What else do we have going on?"

"Alex and I are going to open the gallery around noon and keep it open until five. You could go for a bike ride, come by, and we could walk to Ted's. Maybe the four of us could go back to my place after, and you and I could spend the night there. You haven't spent the night at my place yet. What do you think?"

"I like that idea."

WHEN I arrived at the gallery around four thirty, both Guy and Alex were behind the counter. It looked like they were finishing up a sale, with Alex busy wrapping up a canvas that looked to be about three feet high and four feet wide. The buyer, a well-dressed, thin man with glasses and brown hair streaked with gray at the temples, was deep in conversation with Guy. He looked familiar.

Guy didn't look away from their conversation, but Alex came toward the door to greet me. "Hey, Connor. We're finishing up our last sale of the day, I think."

I smiled at his use of the word "we." "Last one, huh? Been a good day?"

"We've had three sales. This is one of Guy's." Alex dropped his voice to a conspiratorial whisper. "His most expensive one."

"That's great." We'd reached the counter, and Guy and the buyer turned toward us. I still couldn't place him, but I forgot him entirely when Guy grinned at me.

"Connor, you remember Father Stevens? From the hospital?"

"Walker, please," he said as he held out his hand. His grip was firm and warm.

"Nice to see you again, Walker, especially if you're buying one of Guy's paintings."

He laughed, and it made him too attractive for a reverend. "I've admired this painting for months. I decided I had to have it after I met Guy. It is exquisite."

Guy blushed. "Walker, I'm amazed you want it now that I've heard about your art collection. You've got works that are museum quality."

He laughed again. "That's why I'm buying this one. Your cowboy paintings are as good, Guy."

Guy tipped his head in a manner that should have appeared humble. I hoped the reverend thought so. To me, he looked damned sexy. "Would you like me to come over and help you hang it tomorrow?" he asked Walker.

"That would be great. Do you two want to come by for lunch after church?"

Guy looked at me eagerly. "Connor?"

"Are you sure you want me there? I don't know anything about art."

"Connor was a literature and psychology major," Guy told Walker. The pride in his voice vastly overmatched the simplicity of the statement, but it made me feel good. He wanted Stevens to be impressed.

"Great. We'll each have something to pontificate about when we get together," Walker said, laughing at his own joke. "You've got my address on the sale bill, Guy. How about you come by around one?"

"Do you want us to bring anything?" I asked.

He shook his head. "No need. The church ladies make sure I'm plenty stocked up on food. One of the perks of being a single priest. Just bring your appetites. Oh, and our last service is at eleven if you'd like to make that. No pressure, though."

Guy prodded Alex to help Stevens carry the painting to his car. As soon as they left, he went to the front door and switched the Open sign to Closed. "You okay with having lunch with a minister tomorrow?"

I chuckled. "Aren't we the social couple? Last weekend with Nate and Jenna. Tonight with Josh and Ranger, and now lunch. Did you want to try to make church too?"

"What do you think?"

I must have looked as stunned as I was. Guy rushed to assure me we didn't have to go. "I was kidding," he insisted.

I shrugged. "We can see how things go. I haven't been to church in decades."

"Decades?"

"Since I was, like, eight. And I'm thirty-three now so, yeah, decades. How about you?"

"Do my parents' funerals count?"

"Sure."

He cocked his head, doing the math. "Then it's been six years. The funerals were in the same church where Walker is a priest. I grew up in that church."

"Did you go regularly?"

"Yeah, until I started college. It's a nice church. Pretty inside. Walker wasn't one of the priests then, or I'd have kept going."

"Because he's gay?"

Guy laughed. "No. Because he's younger than sixty."

"He's a priest. So you're Catholic?"

"No, Episcopalian, but we say priest too. You call them Father or Reverend. But Walker likes to be called Walker."

"It sounds like you've had several conversations with him." I felt jealous, and foolish about that.

Guy frowned. "You know he visited me in the hospital both times." He crossed to the counter and started pushing papers around, not looking up at me. "And I've talked to him a couple of times since I got out, about stuff related to the attack. And he came by the gallery on Wednesday to say he was glad I'd reopened. I told you that."

"It's okay. I'm just trying to figure it all out. I didn't realize you grew up going to church. I didn't. That's all."

He nodded. "We can head over to Ted's as soon as Alex gets back."

SEVENTEEN

WE WERE a few minutes late to the restaurant, and Brooks and Keller were already seated at a booth. They'd ordered a couple of appetizers. Guy was tired—the big energy rush after selling his painting was wearing off—so sitting right away was good. So was getting a few onion rings and bison nachos in him before his straight-up martini arrived. Fortified with a little bit of each, he launched into an excited discussion of his sale.

"It was *Hector's Paces,* Josh," he said excitedly.

"That's great," Cowboy exclaimed. "You had a five-figure price tag on that one."

"I sold it to a minister with quite a Western art collection already. We're going over to his place tomorrow so I can help him hang it."

"Where does a reverend get thousands of dollars to spend on art?" Keller asked. "And do you think he'd like some furniture? I could give you one of my brochures."

Josh and Guy laughed, and he joined in. Me, not so much, because he'd asked something I already wondered about. I was glad Guy had sold the painting. He needed the sale. But priests didn't usually have big incomes. And this one was spending significant time with Guy too.

When I realized everyone was quiet, I tuned back in. Guy stared at me and drained his martini glass. Time to quit playing cop, or jealous boyfriend. "Maybe he's got a trust fund?" I offered.

"Entirely possible," Keller agreed, tossing me a bone. I nodded my thanks, and he touched his fingers to the brim of his ball cap.

Brooks, of course, was wearing his cowboy hat. He looked fine in it. Maybe I should get one. Guy, who was seated across from him, gazed his way a little too often.

"So what is *Hector's Paces*?"

"It is an incredible painting of one of my horses," Brooks answered.

"Josh has trained Hector to do some amazing footwork, and I painted a picture of him putting Hector through his paces. Hence the name."

"Guy makes it look like Hector is dancing. He looks so alive it's like a photograph. It's beautiful."

"You look alive too?" I asked.

Keller snorted. Guy glared at me.

"Hard to say," Cowboy answered. "One of the best things about the painting, I think, is that my hat covers my face."

Keller reached over and playfully pulled his partner's hat down over his eyes. "Like this, you mean?"

Brooks rushed to lift his hat. Now he was glaring at Keller—with a look full of enough sexual heat to start the tablecloth on fire. Poor Guy. He didn't stand a chance of regaining Brooks's affections. How long before he realized it?

Keller continued, "I'm sorry I'm not going to get a chance to see this one, Guy."

"Oh, I have a picture of it. I can e-mail it to you."

"I'd like that. You have any other paintings of Josh?"

I pictured *Cowboy and Cat* and that notebook filled with nude drawings and bit my tongue before I said something I couldn't recover from. Instead, I replied, "There's another painting of Josh working with horses in the gallery right now. It has a couple in it too."

Brooks turned to his partner. "Jesse and Sarah."

"Josh's brother and his wife," Guy said to me.

"We have to get you out to our place, Connor, so you can meet everyone," Brooks said. "If you make it after September 12, you can stay overnight at the ranch. We're done for the season on the eleventh."

"That's late for you to finish," Guy noted.

I marveled again at how much he knew about Brooks's life. I didn't know that kind of thing about anyone, though with Nate and Jenna and Alex and Kellie, that was changing. I was collecting my own little family around me, and I liked that idea. Maybe Guy and I could have that together. I wanted to—if he could get past his college roommate.

"What do you think, Connor?" Brooks asked. "Can you get a couple of days off in September?"

"If we make it midweek."

"You let me know the dates," he said. "We can get you riding too."

Our food came, and we ate, talked, and joked like real friends. Eventually, Brooks and Keller had to begin the drive back to their valley. We split up on the sidewalk, and Guy and I walked back to his place. I had hoped we would make love, but he fell asleep as soon as he hit the bed. I lay awake awhile, wondering whether he was truly tired, he'd had too much to drink, or being around Brooks had made me look less desirable.

THE NEXT morning, we went to church. Guy wanted to, and he wanted me to go with him. Walker wasn't surprised to see us. Several people recognized Guy from when he attended as a kid. They knew about the attack and came up to say how pleased they were that he was recovering. No one seemed surprised to see him with a man, or bothered about it either. Walker preached a sermon on the Prodigal Son, a story I'd heard despite not going to church. You can't be a lit major without knowing it. But Walker suggested that while we were all sometimes the prodigal, we were also the older brother who didn't run away. And like him, we weren't pleased to see the spendthrift, loose-living brother come home or be forgiven, let alone celebrated. Finally, he suggested we could also be like the extravagantly forgiving father— if we wanted to. The interpretation was interesting, and I saw the wisdom in all his points. But as a cop who had seen people escape justice, I could sympathize with the angry older brother.

Guy, on the other hand, thought the sermon was the best he'd ever heard and told Walker that with profuse praise as we ate a lunch of lasagna and green salad at his house. The reverend steered the mealtime conversation to questions about Guy's background and mine, taking care not to say anything too personal unless we answered his questions first. The man was a skilled interviewer, but I kept my revelations to the minimum that my dad was a cop, Mom was a school secretary, and they were both gone.

Through Walker's questions, though, I learned more about how Guy felt about his parents—grateful for a good upbringing and finances that comfortably set him up for life, but distressed to the point of bitterness that they didn't love him. And he had no idea how obvious his feelings were to others, or that he might easily go through the rest of his life with his heart as permanently damaged as his right shoulder was now. I wanted to wrap my arms around him and try to make up for all of it.

Walker had a more practical suggestion. "You know, Guy, I've been a psychotherapist for more than a decade. I'm available if you ever want to talk more about this."

Guy blinked in surprise, like counseling hadn't occurred to him.

"The offer's always open," Walker said conversationally.

The guy was so serene. Had he spent time in a Zen monastery too? But what I asked was where he'd gotten the money for his art collection.

He gave me a "you got me" smile. "Trust fund. My parents are wealthy on both sides for generations. It's allowed me to do whatever I want all my life. I wish everyone was so lucky."

With that, he offered to show us the collection. We hadn't seen much of it yet, since we hadn't gotten out of the eat-in kitchen.

"I've got paintings throughout the place," he said. "One good thing about being a single guy staying in a house this big is having a lot of wall space." He laughed at himself, a genial quality that made you like him more rather than be angry or envious.

He walked us through the formal dining room, living room, and entryway, a separate study, and three upstairs bedrooms—all painted in muted shades of blue, green, and gray so you'd focus more on the paintings than the furnishings or the rooms themselves. It worked, because all you remembered were the striking Western landscapes or cowboy scenes or visions of wild horses. All were originals, and while I didn't recognize any of the artists' names, Guy did, and he was impressed and thoughtful.

When we'd seen the last bedroom, Guy asked, "So where did you think you wanted to hang *Hector's Paces*?"

"Oh, I've already hung it," Walker said, smiling brightly, "and I love it where it is. Come see."

He took us down a hall and stairway we hadn't seen yet, to the back of the ground floor. But instead of turning into the kitchen, he opened two glass doors and took us into the large, rectangular family room, done in shades of cream and tan. *Hector's Paces* had the place of honor on the stone fireplace above the main grouping of leather furniture.

Guy sucked in a big breath, and I grabbed his hand without thinking. "It's perfect here."

"You like it?" Walker asked, beaming not with pride but joy. "I knew this was the place for it."

"I can't believe…," Guy said, his voice fading as he took it in.

"I can. It's like the space was waiting for it."

"It was, Connor," Walker enthused. "I'd been looking for the painting for this space for a long time. To me, Guy's painting pulls together or encapsulates parts of everything I've bought so far." He turned to Guy. "What do you think, Sir Artist?"

"I'm speechless, Walker," Guy said. Truly he was. Tears came to his eyes, and he brushed them away with embarrassed awkwardness. "Sorry. I've been overly emotional since I was attacked." He pulled away from me and turned his back on us as he struggled to rein in his feelings.

"I think it's beautiful here, Walker." I couldn't think of enough right words, but I wanted to get the attention off Guy for a minute.

He nodded knowingly. "I'm so pleased you both like it here. I can't wait for my parents to visit me and see it."

"Are your parents collectors too?" I asked.

"Oh yes, but Mom likes Impressionists while Dad is partial to the portraits of Frank Duveneck."

At that, Guy giggled, turned around, and joined the conversation again. "How in the world did you get interested in Western art?" he asked. "You're from the Midwest, right?"

"Born and educated in Chicago and lived there until I came to Bozeman a few years ago," Walker acknowledged. "But when I was a kid, we spent every summer on a ranch in Paradise Valley."

"Do you know the Brooks family?" Guy asked excitedly. "Josh is a friend of mine."

"I do. Jesse and I hung out together. Josh was too young, as I recall. But their dad gave me my first riding lessons, and Karl helped my dad choose my first horse."

"Amazing," Guy said. "Have you seen them lately?"

"Not for years. My folks sold the ranch when I was a teenager. Since I moved to Bozeman, I've been through the valley, of course, but never stopped by. I didn't think they'd remember me."

"I'll call Josh and ask him about you," Guy promised.

The conversation veered back to Walker's art collection, and I drifted away from the two of them to stand in front of *Hector's Paces* again. Masterfully done, the painting could hold its own in any art museum.

Once we were back at Guy's, I told him so, adding, "It sure has found a good home."

He blushed. "Walker has an incredible collection of modern Western painters. I'm amazed I'm in it." He was too. For all of the confidence he'd shown when we first met, Guy was self-effacing about his talent now. Was it because his parents hadn't loved him enough? Or had the attack shaken his confidence that badly? Thinking about it like that, I wasn't sure I liked this humility.

"I'm not surprised. You're a great painter, Guy."

"I was."

"You are."

EIGHTEEN

FOR THE next couple of weeks, I watched for signs the visit with Josh might trigger a drinking episode, but I didn't actually see Guy that much. Summer was in full swing, with plenty of events and tourists in town, and some officers diverted to the bike squad. I picked up more hours. Guy's physical therapy sessions and gallery hours kept him busy when I was off, and we became two lovers passing in the night— mainly on my lunch hour.

Toward the end of June, he got rid of the sling. He was doing stretching exercises faithfully five times a day. He even started drawing again. I heard about it at his place one night over sandwiches.

"It was slow in the gallery this afternoon, and I did some sketches of Alex." The kid worked every day now.

"That's great."

"I was rusty. Everything looked like shit." He scrunched up his face in disgust.

"I'll bet not. What did Alex say?"

"He said it looked like him."

I put down my sandwich. "Come on. I know he said more than that. The kid talks lots."

Guy giggled. "He thought I was doing a great imitation of Picasso in his Cubist period."

"And were you?"

Guy punched my arm. "No. And that's not what he said. He said I did a great job capturing him in natural poses."

"Natural poses?" The words came out like two squeaks as Guy's notebook images popped into my head. "Please tell me the kid had all of his clothes on."

"Connor!"

"I've seen your natural poses."

He punched me again. "And you like them, as I recall. Speaking of which, are we ever going to be together long enough to have sex again?"

I captured his hand in mine. "You miss me too?"

"I do." He pulled my fingers to his mouth and nibbled on them. The sensation went straight to my dick. "I really do."

"If it's any consolation, Nate says Jenna is getting tired of his schedule too."

"I know. I'm babysitting for her Thursday night so she can go out with some girlfriends."

"You are?"

"Uh-huh. Alex said he'd help me."

"I'm sure she's grateful. So, when do I get to see these sketches of Alex?"

"When I start to paint them, okay? I'm still rusty."

I ruffled his hair. "I doubt that, but okay. And you let me know when you want me to pose."

"Oh, I've got lots of things I want you to do, but posing isn't one of them." He came around the table and sat in my lap, grinding his butt around some before he settled down.

I retaliated with tickling, taking care to grab onto him first so he couldn't shoot out of my arms. In seconds, he was a squirmy, shrieking mess.

"Not fair! Not fair at all! I'm calling the police!" he cried.

"I am the police."

"Oh, please, Officer," he said between giggles, "stop tickling and handcuff me, won't you?"

I groaned and pulled him close. "I'd love to. But I have to head back to work. I'm sorry."

Reluctantly, he stood up. He pulled me up, and we headed toward the door. "Any news on Jimmy Mitchell?" he asked.

"He still hasn't surfaced, but he will soon. Haney's putting pressure on some of his old associates, and something's going to pop. You and Alex aren't worried, are you?"

"No," he replied vaguely.

I stopped. He wasn't telling the whole truth. "What do the two of you talk about all day?"

"Art mainly, art schools, and drawing techniques he'd like to try. Girls. And we've talked some about the attack. I still don't remember anything, not even what Mitchell looked like."

"That's not so unusual, Guy. The mind is good at blocking out things that hurt us."

"Yeah." He looked up at me. "The thing I still don't understand about that night is how Alex was brave enough to walk in and save me."

"He is a rare kid." What I wanted to say was that I still couldn't believe Guy hadn't mentioned one thing about his meeting with Mitchell being about *Cowboy and Cat.* I knew the investigators had asked him about it, and he'd told them no more than what was in the *People Magazine* story. I was waiting for him to say something so I could come clean about having it under the bed. I no longer believed Guy would discover it there, but the thing haunted me like the dismembered body under the floorboards in Poe's *The Tell-Tale Heart.* One of these days, I might blurt out that I had it. Then what? Would Guy demand it back, dump me, and spend the rest of his life looking at it and longing for Brooks?

I tuned back into Guy's comments as he was saying something like "She's pretty incredible too."

"Huh?" I felt my face growing warm.

Guy turned on me. "Where did you just go?"

"Thinking about work. I guess I should get back." He didn't look like he believed me. "But tell me again what you were saying. Please."

"I was talking about Kellie. She's the reason Alex is so amazing. He's as thoughtful as he is because of her, I can tell. Look at all she's doing for me. She takes me to and from therapy appointments and barely lets me pay for the gas, let alone do anything else to help her. And I'm the one who owes her son, not vice-versa, no matter what she says." He shook his head.

I knew that frustrated him. We'd talked about ways to help her that she couldn't refuse, but we hadn't come up with anything yet.

"I owe her and Alex everything," Guy whispered.

I took him in my arms and rested my chin atop his head. "Don't worry. We'll come up with something special, Giggles. We both owe them. How about I come by here first thing if I get off work on time?"

"Come even if you don't get off on time." He smiled devilishly. "I'll make you happy you did."

HE MET me at the door in nothing but sleep pants.

"You look amazingly cute this morning."

"Just amazingly cute?" He pouted.

I studied his honed chest and his biceps and shoulders, not seeing the scar for all the muscle sculpting he'd achieved with his therapy. He looked yummy. I moved to kiss him, but he turned his head. I nibbled at his ear and caressed his hip through the thin pants. "Buff, damn cute, and sexy too?"

"Now you're trying to come on to me?"

His sideways glance through half-closed eyes made my pulse jump. I slid my hand to the bulge in his pants and ground against him. He stiffened. "How am I doing?" I teased.

He thrust at me, tossed his head back, and moaned. "Definitely coming on."

"Time to find the bedroom?"

"Oh yes."

But I didn't move right away. I explored his lips with a long kiss and tasted toothpaste—thrilled to realize he hadn't just woken up. He'd been waiting for me. I picked him up, and he wrapped his legs around my waist. I ran my hands up and down his back, up and down warm, smooth skin that smelled like bedsheets, and I ached to have him, to lose myself in him. When he kissed me, I opened my mouth and felt him suck my tongue and all my air inside himself, until I had to break away to breathe or die.

"Connor, I can't wait," he gasped, his breath tickling my ear and fritzing my brain. "Bed. *Now*."

I loosened my hold on him and felt his thighs slide down mine, burning my skin. As soon as his feet touched the floor, he slipped away into the living room.

"Start taking off those pants," I called as I stalked him.

I caught up to him at the bedroom doorway, and he squealed when I pulled him into my arms. He trembled against me as I kissed him long, slow, and tender, all the while steering us toward his gigantic bed and fumbling to remove my utility belt and holster, and my shirt, with one hand. I couldn't let go of him completely. He managed to wiggle his pants down to his knees, but I'd gotten nowhere with my stuff.

"Faster," he hissed, thrusting at me.

I pulled off his mouth. "Stand still."

He giggled and obeyed, and I released my belt and holster and dropped them to the floor. His fingers fell on my shirt buttons, making short work of them and pushing my shirt off my shoulders and down my arms. I felt trapped in too many clothes.

"Maybe I leave it like this?" Guy teased. "With a twist or two, so you can't use your arms?"

"Forget that. Help me get rid of my pants," I hissed as I toed off my shoes.

"Oh, right." He bent his head to concentrate on my zipper, then lowered himself to the floor along with my pants and briefs. I stepped out of them and raised him up again, half carrying, half waltzing him to the bed.

He shook with silent laughter, but I kept my lips on his as I moved him onto the bed. I slid down beside him and kissed little circles across his chest. His shaking stopped. "Oooh, do that some more."

I did, eventually kissing my way to his mouth again. He sighed and grinned and kissed me back. Then he slid his hand down my chest to tease my nipples, which suddenly seemed connected to my balls by a zip line of electric sparks. I moved on top of him, my hands flat on the bed alongside his arms to keep my weight off him. He wrapped his legs around me, trapping me against his hardness, and our grinding and thrusting quickened until we lost all friction to the slickness of feverish heat and sweat and precum. I thought I might self-combust before I got inside him.

"Mmm, mmm," he groaned, like he was eating all his favorite chocolates at once. "So good, Connor. Fuck me."

I knelt between his legs. "Condom?"

"In the drawer under the lamp. Hurry." I fumbled the drawer open. He watched with lust-glazed eyes as I put it on. No one before, not in life or in the movies, ever looked as beautiful as he did. The thought stopped my heart.

"Going to do this slow." I pressed soft kisses to his cheeks and lips. "I want to savor you and make you scream."

His eyes widened and closed tight. He tossed his head against the pillows and gripped my waist, but I wouldn't let him hurry me. With gentle fingers, I stroked and played against him, taking my time, feeling him yield, open, then finally surrender.

"That's it, baby. Give yourself to me. Let me in." I sank into his heat and we melted together.

"Please," he whimpered, and the sibilant sound of the word never died as I posted in and out, savoring every slide of his skin, each grip of his muscles. Jolts of pleasure rocketed up my spine.

"So good, baby," I crooned, kissing his lips, his nose, his cheeks. I thrust slowly, dragged hard as I pulled back, over and over again. Desire moved across his face, making him smile, grimace, then smile again. I felt like the world's most powerful man. I wanted to give him the universe.

He gasped out a breath, part sob and part laugh, and his eyes flew open. His mouth rounded in a silent cry, he clutched me and climaxed. I followed with a shuddering explosion that made me holler.

When I opened my eyes again, he was smiling at me. "That was... the best."

I rested my forehead on his. "It was."

"We're good together," he whispered, and I knew I would remember this moment forever.

NINETEEN

THE CALL came in the night after July Fourth, about eleven o'clock.

"All units, watch for a blue late-model Ford 150, four doors, going west on Peach, headed for Rouse. One suspect, adult male, wanted in connection with a double assault on Plum Street. Approach with caution."

Alex and Kellie lived on Plum. The hairs on the back of my neck rose in that way I'd learned over the years meant I should pay attention and get involved.

I was on Church Avenue. If the suspect made it past me, he stood a good chance of making it to Seventh and the freeway. I sped up and called in my intention to block him at Church and Peach.

The intersection was quiet and dark as I approached. Seconds later, a light show of high beams followed by flashing red-and-blue roof lights raced toward me.

Night Sergeant Nash's voice came over the radio. "Maclean, intercept with caution. We have confirmation that it's Jimmy Mitchell. Armed and dangerous. Davis, back off your speed and be ready to assist."

I hit my lights and pulled into the intersection, effectively blocking it to the oncoming truck. The squeal of rubber skidding on pavement cut the air as Mitchell turned sharp and fast, trying to avoid my cruiser. The rear of the Ford swerved, missing my front bumper.

He must have hit the gas immediately after, because the truck jerked forward like a sprinter sprung from the starting block and slammed into a car parked on Church, sending it into another car. The screechy sound of crunching metal was loud, violent, and short-lived. Then everything was still, including the truck.

I jumped from my vehicle, drew my gun, and approached the driver's door from the rear, calling loudly, "Mitchell, come out with your hands up." I spotted Davis sprinting toward the passenger door, pulling his gun as he ran.

Inside the Ford, the driver was upright and unmoving, held in place by his seat belt, his head resting on the steering wheel. As I watched, he began to move, barely rolling his head from side to side like he was trying to clear it.

"Hands up. Get out of the truck," Davis yelled.

Mitchell looked at Davis, then turned his head toward the driver's side window. His plan to run died when he saw me.

"Put your hands on your head and come out slowly," I repeated, watching his hands, sure I saw no gun. Once they hit his head, I opened the truck door, took a step back, and waited, keeping my gun pointed at his chest as he moved. When his feet smacked the pavement, I spun him around and pushed his chest into the truck bed panel.

He was about six feet tall, with some weight on him, and he perfectly matched the picture Alex drew the night Guy was attacked. When that reality clicked, I gripped his arms tighter, mainly to keep from punching him. A queasy feeling roiled my stomach again. Who were the victims on Plum?

Davis came around the front of the truck to stand about ten feet away. He closed the truck door and trained his gun on Mitchell. I holstered my weapon and put cuffs on him.

"You got no cause to stop me," he spat out over his shoulder. "What's this about?"

"Jimmy Mitchell, you are under arrest," Davis said, not moving from his firing stance.

Mitchell jerked his head around to glare at him, and I got a close look at three bloody, parallel scratches on his cheek. "I ain't—"

"You are. The kid's drawing was good enough to be a photo." I peered into the truck, where the dashboard lights cast a green glow over the bench seat, illuminating some kind of pipe. I felt a prickling across my scalp. "Looks to be a pipe on the front seat," I called to Davis.

"You can't hold me," Mitchell insisted, jerking halfheartedly against my grip on his arms.

"Quit moving," I ordered, pushing him hard into the truck again.

We all stopped moving as an unmarked car with a flashing dash light pulled up. The passenger door swung open, and Detective Haney stepped out. He looked grim as he came toward us. "James Rodney Mitchell, you are under arrest for the attempted murders of Kellie and Alex Whittaker."

Cold fear zipped down my spine. I stared at Haney, waiting for details.

"On their way to the hospital," he said. "The kid is going to be fine. She's in bad shape. It looks like Mitchell attacked the kid first, on the front lawn. The mother arrived and he turned on her, hitting her hard across the neck with something. Hamilton is on his way to finish up here. You're needed at the hospital. Nash says you're done for the night. We've got this."

Davis moved in to take hold of Mitchell. Haney pointed his finger at me. "Go. Tell the kid we're thinking of him."

I hurried to my patrol car. Hamilton's cruiser passed me on the street.

AT THE emergency room desk, the nurse gave me grief as soon as I asked for Alex. "He can't be interviewed right now," she snapped.

"I'm here as a friend of the family. Where is he?"

She eyed me suspiciously. I stared back. She backed down. "Room Two." She waved her hand toward a door to my right. "But if I hear any untoward noise from that room…." Her threat to call security faded away behind me.

Alex sat on an examination table, a large bruise purpling his cheek, a butterfly bandage on his forehead holding a nasty gash together. Drops of blood splattered his jeans and T-shirt. He clutched at a blanket wrapped around his shoulders, a bandage binding the knuckles of his hand. Guy stood beside him, staring at the floor. They both looked like they were in shock. I took a deep breath, a poor attempt to calm my pounding heart.

Alex talked first. "Jimmy Mitchell came to my door—"

"We got him." I moved to stand in front of him and put my hand on his shoulder. "How are you feeling?"

"My mom…."

"I know." I pulled him close, and he went limp in my arms. I looked at Guy. "What are they saying?"

"Nothing. Why haven't they told us anything?"

"Connor, I'm so scared. My mom…. She couldn't talk or breathe."

"Guy and I are here for you, Alex. We're not leaving. We'll figure this out."

"That's right," Guy whispered, his voice shaky. Being here had to bring back memories he didn't want to have.

"We gotta wait a little longer, buddy," I said to Alex.

He made no move to leave my arms, and I kept them around him. The image of my fifteen-year-old self in a hospital waiting room flashed in my mind. My mom sat on one side of me, shaking and sniffling, Dad's patrol partner perched on the other, one foot tapping the floor as a gray-haired, Indian doctor came in and told us Dad was dead.

The doctor who walked into this room was young and female, her blue surgeon's cap smashing short blonde curls close to her head. Her sorrowful look made me grip Alex tighter. He looked up at her and his face crumpled. He howled like a wounded animal. Guy jumped. My mind went blank except for random swear words I didn't utter.

She reached Alex in two strides and put a slim hand that smelled of disinfectant on his back. He shrank into me, hunching his shoulders away from her, but she kept her hand on him. When his cry died away, she spoke into the silence. "My name is Doctor Harrison, Alex. Your mom's windpipe was crushed. We tried everything we could. I'm sorry."

Alex buried his face in my chest, quaking with great, silent sobs. I held him up. Guy gripped his hand, and the doctor softly kneaded his shoulder.

After a long while, she spoke again. "I know your mother loved you very much, Alex. She was very brave. Would you like to see her now?"

Alex jerked at her words. Guy groaned in pain. I wanted to.

"It's your call, Alex. Either answer is the right one," I said, using the same words the old doctor said to me.

"Yes," Alex gulped out, the word thick and slurred with tears.

Doctor Harrison squeezed his shoulder once more. "I think that's a good idea, Alex." She took his hand as he slid off the exam table, his blanket falling away like a cast-off shroud. He slipped his other hand from Guy's grasp and followed her out of the room like a trusting child. Guy and I fell in behind them. He trembled, and I gripped his cold hand in one of my own. He resisted slightly, then followed me with slow, hesitant steps.

The doctor led us through a bright hallway and a swinging door, then down a dim hall of closed doors toward the only open one. A pale yellow light leaked from the room, falling across the floor, pulling us all where we didn't want to go.

One lonely gurney stood in the middle of the small tiled room. Kellie lay on it, a single light casting a low, otherworldly glow over her still form. A sheet covered her up to the chin, hiding any sign of the trauma she'd been through or the doctor's struggle to save her. Her face was unblemished. Peaceful looking. She could have been sleeping, except that her chest didn't rise or fall. Someone had combed her hair, placing it round her face with great care, a kind last image to leave a child. Her son's breaths, fast and shallow, made the only sound in the room.

He and the doctor stopped beside her, and Alex sucked in loud, ragged breaths and swayed on his feet. I stepped up beside him and put my arm around his waist, ready to bear his weight. Guy stayed at the foot of the bed. He wouldn't move closer.

Alex swiped at the tears on his cheeks and looked a long moment into his mother's face. His lips quivered. He blinked rapidly, trying hard to be brave. He did a good job until he reached out a shaky hand and touched her cheek. He wrenched it back like he'd been shocked, collapsed across her chest, and began to weep again. When a tortured "Mama" escaped his lips, Guy burst into tears. I had to choke mine back.

I rubbed small circles on Alex's back between his shoulder blades. The doctor placed a soothing hand on his hair. I felt Guy's hand slip into mine again, and I squeezed it.

We stayed that way until Alex stopped crying and the room grew still. Then we stood that way some more. I watched him, feeling all the while that somehow I stood outside the picture, seeing another boy, his hair dark instead of red, caressing his weeping mother's back. Like Alex, that boy seemed so very small and young and alone. I glanced at Guy, who stared at his feet again. He looked small too.

In my head, I heard my father's voice. "This is *your* family, son," he said. "You and Guy taking care of this boy, taking care of each other. Time to step up now, Connor."

TWENTY

GUY AND I remained at the hospital for another hour with Alex, waiting for a caseworker from Children's Services to show up. The woman at the desk when I first came in was kinder now, concerned for Alex. She put us in a sitting room by ourselves and brought us coffee, tea, and hot chocolate. We didn't touch them, and the smells mingled into a sick, chocolaty mess that soon had me breathing through my mouth. She couldn't have known that would happen, but the room was claustrophobic tiny, and it did. We stared at the door, waiting for it to open on whatever bad thing would happen next.

Alex sat in his chair, gripping the arms, not saying a word. About twenty minutes into the wait, he began to tremble. Guy disappeared to find a blanket. I wrapped my arms around him and held on.

I wanted to say something reassuring, but no words came. All I remembered of what people told me after Dad died were the stupid sayings, like I'd get over it, or he was in a better place. I would not say them to Alex. So I held him and told him Guy and I would be there for him no matter what. He didn't say anything.

The door opened, and Alex jumped up in fright. It was Guy, back with the blanket, and Alex collapsed into his chair again. Together, Guy and I wrapped the blanket around him and held him. Guy petted his back and promised nothing about their relationship or Alex's job would change. Still, Alex stayed mute.

When the door opened again, the three of us looked up in unison, our anxiety so palpable we should have been able to smell it.

A round middle-aged woman in a navy blue sweat suit, toting a gigantic, beat-up black leather bag that might have held a bowling ball, entered the room. Her short brown hair stood up every which way, like she'd been roused from bed, but she was kind and gentle with Alex when she introduced herself as Mrs. Sydler.

He started to shake again. "What's going to happen to me?" he whispered, his teeth chattering so he could barely get the words out.

She pulled a chair away from the wall and sat down, centering herself in front of him. She put a soft hand on his arm and looked him in the eyes. "Right now, I want to tell you, Alex, that I'm so very sorry for your loss. It's awful, inexplicable. Your mother was so brave."

I thought she was going to continue with some revolting lecture about how Alex needed to be brave, too, but she didn't. She was a pro.

"I'm going to take you to the home of Mr. and Mrs. Jameson for the night. They're a wonderful couple, with a home near Montana State University. They're waiting for us to arrive."

"How long?" Alex's voice was barely audible. He had fallen back against Guy and me, away from the caseworker, but she kept her hand on his arm, patting him every few minutes.

"How long will you stay with the Jamesons? All day tomorrow for sure, and for the next few days after that, while we examine your options together, Alex."

"Options?" Alex asked.

"Do you have other family?" she asked softly.

He sniffed and shook his head. "It was just Mom…."

He choked off a sob, wrapped his arms around his waist, and fixed his gaze on his sneakers. I looked at them, too, and noticed blood on the left one.

I snapped my head up. "What do I need to do to become Alex's guardian?" Alex's and Guy's heads swiveled toward me. Guy's face was a startled, guilty mess. Alex was confused.

"There's an easy way to get that started"—Mrs. Sydler glanced at my metal name tag—"Officer Maclean. Because Alex is older than fourteen, he can go to court with a Nomination of Guardian petition, asking that you or anyone he wishes be named his guardian. The court generally grants it if at all possible."

Alex stared at me, then looked at Guy, who had managed to banish every trace of his initial reaction. He nodded encouragingly, and Alex turned to me again. His eyes shone with a hopefulness that was naked and painful.

"I'll get a lawyer first thing in the morning, Alex. I promise." I turned back to Mrs. Sydler. "I've known Alex for a couple of months. We cycle together. And I know—knew—his mom."

"That's very good," she said. She leaned toward me and lowered her voice. "You didn't hear this from me, Officer Maclean." She smiled briefly. "But you'll want to call attorney Heather Fox. She's good."

"Thank you."

She nodded, then turned to Guy. "And you are?" Her question was friendly, supportive.

"Guy Gustavsson. I'm Alex's employer. I own an art gallery."

"How kind of you to be here for Alex, Mr. Gustavsson."

He sat up straighter, instantly looking like the businessman he was. "Alex isn't just my employee. He's my friend. He saved my life."

Her eyes widened appreciably, and she patted Alex's arm again. "Then Alex, we will get your case settled quickly so you can be back with your friends. I'll call in the morning, Officer Maclean, so we can get the paperwork going."

For the first time, something like light glimmered inside the black hole we'd fallen into. "Thank you, Mrs. Sydler. I'll do whatever you need."

She pulled her huge purse off the floor, rummaged around in it, and eventually pulled out a notebook, pen, and her business card. She handed that to me and took down all of our phone numbers. Then she took back her business card and jotted a number on it.

"That's the Jamesons' number. Feel free to call them and to visit Alex at their home. I'll give them your names. Do you have a phone, Alex?"

"We need to bring him a new charger tomorrow," Guy said.

"Good. I'm sure Alex will want to see you both tomorrow. Call first so the Jamesons know to expect you. They're good people."

She stood up slowly, so as not to startle Alex. "Shall we go, Alex? The Jamesons have a very comfortable room ready for you."

He shrank back in fear and grabbed my arm hard. "Connor?"

I gently helped him to his feet. "It's okay. Guy and I will walk out with you, and we'll see you again in a couple of hours, I promise."

"Promise?" His voice pitched high, overly loud in the tiny room, his panic taking up all the space.

"When does Alex need to be back to work, Mr. Gustavsson?" Mrs. Sydler asked as she put her chair back in its place along the wall.

"What?"

"We want Alex to get back in his regular routine as soon as possible," she told him, speaking slowly, trying to keep us all calm before the separation.

"He works ten to four most days," I offered, "except Sundays and Mondays."

"Maybe he can be back to work the day after tomorrow, or even for an hour or two tomorrow. We'll see how that goes, Alex?"

"Great," Guy said quickly, catching on to her strategy.

"Great," Alex echoed, but his voice was empty of emotion and energy. He was fading. He needed to get out of here.

Mrs. Sydler gestured toward the door, and I moved us all out into the hall.

Alex gripped my arm. "What… what about my mom?"

I put my hand on his shoulder again. "There's the autopsy first. That will take a few days maybe."

He winced. "Then the funeral?"

"We'll help you with that," Guy said.

We walked the two of them to Mrs. Sydler's car, hugged Alex, and promised him again that we'd call in a couple of hours. He nodded and got in the car, then watched us, unblinking, as she drove away.

I grasped Guy's hand. The parking lot was nearly empty, the moon sunk low in the western sky. The sun would rise in an hour or so. I spotted his car and led him to it.

"How about you head to your apartment, and I'll meet you there after I return my patrol car?"

"Yeah."

A HALF hour later, I parked the Jeep in the alley behind the gallery and called Guy to let him know I was on my way up.

"Door's open at the top of the stairs." His voice was a hollow monotone. I didn't like the sound. I had a bad feeling about it.

I smelled coffee as soon as I opened the door. I found the biggest mug he had and filled it. Then I grabbed a second, made him some tea, and carried the mugs into the living room.

He sat on the couch, curled up at one end of the L, his hands pressed against his sides.

"Here's tea for you." He didn't reach for the mug. I put it down on the coffee table and sat next to him. I felt him stiffen. "Want to talk about it?"

"I don't know what you mean." He didn't look at me.

I picked up my mug, turned toward him, and settled back on the couch. He leaned over the couch's wide arm, away from me.

"What are you thinking?" I asked gently.

He jumped off the couch and began to pace in front of the table, staring at the green rug beneath his bare feet.

"Guy?"

His feet spun toward me. He clenched his fists at his sides, his nails digging into his palms. His chest heaved with noisy breaths. "What am I supposed to be thinking? I had to sit alone with him until you came. I saw her body." He sucked in a huge breath, then said angrily, "That's probably all in a day's work for you."

I put my cup on the table. "It was an awful night," I said evenly.

"Do you ever get angry?" he yelled.

"Of course I do."

"Gritting your teeth is not getting angry," he snapped. He resumed pacing. "Screaming, stomping your feet...." He walked over to one of the chairs, picked up a yellow pillow, and heaved it into the kitchen. "Throwing things. That's getting angry." He turned on me again, his face red with the exertion.

"I don't act out. Sorry." I scrubbed my face with my hands and stood up. "Why don't you tell me what this is about now?"

"*You're* going to become Alex's guardian?" he demanded, settling his hands on his hips.

"Did you want to? I'll back off if you do. I didn't think much before saying it. I figured we'd do it together." I gestured between us. "The two of us."

Guy shook his head. "There won't be an 'us' if you become his guardian."

I stared at him. "Are you going to leave me if I become Alex's guardian?"

"You'll leave me. You won't have time for me. You won't have time for anything." He flopped on the other wing of the couch, his back to me.

I stepped toward him, sat down again, and put my hand on his shoulder. "Of course I'll have time for you. We'll be together all the time, the three of us."

He didn't turn toward me. "No. There will be you and me or you and Alex, but not both and not three of us. There will always be an outsider, and it will be me." His words came fast, from deep inside him, remembrances of his past, but not reality, and not the future.

"I love you." I hadn't thought I'd say the words now, not like this. They came out unbidden, but they were true.

Guy didn't think so. He pushed my hand off his shoulder, jumped up, and turned on me, his face taut with anger. "Don't say that," he cried. "It's not... true. You can't want to be Alex's guardian and love me too."

His eyes rounded in horror at his words, and he ran for the bedroom. I chased after him, blocking the door before he could slam it.

When I entered, he was on the far side of the bed cowering against the wall.

"Get out!"

"Please, Guy, let's sit down and talk about this."

"There's nothing to talk about." His eyes darted around the room as he searched for an exit. I blocked it.

"There is. Did you hear me? I love you."

"No. Stop saying that." He squeezed his eyes shut, trying to erase me, and pulled at his hair. "You're lying. You can't mean it."

"I do mean it. You can't change the truth by calling me a liar."

I moved into the room, and he stepped back, banged into the wall, and slid down it, covering his head with shaking arms. I moved to his side, kneeled down, and tried to gather him in my arms. He stiffened and pushed back, but I held on and began to rock him gently.

"Baby, what's this about? Tell me," I whispered.

"You don't love me. No one's ever loved me. I'm not loveable."

"You are. I do—"

"No," he choked, his voice thick with tears. The verbal vomit poured out of him. "Kellie is dead. Alex is an orphan, and it's my fault. If he hadn't tried to save me…. If I hadn't run that ad to get that stupid painting back…. And now… I'm not helping him. I'm not offering to be his guardian…. I'm a selfish, horrid shit." He exploded out of my arms, knocking me on my ass, and scrambled onto the bed.

I swallowed down my fear at his mention of the painting. Better to think about that later. I followed him onto the bed, pinning him down before he could get away again. We were face to face, and he shut his eyes against me.

"Look at me," I ordered. "If you look at me, you'll see the truth. I love you. Kellie's death is not your fault, and you're not horrid. You've seen horrible things tonight. You're in shock. It's normal. Look at me."

A tear leaked out of one of his eyes. I brushed it away with a kiss, and he blinked and looked at me. His irises were so huge, his eyes looked black. They were filled with shame. My heart ached for him.

"I can see myself in your eyes. Can you see yourself in mine?" But he'd closed his eyes again. I kissed his cheeks. "I love you."

"No," he said through gritted teeth.

"Yes." I kissed his lips. He sucked them in and bit them to try to keep me out. I chuckled and blew a warm breath over them.

"No," he whimpered.

His lips parted and I attacked, pushing my tongue in his mouth, tasting his salty tears. I released one of his hands, brushed my fingers across his cheek and jaw, and kissed a trail to his neck and collarbone, pushing my chest against his, willing him to match his ragged breathing to mine.

"I do love you. Connor loves Guy. Say it." I licked and nibbled at his neck until his chest rose and fell with mine and I felt him harden. "Say it."

He kissed me back instead, wormed his free hand between us, and began to claw at my shirt buttons. I raised up and released his other hand. "Faster," I encouraged. "Then undo yours." I rolled us over so he was on top. "Take off all your clothes."

He had us both naked in a minute, and he'd pulled a condom and lube from the nightstand in another. It couldn't be right to want sex after what had happened tonight, but we both needed to feel alive. He needed to know I loved him, and I wanted him to forget what he'd seen and said. I ground our cocks together. "Get me ready."

He ripped the condom package with his teeth, rolled it on, and squirted me with lube. I rolled him on his back again, slid my fingers through the slick, and slipped one inside him until I hit his prostate and he yelled. I did it again and again, then replaced my finger with my dick and pushed inside him. He clasped his arms and legs around me, I sank deeper, and he groaned my name.

"Connor loves you," I whispered. I pulled back and thrust in hard. "Connor loves you. Say it."

His eyes flew open and focused on my face, searching it until wonder dawned.

"Connor loves you. Say it."

"Connor...." He stretched my name into countless syllables and humped against me.

"Say it!"

"Connor loves me."

"Yes." I captured his lips and kissed him until my lungs ached. I pulled back gasping.

"Connor loves me," he shrieked. "Connor loves meeee." He came like a geyser, his last word not ending until he stopped spurting. I came as the silence descended around us, then collapsed beside him, my lips settling near his ear.

"That's right," I whispered. "Don't you ever doubt it."

He grabbed me hard, and I held him close, petting him and brushing kisses across his face. I pulled the bedspread over us, and he fell asleep as the morning rays hit the windows.

I stayed awake. He hadn't said he loved me back, and I couldn't quit thinking about that.

TWENTY-ONE

THE NEXT few days were a blur of paperwork, running around to meet the lawyer and social workers, and spending time with Alex and Guy in between. Each day, I picked Alex up from the Jamesons' home and brought him to the gallery, where he worked or crashed at Guy's apartment for a couple of hours before I had to take him back. And each day, the circles under his eyes grew darker. He wasn't sleeping, but he wouldn't talk about it.

He wasn't all I worried about. I watched Guy closely, too, for signs he was drinking. I didn't see any. Instead, he began an odd disappearing act for ninety minutes or so, once or twice each day. He'd mumble something about a meeting and be gone, and he wouldn't say anything else.

The day after the murder, right after I'd gotten Alex to the gallery, Detective Haney called. He needed to interview Alex, and he wanted me there. But he went a step further, asking if Alex needed anything. I decided right then that I would start accepting any offers of help because we needed a lot.

"Can you bring any breakfast food Alex might eat and some chocolate syrup and milk? He likes those in coffee. We don't have anything here, but I don't want to leave him to go get stuff."

"I can handle it, Maclean. I've got teenage boys."

Guy split for some "appointment" as soon as he heard Haney was on his way. Never mind that the gallery was open. He flipped the sign to "Closed" and left. He didn't say where he was going.

Haney went above and beyond. He showed up with the milk and chocolate syrup, a box of Cheerios, and a bag of Egg McMuffins. I led him up the stairs to Guy's apartment.

"Joe, this is amazing. Thank you. What do I owe you?"

He frowned. "Hey, I can do something nice once in a while."

He spread everything on the kitchen table while I poured three mugs of coffee. Alex came in and wordlessly helped himself to the milk and chocolate syrup, pouring large amounts of each into his cup, and we all sat down.

Haney pushed the McDonald's bag toward Alex, and after the kid had eaten one breakfast sandwich, he turned on his recorder. Staring into his milky brown coffee concoction, Alex described how Mitchell knocked at his front door around ten, jerked him into the yard, and began swinging at him with a pipe, knocking him in the head and torso and bruising his hand. All the while, Mitchell swore he'd kill him if Alex didn't quit helping the police.

Alex told the story straight, no tears or hiccups. Kellie arrived around ten thirty. She drove her car onto the lawn, jumped out, and ran at Mitchell, yelling for him to leave Alex alone. Mitchell whirled around, swinging the pipe hard. It crushed her throat and she hit the ground, already dying. Mitchell drove off.

"I ran into the house, found my cell, and called 911. I came back outside and stayed with Mom. She couldn't breathe. She kept mouthing 'Love you, Alex.'"

He lifted the coffee mug to his lips but put it down without taking a drink. "She turned blue, and the EMTs arrived." He gripped it with both hands and looked at Haney.

The detective blinked hard as he made notes in his small black book. I wondered how many kids Haney had, and their ages. I bet he was a good dad. When he finished, he turned off the recorder and looked at Alex. "You did well just now, Alex. So did your mom. She saved your life."

"I wish she hadn't." He stared into his coffee for another minute, then jerked his head up. "Did Mitchell say anything? How did he find me? You said no one was going to know my name."

Haney met the kid's angry gaze. "Nobody said anything, Alex. Mitchell told us he followed you home from the art gallery. We were getting close to him, and he smelled it. He got the idea to see what Guy was up to, spotted you, and figured you must have provided the ID. He went to your house to scare you. When your mom came after him, he got angry. We have it on tape. He's going to prison for a long time, I promise."

"It won't bring her back," Alex whispered. He swallowed hard and closed his eyes. "I stopped him from hurting Guy. Why couldn't I stop him from hurting Mom?" His voice cracked into a higher octave, reminding Haney and me that this was a boy talking.

"Nobody could have stopped him." Haney put his hand on Alex's arm and shook it gently, forcing the kid to look at him. "He said he swung hard and fast, and your mom ran into the blow. Your mom scared him off. That's what saved you. I know that's what she would have wanted. Any parent would."

Alex shook his head. Instead of arguing, Haney squeezed his arm again.

"I need some things from my house," Alex said quietly.

"I can arrange for Connor to visit the house and get what you need…. You finish your sandwiches now, okay?" Haney frowned like a parent who desperately wants to fix everything but can't. He stood up and nodded good-bye, pulling out his phone as he headed for the door.

"Do you want to make a list of things for me to get? Or do you want to come with me?"

"I'll come," Alex said hesitantly.

"Maybe Guy will be back before we leave."

He wasn't.

AT HIS house, Alex couldn't get out of the Jeep. I wasn't surprised. The whole front yard was cordoned off with yellow tape. Tire ruts marred the lawn, and Kellie's car sat where she'd left it. Another patrolman met me on the sidewalk and let me inside.

Much as I'd done for Guy two and a half months before, I made my way through a strange place collecting what was on a list and talking to Alex on the phone when I needed directions.

He answered in monosyllables. I went as fast as I could. Sitting outside he was looking straight at the murder scene. I wished Guy could have been here with him.

Kellie had been a neat housekeeper. I had no trouble finding things, except in Alex's bedroom. Messy dishes and piles of clothes clean and dirty littered the floor. When I opened the blinds to let in some light, dust particles floated on the sunbeams. It gave me an idea what the spare bedroom in my apartment was going to look like soon.

I sorted things into two piles as I gathered them—what Alex needed at the foster home and what would stay at the gallery until he came to live with me. It took five trash bags and three trips for me to move everything. His bike, clothes, four pairs of shoes, blankets and two pillows, an iPod and an old computer, books, even a couple of specific dishes were on his list. All the while, he sat in the Jeep, hunched over in the passenger seat, hoodie pulled tight over his head, staring at the floor.

"Sorry. I worked as fast as I could."

"It's okay," he mumbled.

"I got everything."

"Thanks."

"You want anything from the grocery store?"

"I'm not hungry."

Guy's car was back behind the gallery when we returned. Alex and I moved everything into the room behind the showroom, and Guy joined us a few minutes later.

"So where'd you go?" I asked as pleasantly as I could.

Guy rolled his eyes at Alex. "I'm going to be glad to share some of this cop grilling with you," he quipped.

"I'm not grilling anybody."

"Yes you are," they answered in unison.

"Is this how it's going to be now? You two ganging up on me?"

That brought the first hint of a grin back to Alex's face. But he seemed to realize it, too, and it vanished.

"My dad died when I was fifteen, Alex, so I know a little about this stuff. It's okay to smile and laugh. Your mom would like that."

"Sure." He separated out the one bag that would go with him to the Jamesons, neatly stacked the others and his bike in a corner, and headed into the showroom, muttering something about cleaning things up. He made sure to shut the door firmly behind him.

I sat on the corner of Guy's desk. "You got any ideas?"

"You're the one with the expertise," he answered too brightly.

"You're going to help me with this, aren't you?" When he didn't answer, I repeated my earlier question. "Where did you go before?"

"Connor, I'll be here for Alex. I'll do what I can to help you. But I need my space."

He didn't look at me, and I felt a stab of panic. Was he running out on me? Because I'd told him I loved him? Because he didn't want to be a parent figure and didn't want to date one? Was there someone else, besides Josh Brooks? He didn't say anything more.

"Sure. You need your space. No problem." I stood up. "I'm going home to sleep some before work. Tell Alex I'll be back in a couple of hours."

MRS. SYDLER was true to her word about rushing the paperwork and inspections for my temporary custody of Alex, pending the formal guardianship hearing. He came to live with me three days later.

He still wasn't sleeping, and he moved like a zombie as he helped carry his clothes and belongings into my apartment. Once we'd moved everything inside, he disappeared into the spare bedroom, now his, and shut the door. Nate and I had already moved his bedroom furniture and some chairs, end tables, pictures, and even dishes from Kellie's house so he'd have familiar things around him.

Guy agreed to spend nights at my apartment for a while when I was working, so Alex wasn't alone. He showed up as I called in an order to Alex's favorite pizza place.

"Did Mrs. Sydler say anything about helping him get some sleep?" he whispered. He didn't need to be quiet. Alex hadn't left his room.

"She's hoping being in a place he's been in before will make it easier for him to sleep. You got any ideas?"

"No. The past two days, he's gone up to the apartment to sleep. But I don't see how he gets any. He cranks up my sound system. I've let him do whatever he wants, but maybe I shouldn't."

"What do you mean?"

"Each time, he's come back to the gallery looking worse, haunted almost. Maybe I shouldn't let him be alone? He hasn't cried in front of me. And he hasn't talked with me about any of it."

"Me either."

Guy was quiet as he got some plates out of the cupboard and put them on the dining table. "Walker says he's going to need a lot of time," he said at last.

"How is the priest?" I was almost afraid to hear the answer. I hadn't realized Guy talked to him more often than at church on Sundays.

"He wanted you to know he's praying for you and Alex, and he'd be happy to talk with Alex if you think that would help."

Right. Walker was a psychologist besides being a priest. Another reason to watch what I said around him and about him. "That's... nice." Maybe that didn't sound sincere.

"Walker is a good guy, Connor."

I bit my lip to keep from asking if Guy was constantly taking off to see Walker. Luckily, the lobby buzzer sounded, indicating the pizza had arrived. When I returned from paying the deliveryman, Guy and Alex were seated at the table.

I gave everybody two big slices, but neither of them dug into theirs. I wasn't all that hungry, but I made an effort, hoping it might encourage Alex.

It didn't. He toyed with his food and his can of soda before giving up and settling his hands in his lap.

I tried to study him without being obvious, but he was closed up tight. When my dad died, I cried a lot. But I still had a parent to help me, and despite her alcoholic benders, Mom did comfort me. Who was going to do that for Alex?

His voice, thin and shaky, broke into my thoughts. "What's going to happen now?"

"Do you mean what's going to happen tonight? I'm off. Guy and I will be here with you."

"And I'll stay here with you on nights when Connor's working, unless you want to stay at my place," Guy added.

Alex shook his head. "My... mom," he breathed. "What about my mom?"

Guy looked at me in panic.

"Detective Haney called about an hour ago. I was going to tell you after supper. Kellie's body will be released tomorrow."

Alex's eyes grew round with fear. "What does that mean?"

"We can plan her funeral now."

Alex looked from me to Guy, and he, thank God, was ready with a reply. "Walker—you remember him, Alex. My friend the priest. He suggested a funeral home to me. Would you like to use that one?"

"What does it cost? Mom and me...." He sucked in a breath and swallowed hard. "There's not a lot of money."

Guy nodded. "Walker said he can get us help with that too. He could do the service, and there's a fund at his church that could help with the cost." He paused to let that sink in. "Would you like that?"

"We can call the funeral home first thing tomorrow," I offered.

Alex nodded. "Thank you. Can I be excused?"

"Sure. I'll put the leftovers in the fridge. Help yourself if you get hungry later."

He was already halfway to his bedroom. In another minute, the radio blared through the door. Guy arched his eyebrows. I shrugged back. I didn't know what to do.

"That's a good idea you had, getting help from Walker with the funeral planning." I picked up the pizza box and took it to the fridge.

"Once in a while, I can fix things too."

"What do you mean by that?"

"Nothing."

"Bull." I slammed the refrigerator door closed. "Say what you mean, Guy."

He glanced at the clock on the stove. "Sorry. I gotta be somewhere. I'll be back in a couple of hours." He put down the plates he'd picked up and headed out the door.

I finished the rest of the cleanup without banging doors or dishes and tried to figure what Guy meant about fixing things. Did he think I fixed things too much? I was trying to restore order, like I was trained to. I was good at it. What was Guy's problem? What was I not understanding?

A fearful cry split the air: Alex, screaming. I headed for the bedroom door and cracked it open.

"Alex? Can I come in?"

He answered with a moan that I took as a yes. I stepped inside.

He sat up on the bed, on top of the covers, his back against the headboard. He had that haunted look like he'd been awakened from a nightmare. "My mom is dead, and it's my fault," he said without looking at me.

I killed the radio and sat down beside him. "I know you think that, but it's not true. Jimmy Mitchell did this. He's the one responsible. You and your mom are the victims."

"If I hadn't helped Guy, if I hadn't drawn that picture of Mitchell, if I had protected my mom—"

"Stop." I put my arms around him and held on even as he stayed stiff. "It's easy to think this way, but it's not true. You saved Guy's life."

"And killed my mother," he wailed.

He pulled away from me, but I hung on. "You didn't kill your mom. She was proud of what you did for Guy. That took real bravery. She taught you that. You honored her when you saved Guy. I'm very grateful you did."

He shook his head. "It's my fault," he mumbled.

"We'll keep talking about this until you quit thinking that." I pulled him close again. He collapsed against me and began to cry body-shaking, noisy sobs.

I let him, biting my lip to keep from shushing him or telling him things would be all right. People had said that to me. They'd been wrong. Things were painful and lonely and different after my dad died. After my mom died too. While the pain eventually disappeared, and a new normal emerged, some part of me was always alone right up until I realized I had a new family with Nate, Jenna, and Andy. Now I had a chance at one of my own with Guy and Alex. Either could say no, or leave at any time, or open up to the possibilities. I would have to wait for them to see that for themselves.

Alex stopped crying. He pushed out of my arms and looked at me. "You said your dad died when you were fifteen? How?"

"He was a cop. He was killed in the line of duty."

"How?" he repeated.

"A psychopath hijacked a school bus, one of those mini ones, with six kids on it. They all had Down syndrome. My dad was the first officer on the scene. When he got there, the man grabbed a ten-year-old and held a gun to his head. Dad tried to talk the guy down, but he turned the gun on Dad. They fired at each other at the same time. Dad killed him with one shot and died two hours later in a hospital."

"Your dad was a hero."

"So are you."

He shook his head. Tears filled his eyes again. "I don't want to be…. I want my mom back."

He leaned into me, and I wrapped my arms around him as he cried again, hard and long until only hiccups remained.

"Can you try to sleep now? You need to sleep."

"No! I might wake up screaming again. I did that at the Jamesons'. I woke up all the kids. I don't want to do that anymore."

"It's okay if you do." I pushed him gently toward the pillows. "I'll stay here for a bit if you like, and I'll come back if you start screaming. It's okay, Alex. You need to sleep."

He shook his head, but eventually he rolled over, curled up tight, and drifted off. I sat with him until the sun went down. Then I went to bed. Alex didn't wake me again, and Guy didn't come back.

TWENTY-TWO

FIRST THING the next morning, I set up an afternoon appointment with the funeral home. I called Guy to tell him. Neither of us said a word about his disappearing the day before and not coming back. He volunteered that Walker would join us at the funeral home. Then he said he had to get back to work and hung up. That was it.

I moved to the next thing on my agenda and was no more successful. I wanted Alex to grocery shop with me so we could buy things he liked. But he asked to be excused and didn't offer suggestions.

"I'm not hungry anymore," he mumbled. Wandering the aisles alone, I had no idea what to put in the cart. So I called Jenna. She'd begun working again, part-time now, at the yarn shop.

I could hear the smile in her voice as soon as she recognized mine. "Are you okay? How are things going?"

"You're not busy now, are you?"

"Nope. I'm in the lull before the lunchtime rush. What do you need? I can send Nate over."

"Thanks, but I don't need his help. I need yours. I'm in the grocery store trying to figure out what to buy for a teenager."

"These days, I'm more familiar with the baby aisle, but I'll do what I can. What aisle are you in?"

"Sodas."

"Cans are probably your best bet. You waste a lot when the bottles go flat. Do you know what he likes?"

"Diet Coke. He orders it at every restaurant, and Guy has taken to stocking it at the gallery for him."

"Thank goodness he drinks the diet variety. Buy…. two cases to start. Does he like chips or pretzels?"

"Not that I've seen. He's not a snacker."

"Great. Stroll down the snack aisle anyway and pick up a couple of cans of unsalted mixed nuts. Those will be healthier. If he doesn't eat them for snacks, you can throw them in salads. And if he doesn't eat salad either, bring them to my house. Do you have any idea what he eats or what else he drinks?"

"Coffee with milk and lots of chocolate syrup."

She chuckled. "He's a sugar fiend. Head for the dairy aisle."

Once I was there, she instructed me to grab two gallons of two percent milk and some yogurt with fruit on the bottom. "Lots of sugar in that, but some calcium too. How are you on eggs, bacon, butter, and bread?" We continued like that through the store until I'd been everywhere but the baby aisle. The cart was full.

"You must have some customers by now."

"They've been waiting patiently, and offering their own suggestions. One of the ladies has teenagers," she answered. "They've enjoyed helping."

"Thank everyone for me."

"I will. Call again as soon as you need to, and you three come over for dinner tonight. I put a meatloaf in the slow cooker this morning."

"You sure? Alex says he's not hungry anymore. And we're going to the funeral home late this afternoon."

"You and Guy will still need to eat, and you won't want to cook."

"Thanks, Jenna. I think I'm going to be saying that a lot in the next few days."

"That's all you have to do every time, Connor. You're family now. Alex and Guy too. We're here to help any way we can."

I BEAT Alex and Guy to the funeral home, but not Walker. A receptionist led me to the soothing green conference room where the priest already sat in one of the leather swivel chairs that circled a table for six to eight people. He wore jeans, a pale blue polo shirt, and sandals. A bar with a minifridge, an elaborate coffeemaker, a huge carousel of coffee pods, plus lots of glasses and mugs, lined the wall behind his chair.

He stood and shook my hand. "How are things going with Alex?"

I shrugged. "He doesn't sleep well. He wakes up screaming sometimes, and he says he's not hungry anymore."

"Nothing unusual there, considering. I can talk to him if you think that will help?"

I studied him for a minute. He was nothing but sincere. No hidden motives, no hidden anything that I could discern. Nothing about Guy. So I brought him up. "From what Guy says, you're already helping more than I can ever thank you for."

He shook his head. "You're doing a commendable thing becoming Alex's guardian, Connor. I want to do anything I can to help. Even testify in court if you need it."

"Thanks. That could help a lot. If Alex is willing to talk to you, I'll be glad to bring him around too."

The door opened, and the receptionist led Guy and Alex in and offered us all something to drink. Guy asked for tea. Walker and I both took a bottle of water, but Alex passed. He clasped his hands on the table and stared at them, flexing his fingers again and again. A few minutes later, a young man in a dark suit came in. He introduced himself as Jamie Schilling, the funeral director who would be helping us.

"How old are you?" Alex demanded.

Schilling smiled. "Twenty-seven, but I know what I'm doing, Alex."

"I've worked with Jamie before. He's quite good," Walker offered.

But Alex had turned back to Schilling. "Why would anyone young become a funeral director?"

"It's been my family's business for three generations." Jamie answered like he'd been asked the question lots of times. "And I like helping people. Are you sure I can't get you anything to drink?"

Alex eyed the coffeemaker. "Can you make a mocha cappuccino?"

Jamie nodded. "I like those too." In a few minutes, he handed Alex a full cup.

Alex took it and leaned back in his chair, like he was trying to distance himself from the conversation that was about to start. Or maybe he needed room to bounce his knee. It popped up and down like an engine piston, the nervous energy like a sixth person in the room.

At last, the kid took a long drink, then swallowed hard. "My mom wanted to be cremated."

"That's a good choice." Schilling began to make notes on the legal pad he'd brought in.

With Walker's guidance, we planned a funeral at his church for three days off. Alex made every decision, sometimes looking to Guy or me for advice, sometimes simply agreeing to Walker's or Jamie's suggestions. A couple of times, his response was a brisk, "Whatever's cheapest." He didn't falter or get rattled, he kept drinking the mocha. Jamie made him a second as soon as he finished the first.

"What's the total cost?" Alex asked once we were done with the decisions.

"I think we'll be able to get some help from a church fund," Walker answered. "You don't have to worry about that now, Alex."

"But we do need to think about the media," Jamie said.

"You're kidding." Guy slumped in his chair.

"Media?" Alex asked in alarm.

"Unfortunately. Because this was a violent death that made the news," Jamie answered. "You can probably avoid the cameras by getting to the church early, Alex. And I'd suggest a private burial at a later date, one that's not announced in the newspapers."

That's what we did. A TV crew did show up, and they filmed people arriving at Walker's church, but they never got a lens on Alex. Walker conducted a great service, with kind words about Kellie and her sacrifice for her son. He quoted a Bible verse about how she showed the greatest love, and said we shouldn't see her death as a tragedy but view her life as an example of how to love and something to aspire to.

He spoke directly to Alex, too, telling him not to feel responsible for Kellie's death, because he wasn't, and not to feel responsible for not being able to stop it, because he couldn't. He wasn't to blame, and he wasn't being punished, because God was on his side. God was on all our sides.

I hoped Alex could believe that. I wanted to. I promised myself I'd repeat some of the words to him later, because if the kid was going to move forward, he needed to come up with some positive way to make sense of things.

Haney and Sergeant Nash came, and Nate and Jenna, and a couple of Kellie's friends. So did some of Alex's school friends, along with their parents, plus several of Alex's teachers, the band director, and the principal. They all stayed for the lunch the church women's society arranged. The director and principal, and a couple of the parents, gave me their phone numbers in case I needed anything, which was nice. And Walker said he'd be in touch with me about the bill. The Schillings, who were church members, had given us a discount, a church committee would pay part of it, and I could make payments on the balance. I told him I couldn't thank him enough, and I meant it. All these years later, I still didn't know what my mom's funeral cost. My dad's friends took care of it, and I wanted to do the same for Alex.

The urn came home with us, and Alex put it on the dresser in the bedroom. He didn't seem to be in a hurry to do anything with it, and that was okay with me. We'd managed the hard part, and he'd made it through with clenched teeth and a few tears. He was sleeping without waking up screaming, at least for now. I told him his mom would be proud, but he could cry or scream when he needed to. Walker called him regularly. Alex and I went riding a lot, and Guy spent the night whenever I worked.

Guy was there, but he wasn't. He helped Alex however he could, and he did thoughtful things for both Alex and me, but he kept an emotional distance from me. He never spent nights at the apartment when I was there. He arrived after I left for work. And he still disappeared for a few hours at least once, and sometimes twice, every day. I thought about following him to see where he went. But every time my mind went there, I imagined Guy catching me and ending our relationship.

Finally, I asked Alex about it on one of our rides. "I'd sure like to know where he runs off to."

"He'll be back, Connor."

"Do you know where he goes?"

Alex looked off across the fields we were biking. "Not really."

"He never says. Doesn't that bother you?"

Alex shrugged. "He always comes back."

I couldn't argue with that. "You want to go get something to eat?"

We ended up at an Italian place. We both ordered spaghetti. When it arrived, I brought up something I'd been wondering about since the funeral. "Who was the long-haired brunette there that day?"

"Huh?"

"The one who gave you a big hug. In the blue dress."

"Tracy. We're in band together."

"Is she your girlfriend?"

"Just a friend." He wrinkled his nose at me, like the question embarrassed him.

"Just asking." I changed the subject. "The band director told me band practice starts in three weeks?"

"Yeah. We have heavy-duty practice for the football halftime shows. We do some intricate marching routines."

"What do you play? I haven't noticed an instrument around."

"Drums. I've got drum pads in the bedroom, and I've been practicing. They don't make the noise that real drums do."

I nodded. "I don't know if I'll make it to many games to watch you, Alex. I'm not sure how the department shifts things around to cover football yet."

"Don't worry about it. Mom couldn't always make my band events. I don't expect you to. You're doing enough giving me a place to live." He glanced around the restaurant at the others in the dining room. The crowd was sparse. One young family and a couple of tables of senior citizens. Things wouldn't pick up for a bit.

"You can have kids over to the apartment anytime you like, as long as Guy or I are there. You know that, right?"

"Yeah. Thanks."

"You know Guy and I won't do anything to, ah, embarrass you, right?" I felt my face heating up.

He grinned, probably at my discomfort. Still, I was glad to see it. "You mean with PDAs?"

I was definitely blushing. "Yeah, I guess."

"I'm cool with it. And, Connor?" He paused for emphasis. Or was I afraid of what was coming next? "Kisses and hugs are okay around me, okay?"

"Okay. Thanks." *Thanks?* Time to move on to the next few issues. I wanted to raise them like they weren't any big deal.

"Another thing. I'm not sure having a lot of people know about Guy and me will help with the guardianship petition. I'm not saying you need to lie about us, you understand? But if we could keep that between us for now—and Jenna and Nate or Walker if you want to talk to anyone about it—that might be good. Not because I'm embarrassed or anything, and I don't want you to be either. But it might be enough for some people to make trouble for us. Understand?"

He nodded and kept chewing. Or was he laughing at me?

I lowered my voice and leaned toward him. "I don't advertise my sexuality, okay? On account of my job."

He swallowed and dropped his voice to a conspiratorial whisper. "I know. Guy told me you're in the closet at work. I won't tell anyone."

Now I was beyond embarrassed. I couldn't see any way to recover but to be honest. I took a deep breath. "In some jobs, it's not easy to be out. The culture is different, the people are different, and you have to work with that. Is that going to be a problem for you, my not being as open as Guy?"

He shook his head and gave me a serious look that I wasn't sure was on the level. "I understand the macho cop thing. I watch TV." I swear, the kid *was* laughing at me. But he continued. "It's nobody's business, including mine. More of a problem is that you're a cop." Hell, he was trying to kid with me. "But I can live with that."

"Thanks. I guess."

"And Connor? We don't need to have the sex talk, okay? I got that one already."

"Smartass."

TWENTY-THREE

ANOTHER WEEK went by, with Guy still keeping his distance from me. We were more like friends than lovers. I concentrated on everything else I had to do: spend time with Alex, meet with the lawyer about the guardianship, grocery shop. I had to do that nearly every other day. I was cleaning the apartment more often, too, now that two people lived there. And I cleaned out Kellie and Alex's house. Nate offered to help, but I told him to spend time with his wife and baby. Alex didn't say a thing at all about his old house, and I didn't push him. I was avoiding every confrontation I could, I suppose, though I told myself I was being considerate. If I didn't know what to do with stuff, I put it in Nate and Jenna's garage. I filled one-half of it, but they didn't complain.

With all of that, I should have been overwhelmed, but what I felt was lonely. I missed Guy.

I asked Jenna about it, during one of our regular phone conversations about Alex. She started the conversation, like she always did, by talking about Alex.

"I stopped in at the gallery with Andy. Alex told me again how grateful he is for all you're doing for him."

"I wish I could do more."

"He knows that, and he says you're doing all the right things, that there's nothing anyone can do for him."

"He told you that?"

"Yeah. He's opening up more to me now that I see him nearly every day. He's a pretty wise kid. Kind of an old soul, I think. His mother must have been amazing."

"She was. Just like you. You two would have gotten along great."

"You're doing great," she countered. "Keep talking to him. He wants you to."

"I don't suppose Guy told you anything like that?" I was hinting around for any guidance at all about him.

Jenna sighed. She knew what I was doing. "I don't know what to tell you there. Sorry. Guy was his normal self with customers, and he was great with Andy, like always."

"But?"

"I can't put my finger on it." She was quiet a moment. "He seemed distant around me, almost like he was unsure of himself. Yeah, that was it. He wasn't trying to pull away. Does that make sense?"

"Not really. I don't understand him these days. But that sounds like a better description than anything I've come up with."

"I wish I could tell you more. Just treat him like you always do."

"That's what your female voodoo advises?"

She laughed. "My husband's a nut. You know that, don't you?"

"He's a good nut."

"So are you. Hang in there, Connor."

FINALLY ONE Sunday, I made a point to go to church with Guy and Alex and suggested lunch afterward too. I hoped Guy and I might start talking about anything. But all we discussed was Walker's great sermon—Guy went on and on about that—and what was happening at the gallery, and marching band practice. Guy didn't look at me, even though I sat across the table from him and watched him plenty. He looked healthy, clear-eyed, and stronger. You couldn't tell his right shoulder had been injured. But he looked nervous every time he caught me looking at him. I didn't like it.

I tried to talk about us after lunch as we waited for Alex outside a video game store. "What have you been doing with yourself?"

"Working," he replied, looking off across the parking lot. "And being as supportive of Alex as I can, and painting some."

"Anything I can see?"

"Nothing I even want to talk about." He turned his head in my direction but stared at my shoes.

I waved my hand at him, trying to get him to look at me. "I miss you."

He shifted his gaze to his own shoes. "Connor, I... wanted to tell you how—what I mean is.... Damn, I can't. I can't do this yet. I need to get some things figured out."

"Maybe I can help you." I took a step toward him.

He backed away from me. "You can't."

Whatever he'd wanted to say, he'd changed his mind. Numbness settled over me. I tried again. "I've hardly seen you for weeks."

"You see me every day."

"For twenty minutes tops, and never alone." I lowered my voice. "I told you I love you. I meant it."

"I haven't forgotten," he whispered.

"You don't even want to be around me."

He stepped back again, like the words offended him. "It's not that."

"There's someone else." I hadn't known how close to the surface that idea was.

He pulled at his shirt collar. "No, I need time. It's about me. That's all." He looked at me at last, searching for something he wanted desperately, something I couldn't give because I didn't understand, because I was too hurt and angry. But I recognized the moment he gave up looking for it. He glanced around for an escape route.

"Tell Alex I needed to get to the gallery, and he can have the afternoon off to play his new game. I don't think things are going to be busy. I have to go."

"Yeah. You've got a meeting to get to."

Sadness chased the irritation from his features. "Just tell him." He turned and jogged across the parking lot to his car. In a few minutes, he was gone. He didn't look back.

AFTER THAT, I left Guy alone and concentrated on establishing a routine that would help Alex feel comfortable spending some nights alone when I was working. I didn't want to count on Guy as much. Maybe I was petty. I thought I was smart. I arranged times for Jenna to call on nights Alex was alone, I stopped by on my dinner hour, and Alex phoned me before he went to sleep. I called the new arrangement our plan for the start of school, because Alex would need to be in the same place each night to do his homework.

Everyone went along with it. Alex did because it made him feel like an adult, and he was trying hard to make everything easy. If Guy was bothered, he didn't say. He didn't even go out of his way to spend time with me until the first home football game the first Friday of September.

Nate and I had the night off, so he and Jenna bundled up Andy, I picked up Guy, and we all sat together in the home stands. We texted Alex with our location, and he glanced our way when the band marched out for the pregame show, though he didn't wave or do anything anyone would notice. I spotted Tracy, the brunette who had come to the funeral, playing the snare immediately to his right in the second row of the drum section, and they did a fair amount of talking to each other when they weren't playing or marching.

Jenna spotted that too. "Who's the girl who keeps talking to Alex?"

"Tracy," Guy answered. "They have several classes together besides band, and they get together to study."

"Let's hope there's an adult there most nights," Nate muttered.

Jenna gave me the eye. "You know about this?"

"Kind of." I was too embarrassed to say I didn't know as much as Guy.

"What does that mean?" Nate asked.

"It means I noticed her at the funeral and asked him about her, and he said they're friends."

"Friends," Jenna repeated.

"According to the court, I'm the adult who's supposed to worry about Alex," I reminded them. We'd gotten approval of my guardianship the day before. Tonight was supposed to be a celebration, not a commentary on my parenting.

"You're doing a great job too," Guy said. I think he was sincere.

"I don't know why you didn't let me throw a celebration dinner about that," Jenna said again.

"That's nice of you, Jenna, but it's crazy right now with school starting, band practice, football games, and Alex's schedule with work and the school magazine. Who knew teenagers were so busy? I think we'll have time around Thanksgiving."

"Then you're all committed. Thanksgiving dinner at our house."

"Only if you let me buy the turkey," I replied.

"Done." Jenna beamed and turned her attention to her son. "So, Andy, we will have a big, big Thanksgiving for your first one, with our whole extended family. How about that?"

"Sounds great," Guy said enthusiastically.

I looked at him in shock, and he gave me one of his sweet smiles. He was too cute in his black-and-red striped Bozeman Hawks scarf, and I couldn't resist the urge to pull a bit on both ends at once. He giggled and arched his eyebrows suggestively. When the Hawks scored after that and we all jumped up to cheer, he made sure to furtively slide his hand down my thigh as we sat down again. I got his message loud and clear, and though I didn't understand his sudden change in attitude, parts of me south of the beltline definitely liked his attention.

During the first half, the air temperature plummeted. Guy scooted an inch closer to me, and we both heated up. After the halftime show, which was pretty spectacular, Nate and Jenna took off with Andy. A few minutes later, my phone buzzed.

"It's Alex," I told Guy. "He wants to know if he can go out for pizza with some of the kids from band. He's got a ride home."

"Tell him absolutely, as long as he's home by midnight."

"Don't you think I should ask who's driving him home?"

"My money is on Tracy. She has a car." Guy looked at my surprised face and giggled. "What do you think he talks about every day at the gallery? Tracy, her car, and how soon he'll turn sixteen and can drive Kellie's car."

My eyebrows shot up.

"Don't worry. They're both good kids. Tell him you'll be home at midnight, too, so he'd better not be late," he instructed.

"What am I doing until midnight?"

He rolled his eyes, then looked at the scoreboard. "I think we've got this victory wrapped up. Let's beat the rush out of here."

"Sounds like a plan."

Guy jumped up. "Let's go."

I followed him down the bleachers.

"I haven't been to one of these games in years. I had a lot of fun."

"What are we doing next?" I asked once we were in the Jeep.

His left hand landed on my dick. "Going to my place."

"Okay." His hand didn't leave my lap until we parked behind the gallery.

Upstairs, he pulled out chips and salsa. "I've got seltzer, and limes, and flavored water and soda," he offered. No alcoholic choices, and that was fine with me.

"Water works for me."

"Me too." He pulled two bottles out of the fridge and led the way to the living room couch. "You want TV or music?" He pointed out the end he wanted me at and I sat down.

"How about we talk? We haven't had time together in a long time."

"Sounds good." He twirled around, gracefully deposited his bottom in my lap, turned his face into mine, and kissed me. I was hard that fast.

"Mmmm," he moaned against my lips. "You like my idea of sports."

I pulled back and looked into his eyes, which were already lust filled. "I do, but I feel like we ought to talk about a few things first."

He stilled, but he didn't look away. "All right. Do you want to start?"

"We haven't been together—we've barely talked for weeks. What's going on, Guy?"

"It's a fair question." He fidgeted his hands in his lap, but he stayed in mine, and he looked at me again. "I haven't lied to you, Connor. I've been dealing with some of my stuff, holdovers from my attack that came back when Kellie died. I'm making good progress. I want us to be a couple, if you're willing. I'm ready for it again."

"You want to tell me a little more?"

"Not really." He cupped my face in his hands. "I will talk about it, one day soon. But I want to wait until I have more to say and can say it confidently. I know it sounds like I'm playing games, but I'm not. Please trust me. I have some more stuff to get through."

"Are you in counseling?"

"Something like that."

I frowned, not sure what he meant. He frowned back. "Please, Connor. I want… I care for you more than I can put into words. I know how you feel about me, and I don't deserve it, but I am so happy and grateful. I know that doesn't sound fair. When I feel sure that I won't mess up, I'll tell you everything. And it will all be good and wonderful. Please, give me a little more time."

I studied his face, so earnest now, and his hopeful eyes. He looked like a little kid. He looked like the man I'd fallen in love with. "Okay." I brushed my lips across his. He kissed me back hard.

When I opened my mouth, his tongue rushed in. I didn't argue, and that was all the encouragement he needed to push me down on the couch. He made me hot, and he was hotter. I groaned, and he giggled and tore at my fly, popping the snap and pulling hard on the zipper. I lifted my ass, and he pulled my pants down to my knees. He went after my shirt, fighting the buttons first, then pulling the shirt apart. All the while, his tongue teased at mine.

Eventually, I pulled off his sweater, revealing his chest, finely muscled with the trace of a scar on his shoulder. I kissed it softly.

"You've done so well with your recovery." I kissed it again. "I'm so proud of you."

He brushed his fingers down my cheek. "Because of you," he whispered. "I couldn't have done it if you hadn't taken me home with you."

I looked into his eyes, shining bright and clear for me, and he wrapped his arms around my neck, nuzzled my collarbone, and kissed it. "Thank you," he whispered.

I ran my hands down his ribs to settle them on his waist, but he squirmed with ticklish laughter long before they landed there.

"Connor," he squealed.

"Get rid of your pants. Ride me."

He pushed off me, landed both feet on the floor, unzipped, and let his jeans fall around his ankles. He stepped out of them and dashed to the bathroom. "Be right back."

But he wasn't. "Guy!"

"Just a minute. I'm getting ready," he yelled.

He scampered back into the room, a condom packet in hand. He straddled and sheathed me, rose up on his knees, and slid down my length. I felt the slick as I glided in. He had been prepping in the bathroom, and he moaned in delight as he pushed down and I thrust in.

"Again," I gasped. "Do it again."

"Oh yeah. Good. You feel so good," he babbled as he moved. I felt the delicious slide as he came down, followed by a quivering, resistant pull as he pushed back up, over and over, until I was gasping.

"Do it," he cried, covering my mouth with his as he furiously pumped up and down. I stiffened and came with a groan. He did, too, screaming into my mouth until he collapsed on my chest.

I held him close, running my hands up and down his back, laying a line of kisses across his sweaty forehead. "Wow, you're as good as new."

"All of me?"

I chuckled. "All of you. I think you've been exercising those quads too. They were magnificent."

"Magnificent," he echoed. He raised his head and kissed my lips.

"Magnificent," I repeated against his mouth. "You can do that again anytime you get the urge."

He turned his head to look at the clock on the cable box. "Oh, I could get the urge, but you don't have the time, parent figure." He giggled. "You and Alex and Cinderella have to be home by midnight."

I pulled him tight to my chest. I wanted to tell him I loved him, but I didn't. It didn't feel right. As if to confirm the thought, a voice I hadn't heard in years popped into my head, a little girl's voice coming from a young woman's body. I was fifteen, she a much older seventeen. We sat around a table in a church basement meeting of teenagers, many of them brave enough to talk while I held back, too scared to tell my mother's secrets.

"My boyfriend told me he loves me and wants to take me away from all the craziness of my dysfunctional family," she said, clutching her soda can. "I don't even know what he means when he says it. How can someone who's never heard the words understand what someone means when they say they love you?"

How, I wondered, even as I understood why Guy hadn't said anything for all these weeks. Of course he couldn't tell me he loved me. What answer had someone in the group given her? What did she say at a later meeting? I needed to know, but no recollections came. That hadn't been my issue. I hadn't paid attention. Another voice sounded in my head now, saying words I'd heard a million times but never appreciated when I was a kid who wanted everything fixed immediately: "Let go. Let God." Lots of people in the meetings said them. My mom did after she started going to meetings. I realized she was saying them to me now, and I smiled.

Guy raised his head from my chest, his chocolate-brown eyes searching my face. "You okay? Where'd you go?"

I hugged him tighter. "I'm right here."

He gave me a tentative smile. "If we close the gallery on time tomorrow night, can you eat dinner with Alex and me before you go in to work?"

"Sure. Sounds great."

"What days are you off next week?"

"Wednesday, Thursday, and Friday."

"If Alex is heading over to Tracy's on Thursday, and I'm sure he is, do you want to have dinner with Josh and Dane? All the guests are gone until elk hunting starts, and they've invited us. We can be back by ten so you can be at the apartment when he gets home."

"Sounds like fun. Tell them I'm looking forward to it."

TWENTY-FOUR

"THESE MOUNTAINS are so much wilder looking," I told Guy, waving at the sharp ridges and peaks that filled the windshield as we headed south of Livingston, Montana, into Paradise Valley where Josh and Dane lived.

Though we were just thirty miles from Bozeman, the scenery was vastly different. The two-lane road we took off Highway 89 twisted this way and that, bisecting fields now shorn of their crops and sprawling rangelands that fed Black Angus cattle, sheep, and herds of horses. For a moment, we caught a glimpse of the Yellowstone River and its fly fishermen, some standing thigh-deep in the water, others in boats or standing along the shore, all adept at snaking their long lines high over the sparkling surface. On this cool fall day, the sun bathed the landscape with a pale golden light that made everything look like a paradise.

We pulled in to Brooks Ranch with the wind, which had started to blow as we neared Livingston. When Guy opened the passenger door, a great gust immediately slammed it shut, trapping him inside. I ran around the Jeep, opened it again, and held on tight. As soon as he was clear and I let it go, the wind banged it closed again.

"Keep a look out for the Wicked Witch of the West," I yelled, and he laughed, his eyes sparkling. He'd been excited since the minute I picked him up at the gallery. I grabbed his hand, and we ran like two kids to Josh's front door. It flew open, we jumped inside, and Josh shut it firmly behind us.

"Look what the wind blew in," Guy exclaimed, getting the words out between giggles.

Dane groaned, but Josh and I laughed. Guy's giggle was contagious. He was happy to be here, and I was ready for us to have a good time together. I brushed his fine, windblown hair out of his face. He wrinkled his nose at me, and I tweaked it before letting my hands fall away from him.

"Look at you, Guy," Josh exclaimed. "No sling! How's the shoulder doing? Are you painting?"

"Fine, and yes, and that's enough about me," Guy answered, giggling again.

"Is the wind always like this?" I asked Josh.

"Often. It keeps the weather interesting. And it's something the valley is famous for. Now what do you two want to drink? I've got beer, Connor, and fixings for martinis for you, Guy."

Guy froze, like he wasn't sure what to do. "You did that for me?" He sounded astonished, and he paused for a long minute before adding, "I'll do the mixing."

"You're going to have to," Josh answered, and he grinned as he led us into the kitchen. He looked back toward Dane and asked him to get three beers. Ranger nodded, and they held each other's gaze for a long moment, grinning like teenagers, before Dane opened the fridge and fetched the bottles. Josh proudly pointed out the hard stuff, sitting on a counter alongside a shot glass, shaker, martini glass, and small bowl of olives.

Guy's eyes grew round. "You got all of this for me?"

"You bet," Josh replied. "It's been forever since you've been here."

Since at least this time last year, I figured. That's when Josh told Guy he'd fallen for Dane, crushing any hopes Guy had that the man he loved would love him back. Now Dane and Josh were a solid couple, and Guy and I... well, at least we were lovers again.

"Have a seat," Josh instructed, waving toward the set table. He put on a denim apron that protected his front from chest to knees. "We can talk while dinner finishes up."

"You're cooking, right?" Guy asked as he went to work mixing his martini. "No offense, Dane."

Dane laughed as he handed me a bottle of Cold Smoke, then passed a beer to Josh. "None taken. Josh is a great cook, and now I figure I won't need to cook again for the rest of my life." The goofy smile was back on his face as he popped the cap off of his bottle and clinked it to Josh's.

Josh was all grins too. What was up with them? I glanced at Guy. He had noticed.

"What's for dinner?" I slid into a seat at the table. Martini made, Guy came to sit beside me.

"Steaks," Josh answered. "This is a cattle ranch, you know."

"You're going to grill outside in this wind?" Guy asked. "Are you nuts?"

"Nope. I'm using my new range, complete with indoor grill." Josh stepped toward it and waved his hand dramatically. "Isn't it great? It was a gift from Dane." The shiny, stainless steel range was oversized, with two ovens, four burners, and a huge grill area.

"I got tired of grilling out in the cold," Dane explained. "Now we can grill year-round without freezing our asses off."

"Like yours was the ass that was freezing." Josh's gripe turned to a yelp as Dane smacked his butt with an open hand. The crack hung in the air, pouring sexual heat on the horseplay.

"But I work hard to keep your ass warm, Josh." The look Dane gave his partner smoldered.

"TMI!" Guy yelled. His smile was more pained than playful, and it quickly disappeared as he took a gulp from his glass.

"This is an amazing place, Josh," I said, changing topics.

"Thanks." He began to fiddle with the grill knobs.

"I saw the sign saying this was a Centennial Ranch. What's that about?"

"My family has been on this land for over a hundred years," he answered. "Any family that can prove that can apply for the designation."

"Josh's great-grandfather started Brooks Ranch in 1870. He was part of the cattle drive that brought the first Texas longhorns to Montana, and he started one of the state's first horse ranches," Guy chimed in. It bothered me that he knew that detail. I caught his eye and arched an eyebrow. He took another drink from his glass.

"Medium rare okay for you, Connor?" Josh asked as he put four big steaks on his new grill top.

"Sounds great."

"I'll get the salad out," Dane said. "Potatoes are done. We'll be ready to eat in a few minutes."

"How did the guest season go?" Guy asked.

"It ended with a bang," Dane said, putting a clear glass bowl of salad greens, yellow peppers, cucumbers, and tomatoes on the table. "We hosted two special weeks for gay teens and their families, and the second one ended with a wedding." The crazy grin was back on his face.

"A wedding? A gay wedding?" Now I was surprised.

"Well, it was a commitment ceremony really," Josh said, flipping the steaks one at a time so they sizzled and sent a puff of wonderfully aromatic smoke toward the table. My mouth watered in anticipation.

"Two of your teenaged guests had a commitment ceremony?" I grinned at Guy as I said it, but he didn't notice. He was up and headed toward the martini shaker to top off his half-empty glass. His gaze was pinned on Josh.

Dane put his arm around Josh's waist, and his partner turned away from the grill to give him a look of unabashed love. Dane beamed down at him. "Nope," he said, "Josh and I did."

Thank God they were looking at each other. When I glanced at Guy, his eyes were wide with surprise that, in a heartbeat, turned to profound pain. He snapped them shut, like a kid fighting to hold back tears, breathed out a long breath, and blinked his eyes open again. They were absolutely blank. He drained his glass, reached for the silver shaker, and began to make another drink, heavy on the vodka.

I watched it all, until I realized the kitchen was far too quiet. "That is so great, you two. Congratulations." And I meant it. I raised my bottle.

Guy offered a toast, too, holding up the shaker. "To the happy couple." His voice was flat, but he was quick to clink my bottle and Dane's. Then he poured another drink. When Josh raised his beer, Guy tapped it with his glass, but he kept his eyes on it, like he needed to make sure it would connect safely.

"Thanks, Guy. I appreciate that." Josh's smile was huge and sincere. He turned back to the grill. "Sit down now, all of you. Steaks are done."

Guy complied, and Josh brought a platter of steaks to the table, put one on each plate, and took his seat. Dane took the empty plate from him, put it in the sink, and sat down too.

Guy methodically cut a bite and popped it in his mouth. "Mmm. Josh, this is fantastic." But his voice was as detached as his expression.

"It is, Josh," I agreed, trying to cover for Guy, to give him a minute to regain his balance. *This is going to be fine,* I told myself. *You and Guy are solid.*

"Your family was okay with the ceremony?" Guy continued.

"They were. It came together fast, so it was just family and guests," Josh said, sounding apologetic.

"One of our guests was a minister. He did the service," Dane explained.

"It sounds like it was great."

"Must have been nice," Guy said, looking at nobody. He put his glass to his lips and drained it.

After that, the conversation turned to inquiries about Alex and how he was doing and what was new with the gallery. Josh was pretty up to date on our lives, like Guy called him regularly. Now, though, I answered most of the questions. Guy was nearly silent and motionless until he got up and headed for the vodka again.

"Will you get me another beer, Guy?" Josh asked.

"You bet." He fetched a bottle from the refrigerator and brought it to the table, wrapping one arm around Josh's shoulder and leaning in a little too close as he put it down in front of him. He held on too long too.

Dane watched it all, not saying a word.

"Thanks, Guy," Josh said, pulling back from the embrace.

Guy swerved slightly as he navigated his way to his chair.

"I'll clean up in here and put the coffee on," Josh said, rising out of his chair. He stepped toward the sink. "You three go into the living room. I'll join you in a minute."

Dane and I did as ordered, moving into the other room and settling in, me in a leather chair and Dane on the couch. But Guy didn't follow. I looked at Dane. His attention was on the kitchen. An uneasy feeling roiled my gut. My cop instincts lit up.

I heard the clatter of plates being cleared, followed by, "Thanks, Guy," and the sound of water running in the sink. Next came a long giggle and the sudden crash of dishes landing hard, maybe even breaking.

Dane was off the couch and halfway to the kitchen before Josh's harsh tone reached us. "Guy, stop it already."

I followed, and we both hit the doorway in time to see Josh push a wobbly, resisting Guy away from him, then swipe his hand across his mouth. Guy had kissed him. I wanted to back everything up for a do-over, this time making sure I took Guy out of the kitchen with me. But I couldn't.

Dane took a step into the room. "It's time for you to leave, Guy."

Guy had stumbled against a counter when Josh pushed him. Now he stood tall against it and stared up at Dane. "I'm not sorry," he said thickly. Did he think he could challenge the Army Ranger, who outweighed him by seventy pounds and was half a foot taller?

I let out a breath and prepared to step between them. I could do it if I had to. I could do it on autopilot. At the same time, another part of me was running a gut check. Guy had made a pass at his first love. I felt something like hands clawing at my insides, shredding my heart. The hollowness where my brain should be kept repeating, "You've lost him to alcohol. You've lost him to alcohol too."

Then Josh took over, stepping toward Dane and putting his hand on his partner's arm. "It's okay," he assured him. "Guy's had too much to drink. That's all this is."

Dane held his gaze for a long minute, calculating his responses, and nodded. "They're still leaving."

"Yeah, we are." My voice was loud in my ears. I stepped around Dane, grabbed Guy by the arm, and pulled him toward the living room. "Let's go."

I held the front door open, and he walked unsteadily in front of me, not looking up as I fell in behind him. I didn't say anything to Keller and Brooks. I knew their relationship would be fine as soon as we left the property. Mine and Guy's, not so much.

Outside, the wind still blew hard, pushing us along. I moved fast past Guy, who concentrated on making unsteady but determined steps toward the Jeep. I got in, started the engine, and stared out the windshield, waiting. I didn't turn toward Guy when he opened the door. I was too afraid of what I might say. When I heard him sink into his seat and shut the door, I took off. I didn't look at him. I didn't look back. I just drove.

He was silent until we reached the freeway forty minutes later. "I'm not sorry," he said again as defiantly as before.

"I know." And I did. Alcohol had its part in what had happened, but it was a drop in the bucket of Guy's mixed-up feelings. I couldn't argue with something he couldn't get past. I couldn't convince him that his life could be full if he let go of Josh. He couldn't do it.

He remained still and silent, his fingers like talons gripping his knees. What was he trying to hold together? I concentrated on driving. The pain in my chest was sharp, but I stuffed it down like indigestion, not thinking about anything but what was on the road. Another thirty long minutes later, I parked behind the gallery.

I turned toward Guy, hoping for some reaction—maybe an explanation, better yet an apology. He offered neither. He stared out the windshield, frozen in place, like he couldn't figure what to do. Or maybe he was sobering up finally. His fingers grabbed and released his knees obsessively. He wasn't even aware of it. I tried to figure something to say to give him some room to maneuver. Nothing that would sound final, nothing we couldn't recover from.

"Good night, Guy. Call me when you're able to put the past in the past."

He got out without glancing at me, mumbling something I couldn't quite make out. He didn't look back as he walked away, or unlocked the gallery door, or locked it behind him. I watched. A second later, he was gone up the stairs like he'd never been there. That's when I realized he'd said good-bye.

TWENTY-FIVE

HAD GUY meant good-bye? Or had he said the words and he'd be calling me tomorrow? My gut warned me to count on the worst.

I sat on the couch and watched the sunlight dwindle into dusk. Funny how it could still be so beautiful outside when I felt shattered. It should be dark already, and stay that way for months. No way was I going to cry over the mess I'd walked into. I'd seen the signs and fallen in love with an alcoholic anyway. Now I had to live with the results.

I'd get past this. I would. I'd dealt with loss before, and the insanity of alcohol, too, and come out a better, stronger person. But I was likely going to run into Guy regularly because of Alex. I'd imagined a future with him, maybe living with him so we could parent Alex together. This ached like hell and would hurt fresh each time I saw him for a long time. I could blame Josh, or Guy, or alcohol, or myself, but it wouldn't help. I knew that. I had to decide what to do about it.

First, I had to stop wallowing. Now. Alex would be home soon. I had to tell him something, and I had to lose the anger and pain so it wouldn't leak out all over him.

I went into the bedroom and knelt down beside the bed. I needed one of the boxes under it. But I knew what else I was going to find, and I didn't want to touch it.

The clock by the bed said eight thirty. I had an hour to do this. If I could get past that other thing under the bed…. *Let go and let God,* said the voice in my head.

No, this hurt too much. But the voice came again: *Let go and let God.* I dropped my head in my hands.... God.... The voice took over for me.... *God, grant me the serenity to accept the things I cannot change.... The courage to change the things I can.... And the wisdom to know the difference.* How many times had I prayed that prayer since I learned it in those Alateen meetings? I started going to them before Dad died. After his death, they were my lifeline. Mom got crazy before she got sober. Once she stopped drinking, she prayed the prayer, too— out loud—all the time. The words had comforted me after she died. Maybe I should go to a meeting again.

I stretched a hand under the bed and damn, the first thing I touched was that picture frame. What was I going to do with it? I pulled it out, and it came out picture-side up, the glass protecting the beautiful image of the cat and the cowboy I'd had dinner with.

"So," Guy's voice repeated in my head, "why do you like *Cowboy and Cat*?"

"The eyes," I'd answered. "The cat's are almond-shaped, like yours, and it looks like it would tell the man the meaning of life if he would listen."

"There is no meaning to my life." I shoved the picture away from me, hot tears flooding my eyes. I pressed them back with the heels of my palms.

Once, the painting represented the first token of my feelings for Guy. Then it became a painful reminder. After the attack, when I saw how tormented he was that he might not paint again, the thing was like the mocking ghost of a shattered gift. I'd been afraid to tell him I had it, more afraid he might discover it, and too scared to destroy it.

What was I going to do with it? Stare at the image of the real-life cowboy who had everything I wanted but didn't value it? Torture myself with it? Maybe I'd get up the nerve to get rid of it one day. But not now. I was running out of time.

I sniffed back the tears and reached under the bed again, pushing aside the plastic box that held textbooks and diplomas from college and the academy and pulling out the tattered cardboard box behind it. I stared at the frayed gray duct tape that had been laid down and ripped up and laid down again through all my moves from home to college, between my LA apartments, and finally to Bozeman. This box went everywhere I did, even if months passed before I looked in it again.

I pulled back the gray strip one more time, blew off the dust, and opened the flaps. On top were the pictures, three framed collages of them and three albums depicting a happy family of father, mother, and lanky son. We didn't have many pictures from after Dad died—a photo of Mom and me at my graduations from college and the academy and another taken six months before the cancer took her. For too long, taking pictures was painful. I was sorry about that now. I'd make sure I took lots of pictures of Alex.

I removed the albums without looking at them. The shadow box was next. It held Dad's LAPD photo, shield, and hat, the flag that draped his coffin, and his Medal of Valor, awarded posthumously. In the first couple of years after he died, I opened this box a lot—but never when Mom was around. I touched each item and sometimes let teardrops fall on them. Before she died, Mom told me she'd known. Tonight, I simply touched the glass top and put it aside. I skipped over the folder with news clippings and programs from both of their funerals. What I needed was at the bottom of the box.

I settled my back against the bed, pulled my heels tight against my ass, took a deep breath, and fished out the green-and-white hardcover book, secondhand when I got it. I ran my hand over the title, *Al-Anon's Twelve Steps & Twelve Traditions,* opened to Step One, and began to read familiar words I'd underlined, highlighted, and committed to memory: *We admitted we were powerless over alcohol— that our lives had become unmanageable.* Further down the page was the note about how hard it could be to admit being helpless, and another about how our eyes, ears, and hearts opened when we could free ourselves from our determination to have things the way we wanted them.

Damn it. I'd been close to having everything I wanted—the family I wanted, the family I deserved after all those bad years. I closed my eyes against the vision that had slipped beyond my reach again tonight. I closed them against the tears. How had I done the one thing I'd vowed I never would? The signs were there. But I'd pushed them away because I was sure I couldn't make this mistake. Not with all my experience. I'd known Guy was at least a problem drinker, but I loved him too fast, too much. Now I'd have to live with the pain I'd seen too many times on my father's face. If I looked in a mirror right now, I'd see it on my own.

"Damn it, Guy." I looked at the blurry lines on the page again until I saw what I was seeking: the promise that once we were free of the determination, we *began to grow.* I'd done that once. I could do it again. That promise was the way I'd get through this, get past this, and be strong for Alex.

I put everything else back in the box and put the box under the bed. The picture too. I slid the book under my pillow, went into the living room, and settled on the couch, turned on the TV, and waited for Alex to come home.

When he did, I pretended everything was fine. He didn't ask any questions. I didn't have to lie. I'd tell him in the morning. Let him sleep tonight. I asked him about his day and his homework and wished him good night. He closed his bedroom door. I headed for mine, pulled the book out again, opened it, and let it speak to me like an old friend.

WHEN I heard Alex in the shower the next morning, I got up, put on the coffee, and started making eggs and bacon. I also shot a little prayer up to my mom, asking her to help me say the right things and be kind about Guy.

I had to be kind about Guy. As soon as I woke up, I knew I still loved him. He must be feeling physically sick and overall terrible, maybe even ashamed, today.

"What's with this?" Alex pointed at the stove as he emerged from the bedroom.

"You have time for breakfast?"

"A few minutes. But you didn't have to go to all this trouble."

"I know. Have a seat."

He dumped his book bag on the couch, and I filled a plate with the bacon and eggs, added some buttered toast, and brought it to the table. I brought him a mug of coffee, plus milk and chocolate syrup. He dug in while I grabbed my own coffee and sat down across from him.

After a bit, I began. "You working for Guy today?"

"Uh-huh." His mouth was full of food as he mumbled. He swallowed. "This is great, Connor. Thanks."

I nodded. "There's something I need to tell you about me and Guy."

He raised his head slowly, a pained look on his face. He knew what was coming.

"Yeah, we broke up. I don't want to talk a lot about it. And I don't want it to affect your relationship with Guy. But you needed to know."

"Is there any chance you can get back together?"

"I'm not sure. I don't want you to get your hopes up, okay? I want to keep the emotional fallout for you as minimal as possible. You have enough on your plate."

"This isn't about me."

"You're affected, and you might feel like you're in the middle. I don't want that. I'll do all I can to avoid it."

He put his fork down, half his breakfast uneaten. I should have waited a few more minutes to say anything.

"You have any questions?"

"Are you okay?"

"I haven't done this a lot—break up with men, I mean. I haven't had a relationship this serious. I know I'll get over it. I'll make sure you're not caught in any of the mess, okay?"

He glared at me. "I'm not a baby, Connor. You don't have to protect me."

"I appreciate that, Alex. I do. I'm... I haven't been your guardian very long, and we're still new at living together. I'm trying to give you an idea of how I expect I'll behave, so you don't worry too much."

"How's Guy?"

"I don't know." I clutched my coffee in both hands.

He was silent a few moments. "I thought you two went to have dinner with an old friend of his and his boyfriend. What happened?"

"I don't want to go into details."

"Come on." He shoved his chair back from the table, stood up, folded his arms across his chest, and glared some more.

"All I'm going to say is that the old friend is someone Guy once cared a lot about, and Guy had a little too much to drink, and stuff... happened, and things were said."

"It was Josh, wasn't it? The guy in the paintings?"

"It was." *What else would the kid figure out before I wanted him to?*

"Guy must feel like shit."

"I imagine he does." *He should. You wanted to be kind, remember?* I sighed and let go of my cup. My hands hurt. I was ready to change the topic. "It's an away game tonight, right? You're supposed to work?"

"Yeah."

"Be nice to him."

"What if he asks about you?"

"Tell him I hope he's okay. But don't say anything if he doesn't ask. I don't want you in the middle."

"How can you be so calm about this, Connor?"

I ran my hands through my hair. I hadn't let my emotions fly at the ranch. I wasn't going to in front of this kid I was responsible for. *I don't do that ever.* "How about I yell at you to lay off with the questions?" I asked in monotone.

His eyes narrowed.

"Bad joke?"

He rolled his eyes.

I sighed. "I've been trained to respond this way, okay? It's a good way to be. Keeps things from escalating."

"I don't think Guy will be this calm."

"If things get bad for you, you head home early, okay? You're not just Guy's employee here. You two have a deeper relationship, and you are in the middle in a lot of ways. You have the right to leave if you need to. You understand?"

"Yeah." He grabbed his book bag from the couch. "I'm taking off."

"You want a ride?"

"Tracy is picking me up. I'll wait outside."

"Try not to let this bother you too much, okay? Try to have a good day."

"Yeah."

"Call me if you need to."

"Later." He shut the door and was gone.

I DIDN'T feel like eating, so I cleaned up the kitchen and took off on a long bike ride. When I finally got hungry, I returned to town, bought a sandwich at a coffee shop, and headed out into the country again. I stopped every hour to check my phone, but Alex hadn't sent any messages. No one had.

Finally, when my legs burned like they'd been torched, I returned to the apartment. Alex came in as I was getting out of the shower. He stood in front of the open refrigerator, still wearing his jacket, when I came into the kitchen.

"I thought you were working."

He turned to look at me. "Guy texted to say he didn't need me. He wasn't opening the gallery. On a Friday. He must feel awful."

I sat down at the dining table without responding. When I looked up, he still held the door open, but he was studying me now.

"Are you going to call him?"

I shook my head. "That wouldn't be a good idea."

He banged the refrigerator door shut and crossed his arms in front of him. "You're sure?" he demanded.

"If there's a next move to be made, Alex, it has to come from Guy."

He cocked his head a minute, thinking that over, then nodded.

I sighed in relief. "Could you get me a bottle of water, please?"

He reopened the fridge, grabbed two bottles, and shut the door gently this time. "What did you do all day?" He put one of them down on the table next to me and sat down.

"I rode my bike."

"All day?"

"Nearly a hundred miles." I opened my bottle, raised it to him, and took a long drink.

He opened his, took a sip, and swallowed slowly. "This is bad, isn't it?"

"I'm sorry, Alex."

"You don't have to apologize to me."

He let the statement hang there, like he thought I needed to apologize to Guy. But I'd said all I was going to say. I kept my mouth shut.

He picked nervously at the label of his bottle.

I racked my brain, trying to come up with something helpful to say. "You know, today is one of those days I'm really grateful to your mother."

"What do you mean?"

"She raised a great kid."

He blushed. I messed up his hair, and he ducked away from me, but he was smiling.

He took another drink, then cleared his throat.

"What?"

"A bunch of kids are meeting on Nineteenth for pizza, and I was going to ask you if I could join them…. But I can stay here."

"No, you go. What are they doing after pizza?"

"Just pizza right now." He watched me closely for a minute more. "You're sure it's okay?"

"Absolutely. I have stuff to do. I'm fine. But thanks for thinking of me."

"I'll text you if it becomes something else."

"That works. How are you getting there?"

"I'll start walking, and one of the guys will pick me up."

"You got money?"

He nodded again and stood up.

"You got your phone? I'm not working. Curfew is eleven. You call if you need a ride. Got it?"

He rolled his eyes in exasperation. "Yes, parental unit." He grinned like he'd made a joke and was pleased with himself. "Take it easy," he added and left again.

I went into the bedroom for the green-and-white book, then sat down on the couch for a long, lonely night of reading.

THE NEXT day I took another long bike ride, followed by a nap. Neither helped. I must have looked as bad as I felt when I got to work because Nate was on me as soon as I sat down at my desk.

"You look terrible. What happened?"

"Nothing."

"Suit yourself. I'll leave you alone."

But he didn't. He told me to be careful before we both took off on patrol. Four hours later, he asked me to dinner. I declined. Even that didn't do it. As we came off shift, he asked me over to his house for breakfast with Jenna and Andy.

"I have to get breakfast for Alex."

"Which one of us do you think is the stupid one, me or you?"

"What?"

"It's Sunday. He's fifteen years old. He's not even awake yet."

I shrugged. What could I say without proving again that I was the one with the nonworking brain? "All right, I'll come over for breakfast. But I'm warning you, I won't be great company."

"I'm all ears, man."

Before I knew it, the words were out of my mouth. "Guy and I broke up, and I don't want to talk about it. You got that?"

"I'm sorry." He put a hand on my shoulder. "I understand. Jenna and I broke up once. It was awful, but it turned out all right."

"You saying that's going to happen for me too?"

"Not saying anything except this: Don't isolate yourself. We're your family. We love you. We'll come after you too." He grinned one of his big grins, and I ached for Guy—real, physical pain in my chest.

Nate seemed to sense it. He pushed me toward the door. "Come on, let's get to my house and eat."

We were barely inside when Jenna pushed Andy into my arms. "I'm so glad you're here," she announced. "I'm making waffles. He needs a playmate for half an hour."

"I can handle it." The plump bundle of spit immediately made me feel better. He didn't know if I was happy or sad. He just knew I was someone safe, and that was enough to make him squeal and grab for my nose and try to bounce out of my arms. His smile was big like his dad's, and he offered it eagerly. I walked him around the house, asking him about his night and his breakfast and talking gibberish while Nate showered and changed.

He came out of the bathroom as the waffles came off the griddle. I kept Andy in my arms as we sat down so his parents could eat at the same time. I figured that didn't often happen.

"You are coming to our house for dinner next Thursday," Jenna said, making it a statement, not a question. "Figure we'll eat before you and Nate start working. Bring Alex."

She didn't mention Guy, so I knew Nate had told her. She didn't let that sink in much before she started giving me directions again. "You can come over earlier if you like, even before school is out. You can help me figure out how to fix the turkey."

"Turkey? But Thanksgiving is two months away."

"It's a trial run for Thanksgiving," Nate explained. "With enough time for us all to get untired of turkey before the big day rolls around."

"I've never made a turkey before, and I want it to be perfect on Thanksgiving, which you two will come to too," Jenna said.

"Darn, Jenna, these waffles are great." Her husband was trying to change the subject before I could say no and ruin her morning.

"Darn?" I raised my eyebrows. "Now there's a word you don't use often."

He chuckled and pointed his fork at the baby. "Little ears on Little Man, man. You'll learn. Jenna will be rapping you upside the head, too, if you don't fall in line with the Mouth Police."

I turned Andy toward me and raised him up so we could speak face-to-face. "Can you say 'Mouth Police'?" He smiled a pair of bubbles out past his lips and grabbed for my nose again.

"Go ahead and make fun, but I bet you watch your language a bit more now that you have a kid at home," she said.

A timer dinged, and she jumped up. "Your waffle is ready, Connor." She brought it to me, took Andy into her arms, and sat down again. She watched me as I took a bite.

"Darn," I said slowly, and Nate nearly choked, he laughed so hard. "This is good, Jenna. Thanks. Thanks for having me over on the spur of the moment too."

She nodded and waited until I had a couple more bites. Then she got to it. "Tell me what's going on, Connor."

I glared at Nate.

He shrank back as if protecting himself. "She pried it out of me," he insisted.

She ignored him. "Spill. It's not good to keep stuff like this bottled up. You have to vent."

I didn't want to vent. But they were my best friends. Her request wasn't unreasonable. I put my fork down and picked up my coffee cup, holding it in front of me like a shield, keeping my eyes on it so I didn't have to look at them.

"I'm saying this once. Guy and I went to Josh and Dane's for dinner Thursday and found out they'd had a commitment ceremony. Guy started drinking hard, made a pass at Josh, and Dane asked us to leave. I dropped Guy off at his place, and he said good-bye, not good night. I don't know what happens next. This is more than I told Alex, so I know you'll keep this to yourselves. End of story."

They were quiet for several minutes digesting that. Jenna got up and handed her son off to her husband, then draped her arm across my shoulders and kissed my cheek. "I am so sorry. We're both sorry. Let me get you some more coffee."

When she'd done that and sat down again, Nate caught her eye and nodded encouragingly.

"This isn't about you. You know that, don't you, Connor?" she asked. "It's about Guy and lost dreams and fear. But mostly, it's about alcohol."

"Maybe." I picked up my fork again.

"How's Alex taking it?"

"Considering he hasn't seen Guy since it happened?"

"That's why the gallery was closed Friday. What did you tell Alex about things?"

"I told him we broke up. He guessed Josh was involved—he knew we were going out to the ranch, and he's not a stupid kid. He's seen some of Guy's paintings of him. But I skipped a lot of the detail. And I told him he didn't have to be in the middle, that if things got tense at work, he should leave or call me to come get him."

"I can pick him up too," she offered. "Call me. Or tell him to call me directly. Andy and I can be ready to go anywhere in ten minutes. I can even leave work for a short time if Alex needs me. Or he can come over to the yarn shop if he needs to."

"I appreciate that."

"Alex can spend some nights here, too, while you're working," Nate offered.

I looked at him and turned to his wife. She had already pitched in and checked on Alex on nights he'd had to stay by himself. She smiled and nodded at me. "Thanks, both of you. I don't know how that part is going to work out. I'm hoping Guy is going to maintain his relationship with Alex, including at least some of their nights together. That's important for Alex. But it might get in Guy's way if he starts seeing other people."

"Alex can stay here whenever you need him to, even if I'm off," he repeated. "It's no problem. We'll let him take one of the nighttime feedings. It'll be good for him. Help him understand the importance of birth control." He grinned again, clearly pleased.

Jenna shrieked, he grinned more, and I laughed. Then we were all quiet. I watched Andy settle into his dad's arms for a nap and felt a stab of envy. Wouldn't it be wonderful to be that blissfully unaware of life's responsibilities and disappointments for a while?

"Have you talked to Guy at all?" Jenna asked softly.

"No. There's not much for me to say. He was clear right away that he wasn't sorry about anything. He still loves Josh. He may always love him." I shrugged. "I thought he'd get past that, but it doesn't seem like he can. And I don't think I'm a good enough second for him."

She reached out and grabbed my hand. "Give him some time. Give yourself some time. And don't give up hope, Connor, unless you're sure you want to."

THE APARTMENT was empty when I got home. Alex had left a note saying he'd gone to church and he'd text me in the afternoon. I went to bed and slept like the dead, waking just before Alex got home around four.

"How did your day go?" I asked as I entered the living room.

"It was okay. Guy and I had lunch after church. He's okay. He didn't say anything about you except to ask if you'd told me what happened. I told him I knew you broke up but not the details. I think he might have been hungover."

"Did he drink in front of you?"

Alex scowled. "No, Connor, and don't go all cop on me. He wouldn't drink in front of me. But I could tell. I won't mention it again."

"You will mention it if you feel you should," I said too sharply. Alex shut down in front of me. I began backpedaling. "I'm sorry, okay? That didn't come out right. I want you to tell me these things. You need to so I can be a responsible guardian."

"Connor, he's upset too. He handles it differently. Not everyone can be as calm as you." He didn't mean it as a compliment. He headed for the refrigerator.

"How do you feel about his drinking? Are you uncomfortable? Do you feel unsafe? Should I talk to him?"

"No," Alex nearly shouted. "Jeez, I was trying to tell you how he was. He was fine to me. Once he knew I knew, he didn't say anything. He didn't put me in the middle. He was like he always is. But sad." Alex's posture was as close to defiant as I'd seen.

I sat down at the dining table. "Okay. I appreciate the info." I continued calmly as I could, "What are your plans for tonight? I know before everything happened that you were going to be with Guy while I worked tonight. Has that changed?"

He grabbed a soda from the fridge and sat down at the table across from me. "We need to talk about that." He opened the can and fiddled with the tab, not looking at me. "Guy says he's busy tonight."

He looked at me through lowered eyelashes. I made sure I didn't show a reaction. I was angry, but not at Alex. I wanted to call Guy and yell at him. On the other hand, maybe he meant to keep his dates with the bottle private. Great, but Alex still needed adult supervision.

Like he could read my mind, Alex had a reply. "It's okay, Connor. I've stayed alone with no problems. You can have Jenna call; you can stop in on your lunch break—like we've done before. Your plan has worked great." He had to remind me that I'd been the one to figure ways he could stay home alone. "I can do it more often now. It doesn't bother me. I'm old enough. My mom worked some nights, you know."

"Not all night. She didn't leave you alone all night every night."

"I'll be fine. I won't leave the apartment. I'll call and text you like always."

"Do you want to stay with Jenna and Andy? She and Nate told me you can spend nights at their place, even nights when Nate isn't working. And she wants you to know you can call her anytime day or night, and she can get to you in ten minutes. Even if she's working."

"I can stay with them sometimes, but I don't need to tonight. And certainly not every night. Tomorrow's school. I'm going to stay in for the night. Let me do this."

I was quiet, thinking. I took too long.

"For crying out loud, Connor," Alex cried, jumping out of his chair and throwing up his hands. "I'll be sixteen in six months. I can take care of myself."

"It's not you, Alex. I trust you. But most kids your age do not spend lots of nights alone. I'm a cop. I know what can go wrong."

"What can go wrong rarely does. Nothing's going to happen. Give me a chance."

What choice did I have? "Okay. But tell me you're not going to get angry if I text or call too often? And check in with you before you leave for school, to make sure you're up?"

His grin started the second he heard "okay." "You won't be sorry."

TWENTY-SIX

TWO WEEKS after the breakup, I was coming apart. It didn't matter what I read, how many miles I rode, how much I tried letting things go or thinking about something else or doing deep breathing exercises. Or how many cold showers I took. Guy still hadn't called. I missed him more each day. I was irritable and morose. Half of me was missing.

One night when I was off and the gallery was open late—and Alex was at the library—I gave in. I sat down in Guy's recliner and called the gallery number.

My skin and everything else prickled when he answered in his professional tone. "Gustavsson Gallery. This is Guy. How may I help you?"

I almost hung up. I began to sweat. I took a deep breath. "It's me. Can you talk?"

He didn't say anything for the longest time.

"It's Connor."

"I know." His voice was tentative, stiff.

I shouldn't have called. My cold grip on the phone told me how unprepared I was to do this—no matter how much I'd rehearsed. I should say good-bye and hang up. But I blundered on. "How are you? How's your shoulder? Are you painting?"

"I'm painting." He spoke too quickly, nervously, in a voice breathy like he'd forgotten to breathe. "Nothing good, but my shoulder doesn't hurt."

"Good. I'm glad." I paused, hoping he'd say more. He didn't. I filled the painful silence with too much honesty. "I miss you."

"Connor.... Please don't—"

"What's going on with you? Tell me. I can help you. I want to help."

When I finally took a breath, he answered quickly. "I can't do this right now. I'm not ready."

"That's not true," I said without thinking. He had relationships, with Alex and others. I needed to persuade him to put me back on the list. "We had something good. We can again. Tell me what I can do to help you feel differently. I can change."

He groaned. "You are fine. Better than I deserve—"

"That's not true. You—"

"I need time and space right now," he insisted, interrupting my interruption, then taking a deep breath and continuing more loudly. "I need to do this on my own."

"Do what on your own?" I pushed back. "I want to see you, Guy. So we can talk about things. If you're... if you're dealing with alcohol issues, I have some experience there." Now I had screwed up. "I can help you. Please don't shut me out."

"Connor, you deserve better right now," he whispered. "See someone else."

The words hit me like a body blow. I clutched the phone harder. "You don't get to decide that for me."

"Go out with someone who won't make a pass at another man while he's with you," he shouted, his voice thick with shame.

"That wasn't you." I jumped up and paced the living room. "That was the alcohol. I can forgive and forget that. I have. Give me the chance to show you."

"I'm not good for you," he shouted.

"I love you. What am I not saying that you need to hear? Tell me."

"Don't...."

"Don't what? Love you? I can't turn that off."

"Connor... I...." He swore and hung up the phone.

"Guy? Guy!" What had he wanted to say? That he loved me? But he hadn't. He was trying to put more distance between us. I stared at my phone, not wanting to believe its "Call ended" message.

I grabbed my jacket and keys, hastily scrawled a message to Alex that I'd be back soon, and jumped in the Jeep, headed for Main Street. No more than fifteen minutes after Guy hung up, the gallery was dark. The apartment was darker. He was gone. Where did that leave us?

DAYS LATER, I did something I'd been thinking about for weeks. I went to an Al-Anon meeting, in the basement of Walker's church. And damned if Walker wasn't there.

I spent the meeting like most newcomers do, though I knew the drill down to the last prayer. I kept my gaze mainly on my hands, clutched around my paper cup of coffee.

Afterward, a few people greeted me and encouraged me to return. Then Walker was standing in front of me.

"I'd ask if you want to go out for coffee, but I think you've probably had plenty," he offered, smiling. "How about lunch?"

"Sure."

We walked a couple of blocks to a burger place, dodging Saturday shoppers and fall tourists on Main Street and chatting about the weather, football, and our plans for Thanksgiving. But once we ordered, Father Walker slipped into interrogation mode, or what must pass for it for a priest.

"How are you doing with everything, Connor?" His face was open, sympathetic. No tricks up his sweater sleeve.

"Are we talking about Alex or Guy?"

"Who do you want to talk about first? Alex is doing great at church. He's fitting in well with the youth group and having fun."

"I think he is too. He and I are getting along well, adjusting to our new roles. His mom did a great job, and there's not much more I have to do—knock on wood. He's doing fine in school, and I make sure we talk about Kellie and how he's doing with that. It will be nice when the trial has come and gone. I keep hoping the bastard pleads out so Alex won't have to go through that."

Walker didn't raise an eyebrow when I let "bastard" slip. "His job at Guy's gallery seems to be a great fit with his interests, and he and Guy get along well from what they each tell me."

Nice the way he slipped that reference in. "So you're talking with Guy?"

"I am. We've been talking every couple of weeks since I met him in the hospital in April. But you knew that."

"Yeah, I did." I smiled through my lie, hoping he'd go on, and he did—to a point.

"He's still coming to church, to the service before the one you and Alex come to," he offered.

"Good. I'm glad. I wish him all the best."

Our burgers came, and we each took a couple of bites before he continued.

"Do you… wish for something more as well?"

Did he mean something with Guy? Was he saying Guy wanted us to get back together? Counseling me not to get my hopes up because he planned to make a move on his favorite artist? Or simply asking why he'd found me at an Al-Anon meeting?

I took a deep breath and decided to go with the truth, some of it anyway. "I miss Guy a lot." I hadn't said that out loud to anyone but Guy. I was surprised at the pain in my voice. "If you're asking me if I was at the meeting to try to learn how to handle Guy's alcoholism, the answer is no. It's more like I'm there trying to figure out why, with my family background, I didn't pay attention to the signs when I saw them."

He nodded. "Your mom or your dad?"

"Mom."

"That can be a lot harder for some kids."

"Especially only kids whose dads are killed in the line of duty."

Genuine sadness showed on his face. "I'm sorry, Connor. That must have been so tough. Both my parents are still alive, and we're close." He was quiet for a few moments. "So you're checking in with your program again. I'm glad."

"Can I ask you something, Walker?"

"I'll answer if I can."

I took a drink of my water. "Is Guy okay? Mentally and physically, I mean?"

He bit his lower lip, considering his words carefully. "He has good days. He tries to take care of himself. And he's watching out for Alex."

"I knew he'd do that. He's a good man, with a good heart." I picked at my french fries. "I won't put you in the middle."

"I appreciate that. I care about all three of you."

"You're good at what you do, Walker, like you've found your calling."

"I hear the same about you, Connor."

We shook hands when we parted on the street.

A FEW days before Halloween, the high school principal called. Alex had cheated on a math test. He was failing besides. Within an hour, I sat in the principal's office, in civilian clothes, along with the math teacher. Outside the door, Alex sat on a bench by the secretary's desk, his face alternating between grim and indifferent. I hadn't heard his side of the story yet.

The best way to handle this, I knew, was in a detached, levelheaded, "find out what's going on" cop way. I'd decided I'd give Alex a near pass if he handled things right. He'd been through more shock, grief, and change than most people face in a couple of years. I'd expected some kind of problem.

The principal was in her early forties, a trim, professional-looking woman with neatly arranged, wavy brown hair and a friendly face. Her Ph.D., from UCLA, was on the wall behind her, along with lots of photos of students and school events. The math teacher, Mr. Peterson, was a tall, thin man in his fifties, with thinning black hair and Harry Potter glasses. He wore a shirt and tie and a gray knit vest that perfectly matched his gray pants. He was severe and serious.

"Alex wasn't a great student at the beginning of the year, and it's been all downhill since, Ann Marie," he told the principal. He didn't look at me. "Frankly, I'm surprised he cared enough to cheat. But I can't abide the cheating. I won't trust him again. Something must be done."

My crap-o-meter fired with every earnest word he said. I let Principal Carmichael respond. No point in asserting myself until I knew where this was headed. I wasn't pleased with what Alex had done—and I knew with one look that he'd done it—but things could have been much worse.

The principal nodded at Peterson and turned to me. "Alex is not denying he cheated, Officer Maclean, and the usual punishment for a first offense is a three-day suspension and an automatic F on the test with no chance to make it up."

"That sounds fair. Given what's happened to Alex in the past four months, Mrs. Carmichael, what do you think about all this?"

Peterson's eyes widened when the principal used my title. Now he sat up in his chair. "Cheating is never acceptable."

"I agree." I turned my attention back to the principal.

"Alex hasn't been forthcoming with an explanation in my initial talk with him," she said. "You may be able to get him to open up more. I think we were bound to see some acting out."

I glanced at the math teacher, then turned back to her. "Do you advise a math tutor? I admit, math isn't a strong suit for me—"

"What is your strong suit?" Peterson interrupted.

I turned to face him. "Criminal psychology and literature. The degrees are from Southern Cal. I'm a police officer, Mr. Peterson. I became Alex's legal guardian following the murder of his mother in June, and I admit I'm feeling my way through the parent thing. Still, I believe we can turn this around. Alex has had to make a lot of adjustments in a very short time, including moving, so I'm thinking patience and support are the way to go here."

"Cheating is never acceptable," he repeated. "You of all people should appreciate that, Mr. Maclean."

What was up with him? Was he totally lacking in compassion? Did he have it out for Alex? Or did he get so little time with Mrs. Carmichael that he was trying to score points? I'd talked to her a couple of times when I worked football games, and I liked her. She knew kids, and she was supportive of Alex and me.

I shifted in my chair to face her again, not caring what conclusions Peterson drew from my body language. "What do you think, Mrs. Carmichael? A tutor? Counseling? Do I ground him for life?"

She smiled, ignoring Peterson's harrumph at my last question. "I'll set up an arrangement with one of our top math tutors. If you're open to it, an appointment with our staff psychologist is a good idea."

When I nodded, she added, "I'll try to get that arranged while Alex is suspended."

"We can come in any time during the day. I don't work until evening."

"The secretary will let you know what we can arrange. I'll also make sure we get you Alex's other assignments for the days he'll be out." She turned her attention back to the teacher. "Anything else, Mr. Peterson?"

"He'll be getting Fs in my class."

Mrs. Carmichael closed her eyes like a saint searching for patience. "Of course." When she opened them again, a hint of humor showed at the corners where fine lines were beginning to appear. "That will be all, Mr. Peterson. Thank you. I want to speak with Officer Maclean for a few minutes more."

He left without a word. Once the door closed, she leaned toward me, smiled, and whispered, "What kind of criminal do you imagine Mr. Peterson might become?"

I laughed out loud and, for the first time, relaxed in my seat. "You know, cops do evaluate people that way on occasion. I suppose it's the same with educators. You try to guess our grade point averages."

"I'm thinking you got quite a few As, Officer Maclean."

I was astonished at how perceptive she was. "I liked college more than high school, Mrs. Carmichael. Right now, I'm not too upset by Alex's behavior, but I don't want him failing math if we can prevent it. Although I think he's more of an art student than an academic."

She nodded. "The majority of Alex's teachers, especially his art and band instructors, agree with you. And I think you're reading this situation correctly. Try to feel Alex out about what's triggered this behavior, but there's no need to be harsh. We want to figure out why he did it and what he needs so it doesn't happen again." She stood up. "The secretary will call you later today about that appointment. Meanwhile, you and Alex spend some good time together over the next three days, and try to make sure he keeps up with his assignments."

"Other than math."

"Yes." She laughed. "I'll see if a teacher switch might not help the situation. I'll be in touch."

Alex stood up as soon as we returned to the main office area, although his gaze didn't leave his shoes. Mrs. Carmichael shook my hand and turned to Alex. "See you in three days," she told him. "Keep up with your homework, and report to my office first thing Friday morning."

"He will." I looked at Alex and cocked my head toward the door. He followed me without saying a word.

Once we were outside, I slowed my pace so he could walk alongside me. "Did you eat breakfast this morning?"

He shook his head.

"How does IHOP sound?"

"You're serious?"

"You must be hungry by now. I know how much you eat."

He stopped and turned toward me but still didn't look at me. "Connor, I just got kicked out of school for cheating on a math test."

"Thanks for explaining that. I was wondering why the teacher had his briefs in a bind."

Alex's eyebrows banged together as he studied me. "You're not taking this seriously?"

"I am. But not as seriously as Mr. Peterson. Come on, we'll talk about it over pancakes."

He relaxed in relief.

I began the serious conversation at the restaurant once we'd ordered. Alex admitted he had trouble with math and more trouble with Peterson. I could sympathize. He liked the tutor idea and promised to work harder.

"So what do I do for the next three days?"

"Homework, for sure. We'll stop by the gallery when we're done here to see if Guy wants you to spend the three days there or come in at your normal time."

"You're not mad, Connor?"

I sat back as much as I comfortably could in the straight-backed booth. "I'm not happy, Alex. But I'm not angry. How do you think we should handle this?"

He stared down at his plate, which he'd pretty much licked clean, and played with his fork a bit. "Some kids get grounded, I guess."

When he didn't elaborate, I picked up the conversation. "I could do that. Is there something more going on here, though?"

"What do you mean?"

"Look, you're having trouble with math, and we've got a fix in the works. Mrs. Carmichael might even reassign you to a different teacher."

His eyes lit up at that, and I continued. "You're also missing your mom a lot and still getting used to living with me in our cramped apartment. Then you're looking at having to testify against your mom's killer in court, and the two guys you thought were your new family have broken up. You spend some nights with Guy, some with me, some with Jenna and Nate. Or else you're alone all night. None of it is the best, and it has to be stressful. I'm not going to get first shift before you're out of college, and I don't think second shift would be any improvement on what we're dealing with. I'd never see you. What do you think?"

"Everything is okay, Connor. Being with you and Guy, no matter how we're doing it, beats living with strangers. And Jenna and Nate are cool."

"That's a fact. So tell me, why'd you cheat?"

He dropped his fork like he'd been shot, and it seemed to make that much noise when it hit the plate, startling both of us. But he didn't look at me. He couldn't. He pushed the plate away and rested his elbows on the table. "I've never cheated before," he offered.

I nodded and waited.

"Mr. Peterson is one tough SOB, and I don't mean because he's a math teacher."

I nodded and waited some more.

He sighed and looked around the restaurant before returning his gaze to his plate. "I didn't want to be failing. I don't get math, and I was worried you'd be disappointed, or they'd take me away when my report card came—"

"No one's going to take you away, Alex. You're set to live with me unless you don't like the arrangement."

"Really?" He searched my face like he didn't believe me.

"Really. Unless you want things to be different, we're in this together. You and me—"

"And Guy."

"And Guy." Although I no longer saw or talked to him.

I pushed my plate away and mirrored Alex's posture, putting my elbows on the table. "What's new with you and Guy? Things still going good with your job?"

"The job is great." Alex's face brightened. "My friends stop by the gallery sometimes. They think Guy is cool."

"He is cool. Everyone's cool but me."

"That's not true. I mean, I have a hard time getting friends to think your job is cool—except some of the geeky ones. But girls think you're hot. Tracy even says so."

"Have you informed her that I favor the other team?"

"No. Your secret's safe." He grinned. I was happy to see him like this.

"Hot, hmmm? Maybe that's better than cool?"

"Definitely."

"I like it. But you're grounded. Two weeks. No Halloween parties."

He looked up in surprise, then nodded. "I should be."

"I'm glad you agree. You're at home except when you're at school, working, or meeting with your tutor. And we're going over your homework regularly."

"Nothing like this is going to happen again, Connor. I promise."

He was half-right.

TWENTY-SEVEN

THE TWO weeks Alex was grounded passed without problems. While he was suspended, he worked most of every day with Guy, who made sure he kept up with his homework and his tutor appointments. At the end of three days, he returned to school, and a new math class and teacher. Things were looking up.

Guy and I talked about the situation—and nothing else—once on the phone. We agreed on how firm to be and what to expect from Alex. A person listening in would have thought we got along. We were friendly to each other, even kind. Guy offered to do most of the talking to Alex and to watch him at night, so I wouldn't worry at work. I almost felt like I had a partner again.

If Guy felt any stress talking to me, he hid it well. But I was tense. I wanted to talk about us. I wanted him to make the first move, but he didn't. He seemed fine with how things were.

Not me. The longer we were apart, the more I missed his humor and giggle, his enthusiasm and vulnerability, the feel of his hands on me and mine on him. I missed him period, no matter how I tried not to. I reminded myself what he'd done with Brooks, about all my blown dreams, that he wasn't sorry for any of it. None of that worked. We'd had a chance at a good thing. If we talked about it, we could get past this. I was sure.

Because Josh and Dane had gotten past it. I discovered that one snowy night when I picked Alex up after work. He was finishing some work in the office, and Guy and I were standing uncomfortably, and silently, on opposite sides of the showroom counter when Josh and Dane walked in.

"Awesome. You're coming with us after all, Maclean," Keller said.

"Guy, why did you tell us Connor wasn't coming?" Josh asked.

They turned to Guy with puzzled looks that turned to discomfort the longer the stiff stillness continued.

I couldn't think of a thing to say. How had Guy patched things up with them when he couldn't say a word to me?

He was red with embarrassment and staring at the floor. I wanted to shake him. I bailed him out instead.

"Sorry, I can't make it after all." *After all? How about, I was never invited.* "I have to get Alex home so he can do homework. You guys have a good time." I shook their hands and headed for the door. Before I closed it, I called back, "Tell Alex I'm waiting in the Jeep down the street. Catch you later, Guy."

Outside, I half-expected the snow to vaporize as it hit my face. That's how hot I was. Everything was fine between the three of them? How was that possible? Keller was furious that night. How'd he get over it? Had Guy apologized? Why hadn't he apologized to me?

Because he didn't want to. Because he had someone else. I remembered all the times he had to be somewhere. He was still doing that; Alex said so. Now I knew why. I quit thinking about it to save my sanity.

I didn't ask Alex a single question when he got in the Jeep. He didn't volunteer anything. He acted like nothing had happened. I did the same. After we got home and he finished his homework, we spent a couple of hours playing video games. Then we both went to sleep. All I had to do was take enough Benadryl to kill a horse.

The next day, I couldn't help myself. I called Guy. He didn't answer, so I left a message asking him to call. He didn't. Not that day or the next.

When my phone did ring, it was Brooks calling.

"Why haven't you two made up yet?" he demanded in lieu of a greeting.

"You tell me. You're the one who had dinner with Guy the other night."

"He wouldn't talk about it. What is up with you?"

"Me?"

"He was drunk. Are you going to hold that against him forever?"

Cowboy was after me about this? I couldn't believe him. I fired back a couple of questions. "How did Ranger get over this so fast? He threw us out of your place, remember?" I was rolling now. "Second, Guy would have to talk to me before we could get past this—"

"You haven't made a move to talk to him," Brooks interrupted.

"Third, Guy has a serious drinking problem."

"He didn't drink anything but club soda while we were out, and we went to his favorite martini place."

"He's learned not to drink when you're around."

"He's not drinking at all."

I scrubbed at my face with my free hand. "Did Guy put you up to this call?"

"No, moron, and if you don't start acting nice, I'm going to let Dane talk to you. He wants to. Why haven't you two made up? It was a sloppy kiss, nothing more."

"Nothing more? Guy regrets nothing about kissing you. That's the one thing he said during the drive back to Bozeman. When I dropped him at his place, all he said was good-bye. Good-bye. You know what that means, Brooks? Now he only talks to me about Alex. What in that equation has you thinking I should be the one to make a move? Before that night at your place, I told Guy I loved him. He didn't say it back. He hasn't said it yet. He doesn't feel the same."

My comments didn't rattle him, though they embarrassed me. I thought about ending the call. I sure wasn't ready for his response.

"Guy loves you. He's changing his whole life for you."

"Don't tell me fairy tales, Brooks. I don't believe in them anymore."

"It's not a fairy tale. It's the truth. How can you not see it?"

"To see it, I'd have to see him, and I haven't. By his choice. If you want to play matchmaker, you have to talk to Guy. Later." I hung up.

Five minutes later, Keller called. "I ought to come to Bozeman and beat your sorry ass."

"What is it with you two? You're so in love, you want to make sure everyone is?" I was grateful Alex wasn't around. He'd never listen to another thing I said if he heard any of this.

"I told you, we're willing to do nearly anything to see Guy happy. How is it you claim to love him and you're not doing the same?"

"How is it you give a damn about this when you booted us out of your place when he kissed Josh? Weird way to show you care, Rang— Keller."

"I've been waiting for you to call me that to my face."

"I haven't yet. We're on the phone."

Damned if he didn't laugh. "That's one to you, cop. Now go make up with your boy. He needs you to make the first move. You're man enough to do it."

"I'm pretty sure there's someone else, Dane."

"There's not," he replied with all the confidence in the world. "The question for you is, is he the one? Is a relationship with him worth the seeing through?"

Hearing that phrase was like hearing my dad. It stopped me short. It nearly stopped my heart.

Keller noticed. "You there, Connor?"

I gulped and refocused. "Yeah. I... I'm still not sure why I'm talking about this with you, but if you want this conversation to continue, tell me one thing: who made the first overture that got you three back together?"

"Guy did. He called me, not Josh, to say he wanted to make amends."

"Make amends. He used those words?"

"He did. He said he was sorry, he was drunk, it would never happen again, he was happy for us, and he hoped we could get past it. I believed him and said we could. Maybe he can't make the first move with you because he's so afraid of what you'll say. But you're it for him, Connor. I know that like I know my name."

"We've hardly talked since that night at your place, and what we've said has mainly been about Alex." I didn't want to rehash that phone conversation where Guy told me to see someone else, especially not with these two.

"That's another thing. What you're doing for that kid is admirable. But this standoff between you and Guy is not a good example for him. You making the first move, that's an example."

"Thanks for the parenting advice," I snarled. "I know you have lots of experience."

To his credit, Dane's tone was considerate, even helpful. "Maybe we are out of line calling you. All we want you to know is you are the best thing to ever happen to Guy. We're over what happened. We want you two to be. If we can help, you let us know."

"I'll think about it."

"Great. Call if you want to talk some more."

"Right."

I didn't call them again. And I didn't call Guy. I spent the next few days trying to figure how Keller could be so sure Guy wasn't seeing someone else. Guy had called Keller. Keller, not Josh. If he wanted us to be together, he'd call me too. And he hadn't. There had to be something—or someone—keeping him from it.

The thought plagued me every minute I wasn't working—right up until the night Alex really messed up.

TWENTY-EIGHT

I WAS patrolling the downtown bars early Saturday morning when my phone rang. Jenna didn't even say hi before she jumped into what was bothering her.

"I thought Alex was supposed to come to our place after the football game. When he didn't, I called him. He told me I had my nights mixed up. But I heard lots of voices in the background, and I know he's not supposed to have friends over if you're not home."

"You got that right."

"I'm not trying to be a busybody—"

"You're not."

"I don't want to get Alex in trouble."

"It sounds like he's doing that himself. I'll get there fast as I can. And thanks for calling before the neighbors called the police."

"I figured you wouldn't want that."

"Damn it."

"Keep your cool, Connor."

"Be grateful your kid is only six months old."

She chuckled. "I am. Call me later?"

I radioed Nate to tell him what was going on, then drove home. I slowed down as I passed my apartment and counted at least three teenagers inside. I turned the corner, parked, and entered the building through the back entry.

Noise filled the hallway, all of it from my apartment. I was amazed a neighbor hadn't already called 911. I tried the knob, and it turned. I took a deep breath and opened the door.

Three boys and Alex sat on the floor. Pizza boxes, pieces of pizza, and more than a dozen beer bottles, most of them empty, littered the coffee table in front of them. On the couch, a boy and girl I didn't recognize were making out, thankfully with all of their clothes on. Everything would have been fine if they'd all been six years older.

I shut the door with a bang. One of the boys on the floor, a blond wearing gold-framed glasses, saw me first. "Alex!" he yelped.

Alex turned toward me, and his face fell. "Oh shit."

The couple on the couch broke apart. The girl saw me and shrieked.

"Everybody stay calm, hands where I can see them." I stepped farther into the apartment and looked at each kid in turn, making eye contact, memorizing faces. They looked back with fear in their eyes. The black uniform tended to provoke that response.

"Where do your parents think you are?" I turned to the girl, a thin redhead with long curly hair. "Especially you?"

"A friend's."

"They let you stay out this late?"

"They think I'm sleeping over."

"Did you plan on doing that here?"

She blushed furiously. The boy she'd been kissing, a bulky guy who could have been a linebacker, covered his face with his hands. Maybe he thought I wouldn't see him that way. Alex hung his head and didn't say a word.

"Here's what we're going to do." A muscle in my jaw twitched as I spoke through clenched teeth. "You all have cell phones?"

The five heads I wasn't responsible for nodded.

"Each of you call your parents to come pick you up, within the next twenty minutes so I'm not late back to work. Things get worse if this isn't cleaned up before I have to go back on patrol."

"My mom's going to be furious," said the kid sitting next to Alex, who I recognized as another drummer in the marching band.

"Mine'll kill me," said the long-haired boy next to him, looking up at the ceiling.

"Connor, please...," Alex began, looking at me at last.

I pointed my finger at him. "You can talk later. Maybe." I looked at the others. "The rest of you be grateful I'm not taking you home in the patrol car. Start dialing."

The phone conversations were short and pointed. The girl and Alex's friend from band looked like they wanted to cry. Once the calls ended, I pulled out my notebook and took down their names, their parents' names, and their addresses and phone numbers, then moved to the window to watch for their folks. I wanted to throttle someone. We all waited in tense silence.

When the first car pulled up, a father built like the football player got out and came toward the building's front door.

"Don't any of you move while I let him in." Leaving the apartment door ajar, I went to the security door and opened it. The father saw my uniform and blanched. I motioned him into my apartment, propped open the security door, and followed him into my living room. He grimaced when he saw his kid on the couch with the girl.

"I'm Connor Maclean, Alex Whittaker's guardian." I gestured toward the kid I was responsible for. "And this is my apartment. Your child has been here drinking. They've all been drinking. Alex broke house rules about that and having company when I'm not here. How about your kid?"

"He's going to be in trouble with the football coach and then some."

I nodded. "We'll wait for everyone to arrive."

Four more cars pulled up in the next ten minutes. Two were driven by moms, one by a dad. A mom and dad were in the last; I could tell by the mom's red hair that they were the girl's parents. While the other parents shuddered when they saw the coffee table, this pair went on the offensive.

"You let your kid have beer parties when you're at work?" the girl's father asked as soon as he came inside.

"I do not."

"Didn't Alex just get suspended for cheating?" His wife followed up like they'd rehearsed. Maybe they thought putting Alex down would make their daughter look better.

"Yes, he did." I faced them squarely. "Meanwhile, your daughter said she told you she was sleeping over at a friend's house. This isn't it."

I looked around the room at each of the parents. "Your kids have all given me your contact information. I want you to know I'll be reporting this to my sergeant when I go back on shift."

"Can't we pretend it didn't happen?" asked the mother of Alex's friend from the band. Like her son, she was short. She looked tired.

"I can't. My job rides on what I do next." I looked at Alex. He stared at his hands, clasped in his lap. "Alex knew this was wrong, and we'll be dealing with that. Beyond that, my sergeant will decide what happens. I'll let you all know tomorrow. You can take your kids home now."

"I don't see why my kid is in trouble because yours broke your rules," the girl's father started in again.

I stopped him. "This isn't about my rules. They all broke the law. There was no beer in my house when I left for work. You might ask where it came from. I'm going to."

The mother of the blond boy nodded. "Thank you, Officer Maclean. You're being more than fair." She took her son's arm. "Let's go home and talk, Max."

"I'm sorry, Mom," he said softly.

"Tell that to Officer Maclean. You aren't supposed to be at anyone's house if their parents aren't home."

"I'm sorry, Officer," he whispered, shuffling toward the door.

I nodded.

The football player's father pulled him up from the couch and gestured toward the door. He fell in behind his son but stopped in front of me. "Thank you, Officer Maclean." He held out his hand, and I shook it. "I appreciate you not automatically filing a formal report. John won't be getting in trouble like this again."

In another minute, everyone was gone, including the girl and her parents. They'd apparently decided going home quietly was a good idea. Or maybe they knew who brought the beer. That was my hunch.

Alex got up and sank down on the couch once the door was closed. "Connor…."

"Save it, Alex. I still have some cleaning up to do." I wasn't ready to hear his explanation. I couldn't imagine he'd come up with a good one. I pulled out my cell phone and dialed a number I'd phoned once since September. Tonight, he picked up. He sounded like he'd been sleeping.

"It's Connor. I'm sorry to bother you this time of night, but I need someone to come spend the rest of the night with Alex."

"Aren't you supposed to be working? What's wrong? Is Alex okay? Where are you?" Guy grew more agitated with each question.

"It's not life-threatening. Sorry. I should have made that clear. We're at home. I found Alex, five kids, and a bunch of empty beer bottles in the apartment. I have to go back on duty, and I didn't know who else to call…"

"Getting dressed right now." Short fast breaths indicated he was moving in high gear.

"Thanks. Nate is covering for me, but it would be great if you could get here in the next ten minutes."

"Do you need to take off before I get there?"

"No. I'll wait."

"Okay. Hanging up now."

I pocketed my phone and looked at Alex. "Well?"

To his credit, he looked me in the face. "I'm sorry, Connor. I invited Dustin and Max over. I shouldn't have, but we were just going to play video games for a while. Then Colton, John, and Heather showed with the beer, and…." He blinked. "Are you in trouble at work?"

"We'll find out." I walked to the window and looked out into the dark, searching for words and calm. I didn't find them. "I can't believe you did this, Alex. You just got over being grounded for cheating. You're not supposed to have kids over when I'm working. You let alcohol in too. I'm a cop, for heaven's sake. What were you thinking?"

He didn't say anything.

I kept talking. "Was I too easy on you about the cheating? Would you rather go into foster care? I can make it happen if you want, because, honestly, I don't need this kind of aggravation in my life. I get enough of it in my job."

"Connor… no. Please…."

A car pulled up. I cut him off. "Guy's here. I have to get back to work. You clean up the living room and kitchen now, without his help. Get rid of all of the beer bottles so he doesn't have to."

"I will. I promise. I'm sorry," he whispered.

"That's not enough this time." I walked into the hallway and met Guy at the security door. He looked sleepy and so damned good. I wished… It didn't matter what I wished.

"Thanks for getting here so fast."

"You bet." He stuck his keys and his hands in his jacket pockets. "Is this going to get you in trouble at work?"

"I hope not." I shook my head and glanced all around the hallway so I wouldn't stare at him, though I wanted to. I wanted to stare and a whole lot more. "First the cheating. Now this. How could he…." I bit my lip to stop the whine. "I guess I'm not cut out to be a parent."

"It's not your fault, Connor. Alex has had the worst possible thing happen to him. He was bound to do some acting out."

I blew out a breath.

He patted my arm for the briefest second. The touch was gone too fast. "It's not your fault. Be careful when you go back to work, okay? I'll be here when you get home, and we can talk about it if you want."

"I told Alex to clean up the kitchen and living room without your help. Make sure he puts the trash out. Then tell him to go to bed, okay?"

Guy nodded.

I looked at him finally, wanting him to know how grateful I was, that my frustration and anger weren't meant for him. "Thanks. I didn't know who else to call."

"You can always call me. See you later."

THE SMELL of fresh, strong coffee met me when I walked into the apartment after work. Guy was in front of the open refrigerator, bent over at the waist, poking around inside it, his butt flashing me.

I thought of how things used to be, the two of us recovering from his attack. All I had to worry about was his mood. I could manage anything and fix everything. Now, I clearly wasn't cutting it.

Guy turned around then, a grin on his face. "I've been watching for you, waiting all night. I wanted to tell you how—" He swallowed back whatever he was going to say next, his face reddening. He blinked his eyes and started again. "I was going to make some breakfast. Eggs and bacon sound good?"

Whatever he couldn't say, some kind of opportunity had walked out the door. I knew it by the aching in my chest. "Sure." Keep going, the voice in my head ordered, keep this going. I relaxed my shoulders. "Breakfast sounds great. More than I should hope for after the night I left you with."

I gave him a tentative smile, and he returned it. I tossed my jacket on his recliner, on top of the pile of blankets he must have used in the night, and sat down at the table. "Do I even want to ask how things went?"

He poured a cup of coffee, brought it over, and set it in front of me. "Alex and I talked for a long time. Bottom line: the girl showed up with the beer and the other two, including a star football player, and Alex didn't want to look like a wimp. He's sorry. He doesn't want to go into foster care. I think he's willing to accept most any punishment you have in mind. What did your boss say?"

"That went better than I thought it would. He told me he had a similar situation with one of his kids. He suggested I continue Alex's visits with the school psychologist, and talk with her about this. He's going to call the other parents for me, hoping that will make them take it seriously. And he said to come up with a punishment Alex takes seriously."

"What happened with his kid?"

"He became an FBI agent. He's one of the higher-ups in Denver now."

"It sounds like his advice is worth listening to." Guy moved to the stove to start breakfast.

"Is Alex asleep?"

"He's probably awake, but he's afraid to talk to you, Connor. Maybe the smell of breakfast will lure him out." He arranged several pieces of bacon in a skillet and put it on the stove.

"Did you get any sleep in your chair?"

"I love that chair. It was like old times."

"This feels like old times."

His grin disappeared into sadness. I wanted to get it back. "I can't thank you enough for coming over last night. I know I'm the last person you wanted to hear from—"

"You given any thought to how you're going to handle Alex?"

He still didn't want to talk about us. My heart sank into my stomach. I was going to have to put on some act to eat the breakfast he was fixing. I sighed and answered. "I haven't had a good idea yet. You have any?"

He paused a minute. "I think this was about him not being able to sort out his feelings and reactions fast enough. That's why he couldn't tell the kids who showed up with the beer to leave. Now he's worried he's messed up things with you. He's grateful for all you're doing for him. He said that."

"If I'm doing so well, why'd he do this to me?"

Guy frowned. "This isn't about you. Alex blames himself for his mom's death. He thought drinking might help him forget that for a while." He paused again. "Honestly, I think he hates himself, and he's looking for ways to hurt himself. Things aren't going to get better until he decides to get past that."

"But he's not responsible for Kellie's death, we are."

"We?" Guy spun around, waving the giant fork he'd been using for the bacon like a weapon. He looked angry.

I gestured toward myself, and fury I didn't know I had burst out of me. "We. The department. Me," I said too loudly. I stood up and began to pace the living room. "I didn't catch Mitchell soon enough. I should have protected them better."

Guy walked toward me, pointing the fork at me. "Of all the stupid bullshit you could have said…." He blew out a breath and rolled his eyes.

"Don't hold back now. Tell me what you really think."

"That has to be the dumbest, most self-pitying, selfish thing you could have said considering all the pain Alex is in. Tell me you don't believe that."

"Of course I believe that. We knew who we were looking for. I should have found him sooner."

"Connor, you're supposed to be the adult here."

"What does that mean?"

"Think like one. How can you be any help to Alex when you indulge in the same juvenile thinking?"

"What do you mean 'juvenile'?" I marched toward him, settling my hands on my hips.

He didn't back down. "You thinking you should have caught Mitchell sooner is as dumb as Alex thinking he caused his mother's death. Kellie didn't die because Alex couldn't stop Mitchell that night, or because he helped me the night I was attacked, or because I made an appointment to meet with Mitchell, or because you didn't find him soon enough. The person responsible for her death is Mitchell. He could have stopped. He should have stopped. Tell me you understand that, or you'll be no help to Alex."

Guy looked at me and waited, like he was watching for a light bulb to appear above my head.

"Yes, Mitchell was responsible, but—"

"Go on, Alex," he interrupted harshly. "Tell me how you saving my life makes you responsible for your mother's death. Then explain how I'm not the one who's ultimately responsible. Explain that, smart guy."

I stared at him like the light bulb had appeared above his head. At last, I saw his point.

"Do you understand now what Alex is thinking?" His voice dropped to a near whisper. "What I've been thinking?" His eyes widened, like he'd revealed too much. He rushed on. "Do you see how ridiculous it is? What are you going to do to help him?"

"Aw, shit." I rubbed my hands up and down my face hoping to scrape the stupid off.

"Shit is right." He rushed back to the stove.

"What?"

"The bacon is burning." He pulled the pan off the heating element. When he'd inspected each piece, he looked up at me again. "I don't think this is salvageable."

"There's another pack in the fridge."

"Really?"

"I'm feeding a teenager, remember?"

"I have another idea about him."

"Go on. You're doing pretty good so far."

He smiled, and his face brightened. "Maybe instead of the school counselor, you'd consider taking Alex to see Walker today? Walker is a psychologist, remember, and you both know him better. It might be easier to talk with him. This is deep stuff. And he's available today."

"You think Walker can fix this right up?" I stiffened, and my breath caught in my throat. That explained everything. Guy *was* seeing Walker. That's why he could make up with Josh and Dane but not me. The priest had rushed in to help with Guy's drinking crisis. Now he'd help with Alex. He'd repair everything I couldn't.

Guy frowned big time at my sarcasm, then brought the bacon and a plate and silverware to the table and put them down. "Sit," he ordered. "I think this is edible after all." He grabbed his mug of tea from a counter and sat down.

"I think right now Alex can use all the good psychologists you can find him. But if you don't like Walker, you can wait until you can see the school psychologist Monday or Tuesday."

I studied his face, searching for confirmation that he and the priest were more than friends. I saw affection, but for whom?

I swallowed a gulp of coffee, along with some of my attitude. "Obviously you've called him already." I took another drink and surrendered. "Thanks for that. Having Alex talk with him is a good idea. When is he free?"

Guy grinned and damn, he looked happy. I wanted to be the one putting that smile on his face.

"Walker suggested Alex have lunch with him and they start talking. When they're done, he'll call you so you three can talk together."

"Great." I didn't mean it. No way did I want to talk to the priest. But I had to. For Alex. "Can you take Alex to the gallery with you? I need some sleep before I talk to Walker."

"Sure." He looked at the clock. "You want to get Alex moving? You two need to say something to each other this morning."

I nodded.

I didn't hear a noise when I knocked on the bedroom door, so I waited a minute and opened it.

"Alex?"

The shape under the bedcovers moved.

"Can you be ready to go soon? Guy is making us breakfast, then you're heading to the gallery with him and having lunch with Walker. I'll join you later at Walker's house."

Still no noise from the lump.

"Alex? Come on, get up so we can talk a minute, okay?" I walked into the room, to the windows, and parted the curtains to let in some light.

He threw back enough of the covers to show his face. "I'm listening."

I plastered a calm mediator look on my face and turned toward him. "Guy has set it up so you can talk with Walker about last night… and some other stuff. How's that sound?"

"What other stuff?" He sat up against the headboard.

"Your feelings about being responsible for Kellie's death."

"I am responsible." His face was a mask of pain damn close to cracking.

I moved to the bed and sat down. "But you're not. There's nothing you did to cause her death, nothing you could have done to stop it. Same with me. I couldn't have found Mitchell any faster. We did the right things, both of us. You saved Guy's life by what you did. That's heroic in my book."

"If I hadn't done that, my mom would still be alive. Then, when I could have, I didn't save her." He looked like he was going to cry.

I touched his arm. He shrank back, but I touched him all the same. "Sometimes things happen no matter what we do or don't do, or didn't do," I said quietly. "Only Jimmy Mitchell is responsible here. Guy is right about that."

"No!" he shouted.

"Yeah." I slid my hand up his arm and squeezed his shoulder. "I know that still doesn't stop the hurt. Nothing is going to stop the hurt, not for a long time."

He began to shake. I pulled him into my arms. "It's okay to cry, Alex. It's good to cry. It'll be good to talk to Walker too."

He let me hold him as he sobbed. I rubbed his back, repeating "It's okay" over and over for ten minutes—nowhere near enough times for what he'd lost, for what he felt. I never cried enough when I was his age. Probably neither of us would ever cry enough.

TWENTY-NINE

I SPENT a long morning worrying about how Alex's appointment with Walker would go. The good thing was that pretty much pushed my worries about any relationship between Walker and Guy out of my mind. The bad thing was realizing I hadn't done enough to help Alex understand he wasn't responsible for his mom's death. I should have known better.

What a soap opera Alex, Guy, and I were trapped in—each feeling responsible for Kellie's death though none of us was, isolating ourselves in self-blame when we should have been helping each other through our grief. If she were here, Kellie would knock our heads together. Thank God, Walker was both a priest and a psychologist. He'd do a better job answering some of the Alex's questions. If he could fix this, I'd owe him big time.

But was Guy the price I'd have to pay? After we'd gotten together and broken apart twice and now appeared to have one more chance to make things work? Wasn't all of his help with Alex proof that he was reaching out to me again? Or was Walker the biggest part of his life now, and Guy had offered his help because he knew how great Walker was? Even if that were true, no matter the cost to me, I had to accept, for Alex's sake.

I couldn't play the victim. Alex needed help, and I'd do whatever it took. Through the years I'd been a cop, and before that as a kid caught inside my mother's drinking, I'd watched countless victims push away solutions or a helping hand or a happier existence because they couldn't shake free of old behaviors and thinking. I'd vowed, after

I found Alateen, not to do that because I'd learned and I believed that every day, every moment, offered a new chance, a new way of being, a new shot at a good life, if you took that first step. Believing that saved my mother and brought me to a new life in Bozeman. I couldn't slip back into that hopeless abyss where I quit trying to make my life, and other people's lives, better if I could.

Kellie never fell into it, and she raised a wonderful kid as a result. She gave her life to free him from a criminal trying to scare him into a viler, smaller, bleaker existence. As a cop, I'd vowed to do the same for any hypothetical stranger. I had to do the same for Alex. I would, and be grateful. Grateful to Walker if that was required. Grateful for Walker. God sure liked his irony.

The priest called around one thirty to tell me things had gone well. Alex had opened up to him, and the two of them would meet twice a week for a while. He'd have me sit in on one of the meetings soon, so we could all talk together. A few months might resolve things.

"I can't thank you enough, Walker." Saying the cliché made it easier. If I did that a few more times, I might be able to say it in my own, more genuine words. I was going to have to try.

"I'm glad I can help, Connor." His comment was perfunctory, but his tone was sincere. His next words stunned me. "I congratulate you for forming such a strong, positive bond with Alex in such a short time. He's grateful for all you're doing for him. More important, he looks up to you. He feels you're on his side and he can trust you. That means a lot coming from someone his age. It's a real compliment."

A warm feeling bloomed in my chest. "I…. Thank you, Walker. Truly."

"I thought you should know," he said simply. "So, I'll see you at the party tonight."

"Party?"

"This impromptu gallery get-together Guy's got going."

I swallowed a groan. Alex had mentioned it a few days ago, when the idea first came to Guy. I had to be there, he said. It would be a gallery celebration, or something like that. Nate and Jenna were invited, a bunch of other people too. I'd hoped to avoid it if Guy and I weren't back together. Now he'd be there with Walker. But I had to go. I owed Guy that much. What would Walker think if I didn't show?

"Alex asked me to tell you he'd see you there. He's helping Guy set up."

"What time is it again?"

"Seven. See you there."

Yeah, I'd be the one trying to get lost in the crowd of gallery artists and fans, staying away from Walker and the host. I'd get there late and leave early. Fifteen minutes, tops. I could do that.

WHEN I arrived around 7:40, the gallery was dark and locked up tight. Every light in Guy's apartment, though, was on. So much for there being a crowd to get lost in. This was going to be a small party, and I was going to have to interact with Walker and Guy. With a sense of dread heading for the stratosphere, I walked around to the back door and hit the buzzer.

Alex met me at the door, and he was irritated. He expressed it by ignoring me as he opened and relocked the back door, then turned to head upstairs again.

"You're *way* late." He tossed the comment over his shoulder. "Good thing Guy changed his mind about the sit-down dinner or you'd have wrecked everything."

"Sorry." I followed him up the stairs. With each step, I became more aggravated about being here and now needing to apologize. "It's not like I'm the guest of honor," I snapped.

He stopped his climb and turned around to study me. "What is bugging you? You're never like this."

"Nothing."

"Right." He rolled his eyes. "Can you bring back 'always in control' Connor?" Without waiting for a reply, he started up the stairs again. I kept my mouth shut. No way was I taking that bait.

In the kitchen, every counter top was weighted down with delicious-looking party food. On the table were multiple nonalcoholic drink options and a birthday cake—a tall, elaborately iced chocolate concoction. Was it his birthday? Walker's? The cake didn't give an indication, but Guy had gone all out. I grabbed a bottle of water.

In the living room, more food covered the coffee table by the expansive L-shaped couch. Nate and Jenna sat on one side of it, Andy sitting in his mom's lap. He was blowing bubbles at Josh, who sat opposite them. Keller, standing behind Josh, was the first one to see me, and he shot me a look that was more like a dare. I had no idea why.

Then Guy giggled. Keller turned toward the sound, and I followed his gaze to the windows, where Guy stood too close to Walker—the only other guest at this party—giggling and touching the priest's arm. Much like on that first night in LA., he looked like he was performing. The performance was a come-on then, and he was cute. Tonight, it rang false. Walker looked uncomfortable.

Keller looked at me again, that challenge still in his eyes, its meaning all too clear now. And I knew exactly what was bugging me.

Alex had reached Guy and Walker and, apparently, informed them I'd arrived. Walker shot me a hopeful look. Like he hoped I'd come over and save him? Guy made his feelings plain by turning his back to me.

Suddenly, the room felt like an obstacle course. Nate started in on me as I neared the couch. "I thought we'd hear something from you before now," he said sharply. "Jenna's been worried all day." He dropped his voice. "It took some awkward finessing when we arrived to figure out whether Alex was angry with us."

"Angry?"

"Because of my calling you last night," Jenna whispered. She glanced toward where Alex stood with Guy and Walker. We both watched him cross back to the kitchen without looking at us.

"I'm sorry, Jenna. Of course I should have called you. We had a chance to get Alex to a counselor today, and I spent most of my day tied up with that. But I should have called."

"It's okay," she said politely. She should have punched me for being thoughtless, but she gave me an out. "Alex explained, sort of, and we met Walker. He's nice."

"He's going to be a good counselor with Alex," I agreed. I took the cap off my water bottle and took a long drink.

"About that, partner," Nate said, jerking his head toward the back of the room. "You might want to come up with a better idea, huh? Someone Guy isn't so friendly with?"

"Shhh," his wife hissed. "They'll hear you."

I looked again toward the window, then at Nate. His arched eyebrows all but screamed, *what are you going to do about it?*

Keller leaned in and followed up. "I wouldn't let my boy flirt with someone like that."

"As I recall, you drew the line at kissing," I hissed back.

"Is that what it's going to take for you to make Guy quit playing games?" he countered. "To let him know he has your full attention? Because, idiot, I gotta tell you, that's what he needs from you."

I wanted to scream at someone. I didn't. I was too busy trying to decode the weird interior shift I'd felt, like the control I valued so highly had busted loose of its leash. I hadn't felt it in nearly two decades. A kid living with an alcoholic parent keeps his reactions bottled up, because you never know what might set off a drunk. You don't want to trigger a response you can't manage.

All that caution evaporated as I stalked to the windows. My heartbeat hammered in my ears. The other people and noises fell away the closer I got.

"Walker, I think Alex needs you in the kitchen. Can you?" I jerked my head in that direction.

"You bet." He looked at me with something like gratitude, slipped out of Guy's grasp, and was gone.

Guy turned toward me, his eyes flashing. They rounded in alarm when I planted my left hand on the wall behind him and leaned in close. He bumped his head trying to step away from me. "What are you doing?" he demanded.

"Keeping you here so we can talk." When he tried to sidestep me, I grabbed his arm, trapping him in place.

"I need to get back to my guests." He looked around me to the others.

I cast a backward glance. No rescue party would come to his aid. Everyone else, including Walker and Alex now, sat at the couch, studiously not looking at us. Except for Nate, who faced me and flashed a thumbs-up.

I turned back to Guy. "No guests here, Guy. Just friends and family. They won't mind waiting while we talk." I leaned a little closer.

"I have to take care of them," he insisted.

"They don't need anything." I looked him in the eye. "Now, why don't you explain how you could make up with Josh and Dane but not me? Yeah, let's start there."

"Let me go!" He tried to shake me off.

"I can't, Guy. I can't let you go, and you don't want me to."

"I don't know what you mean."

I looked back at the couch. No one had moved. "Let me help you understand. Your days of performance art are over."

"Performance art?" His voice edged up several notches.

"Performance art." I raised my voice too. I liked the sound. I went with it. "What you were doing with Walker. What you're doing now. It's fine when you're the star artist at your gallery or your art shows, but no more flirting with or kissing anybody but me. You got that?"

He jerked his chin up. "Who do you think you are, telling me what I can and can't do?"

"I'm the man who loves you, Guy Gustavsson. You weren't loved as a child. I get that. And the first guy you cared for fell for someone else. That's sad, and I'm sorry. But I love you now. I want to spend the rest of my life with you."

I watched a red flush creep up Guy's neck and take over his face. My face was warm too. Everybody had heard me. I'd never done anything this private so publicly. *They're your friends,* I reminded myself, *your family.*

I brushed my left hand across his cheek. "But you're not that unloved little boy anymore. You're not. Open your eyes and see that."

His chin quivered. "No!" he whispered. "I'm not good enough for you. Not yet. Probably not ever. You deserve better."

Pain seized my heart. He had no sense of self-worth apart from his art. I grabbed his chin and held on hard, forcing him to look at me. His eyes slammed shut.

"You can't believe that." He didn't reply. I waited, far too long I waited, and still he didn't reply. "Look at me!" My voice was no louder than his. Behind us, though, the silence was noisy enough to hurt my ears.

Guy's flush deepened. His eyes opened at last, full of embarrassment and whatever capitulation was needed to end this conversation as quickly as possible. My hands felt clammy. What could I say to guarantee the outcome I wanted? God, help me not blow this.

"You remember that night I made you repeat over and over that Connor loves Guy? Now I want you to say the reverse. You didn't say it then. Say it now. Guy loves Connor. Say it."

"No," he cried. "You deserve better." He bit his lip.

The pain in his words, on his face, brought tears to my eyes. But I swallowed them and gripped his arms hard, nearly lifting him off his feet. He winced and stared at me, begging me to end this.

"You're wrong," I answered. "There is no one better for me than you. There is no one I want but you. You are the bravest man I know. Look how hard you fought to get your arm back, to get your painting and your life back. You're braver than me. More generous too. Look at all you've done for Alex. The reason I was brave enough to be his guardian was because I watched you open your gallery and your heart to him."

A tear slid down his cheek. I wiped it away with my thumb and slid my hand around the back of his neck. "You have to love me. I need you to love me. Please, say you do." My voice was barely a whisper. My arms, holding him tight, trembled. My heart quaked. I leaned into him, hiding my face in his neck, aware of how vulnerable I was. How empty I'd be if he didn't say it. "Please, Guy... I don't want a life without you in it." My arms dropped to my sides.

He didn't move. Tears I didn't know I was shedding wet his neck. I felt like I was teetering on the edge of a black hole, that I'd let everything in the deepest part of me out. And still he didn't say anything. I had no more words, no more moves. I waited.

Painful, long moments passed. Every bit of my skin ached, straining for a response. At last, the ghost of a touch brushed my forearm, his hand, shaky and damp. I raised my head. His fingers brushed my lips, then settled on them like a blessing. A sob I was choking on kissed them back.

He smiled at me and wrapped his arms around my waist. "You… are… everything."

I cupped his face in my hands, my thumbs stroking his cheeks. His eyes were two deep pools of love and longing. I gazed into them in awe, not wanting to move, not wanting to do anything but feel this moment for the rest of my life.

When a sniffle sounded on the far side of the room, though, I was reminded that I'd done this in front of everyone. I froze in panic.

But Guy was fine. He giggled. "It's okay, tough guy. I've got this."

He grabbed my right hand, intent on leading me back to the party, but we were stopped by Alex, who threw his arms around both of us, engulfing us in a hug.

"You're not embarrassed that your guardian has lost all control?" I asked.

He pulled back and grinned at us. "You two are embarrassingly… brave." He turned to Guy. "Birthday Boy, what do you say we get into the cake?" He pushed Guy toward the kitchen, and Guy clutched my hand harder, dragging me with him.

"That's it. You, too, Connor," Alex coaxed, falling in behind me.

As we passed the couch, everyone joined the parade. When I dared to glance up, Ranger waved his hands in a so-so motion, but he was smiling. Jenna wiped a tear from her eye.

In the kitchen, she launched into "Happy Birthday," and we all joined in, cheering Guy at the end. He blushed brightly and giggled some more. Then he cut the cake, plopping pieces onto the plates Alex held and passed around. Soon everyone's mouths were too full to say anything more than, "Great cake" and "Happy birthday, Guy."

Talk turned to Thanksgiving plans. Walker's parents were flying in to visit him. Guy quickly agreed to accompany Alex and me to Nate and Jenna's for the holiday five days off. Next thing I knew, Guy, Alex, and I were going to Brooks Ranch the Sunday after. Keller said something about putting me on a horse named Sugarpie.

"Should I be insulted by this?"

Keller's snicker was the answer.

Josh moved quickly to stifle that. "I think we'll put Alex on Sugarpie. But we've got a good beginner horse for you, too, Connor."

"We're going riding?" Alex asked, clearly liking the idea.

"You bet," Josh answered. "With a few lessons, you'll both be good at it."

"We can place bets on who improves fastest," Keller offered. "My money's on the kid."

"No," Guy countered loudly. "I'm sure Connor can keep up." He looked at me and giggled.

"That doesn't do much for my confidence," I protested.

He giggled again.

We all helped with cleanup. Then people began to leave. I wanted to stay, but I had a teenager to take home.

"You free tomorrow?" I asked as Alex went in search of his coat. He and I were the last of the guests.

Guy shook his head, his frustration clear. "Alex and I are opening the gallery right after church, and you're working tomorrow night."

"Monday morning?"

"How soon can you get here?"

THIRTY

MY HAPPINESS dulled shortly after Alex and I got home. Guy and I might be nearly back together, but I was still keeping a big secret from him, under the bed.

Most of the day Sunday I worried about it, and every moment that night, too, when I wasn't working. I thought about tossing the painting in a dumpster or burning it. But I couldn't. It truly would haunt me if I did that. I had to tell him. By early Monday morning, I thought I had an idea for explaining everything.

I got to the gallery after nine. He was behind the counter when I unlocked the door, his head bent over some paperwork on the desk behind it. I closed the door behind me, threw the deadbolt lock, and double-checked that his sign still showed "Closed."

"You know I don't open today," he reminded me, his amusement clear in his voice. He rose as I approached the counter, a curious smile on his face as he eyed the wrapped package under my arm. "What is it?"

"I want to make a trade," I began, sounding more confident than I felt.

"A trade?"

My heart beat fast as I put the bundle on top of the counter. "I want to trade you this picture."

"Let's see what you've got," he said gamely. He thought I was playing with him.

Cold stabbed my heart as I realized this might backfire spectacularly, irreversibly. I watched with mounting fear as he took a scissors from a desk drawer, carefully cut the paper once, and put the scissors down. One big tear later, he gasped.

"You had it?" he whispered, staring at Brooks looking at the cat.

"I bought it the day you left LA. Paid cash. Wiped out my savings."

"Why…. Why…." With a shaky hand, he pulled the object of so many of his desires from the counter onto his desk, away from me.

"Why did I buy it? To always remember our week together." I searched his face, looking for understanding.

He stared at me, waiting.

My stomach flipped. I wanted to throw up. "I didn't know you wanted it back until after the attack, Guy. Honestly I didn't."

"All these months, you didn't tell me?" His voice rose. He was as angry as I feared he might be. He hugged his arms across his chest, holding it in.

"I was afraid." I brushed my hands through my hair. "For a while, I felt the attack was partially my fault. When I talked myself out of that, I couldn't figure out how to tell you."

I stepped around the counter to get closer to him. He took a step back. My chest constricted. My mind raced, projecting the worst outcome. I looked everywhere but at him and clenched my fists. "You hurt so much when you came home from the hospital. I thought you'd leave if I told you I had it, and I couldn't handle that. I wanted us to be together…. Then I met Brooks, and I knew what the picture meant to you—what he meant to you—and I was more scared than ever that you'd dump me for him." I swallowed hard, steeled myself, and looked into his face at last.

His expression had changed from anger to amazement. "You were afraid?"

"Yes." My voice cracked, but I said the words again. "I was afraid." I shoved my hands in my jacket pockets so he couldn't see the shaking.

"But you're never afraid."

"Not true."

He arched an eyebrow. "And now you want to trade the painting?"

"Yeah," I whispered. "You still want it. Maybe for Brooks. If that will make you happy, I… I want you to have it." I sighed, resigned, not sure at all anymore where this was going. "None of what's happened can be changed, but we have a choice about the future." I hoped I sounded confident.

"What do you want in return?" He bit his lip and watched me and waited.

"For the painting? Nothing. I told you, it's yours. But what do I want? You. In my future for the rest of our lives."

He looked baffled. "You're giving me the painting?"

"I always meant for us to have it together." I broke out in a sweat as he continued to look at me like he didn't understand. "I always meant for us to have it together," I repeated, emphasizing the last word. "To remember how we met. Because I want you in my life for the rest of my life. What… what do you say?"

"Don't you think we have things we need to talk about?"

I watched a dimple tease at his cheek. He was playing with me now. "Sure," I said eagerly. "Let's go up to your bedroom and keep talking. I like that idea."

"We're going to talk in the bedroom?"

"Absolutely. It's a great idea." I took my hands out of my pockets and grabbed his and pulled him close. "You take off your clothes, and I'll listen to anything you want to say."

His eyes grew round. "We're going to talk… while I'm naked?" But he wasn't confused anymore. He was imagining the possibilities.

"I'll get naked, too, if you want. That's a great idea. That'll speed up the conversation."

"You're a nut." He grinned as he said it.

"Come on." I started us moving toward the back of the showroom. "You're all locked up. You can even afford being closed for the day. You just got a painting you can resell for thousands of dollars."

"Upstairs," he agreed. "But we have to talk."

"Whatever you want. You accept my trade?"

He nodded, his eyes glowing.

I took his hand and led him to the stairs. When we hit them, I told him to shed his clothes. His sweater disappeared before we reached the top.

A minute later we were face to face in his kitchen, so close I could smell his sandalwood soap. I unbuttoned his shirt and pushed it down his arms, brushed my fingers down his chest to rest my hands on his waist, and buried my nose in his hair.

"This is good." I kissed his ear, his cheek, and neck. "Now, talk if you want."

"Connor, I...." He pushed his forehead into my chest and his body tensed as he pressed against me. I held him tight, afraid he was preparing to bolt.

"I was so stupid that night in Josh's kitchen." His voice was thick with painful remembering. "I was drunk… but that's no excuse. You and I together were greater than anything I've known. From the minute we met, you drew me in because you were so calm and confident, and you accepted me for who I was—"

"You quit answering my texts," I prompted, knowing that if he told me why right now, we could put the past behind us for good.

Guy gave the slightest nod. "When Josh told me he loved Dane," he whispered into my chest. "I still had strong feelings for him. I'd wanted him… someone… to love me for so long. That longing was stronger than my feelings for him. But I didn't understand that. I was so dumb…."

I raised his chin, but his eyes were closed. I brushed his nose with my finger. "That must have hurt when he told you he loved Dane." He opened his eyes wide in surprise. I smiled back. "I understand."

He sucked in a breath and raced through the rest. "Then I was attacked, and you cared for me and told me you loved me—*showed* me you loved me. No one ever took care of me like you did. I should have understood, but I was still stupid. I heard about the commitment ceremony and thought I had to have Josh that minute. Right or wrong. I was wrong. I didn't want Josh. I wanted what he had. I was too drunk to realize I already did, and I threw it away…. I'm sorry."

His confession proved what Josh and Dane had tried to tell me on the phone. Something was different with Guy. "Are you doing a Ninth Step on me?"

"What do you mean?" He tried to pull back from me, but I held fast to his arms.

"I know about the Steps. They're good things. I like Step Two, about the Power greater than ourselves that can restore us to sanity. But that moral inventory in Step Four is hard. And I never did Step Nine." I recited it from memory. "Made direct amends to all persons we had harmed wherever possible, except when to do so would injure them or others."

"Which program did you do?"

"Alateen. Then Al-Anon. My mom drank. I've been going to some Al-Anon meetings again lately." I put the slightest pressure on his arms, and he let me pull him toward my chest again. I brushed my fingers along his jaw. "It's AA meetings you're disappearing to all the time, isn't it?"

He nodded. "I'd been going off and on since I got out of the hospital the second time, daily since right after we went to the ranch. I have a sponsor. I've been sober for nearly sixty days this time."

"That's wonderful." I pulled him to my chest again and held him close. "I'm so proud of you."

His arms came around me at last. "You are?"

"Absolutely."

"Even though your mom was in AA?"

"Especially because my mom was in AA. I know how hard it is to change. But you'll do it. I have faith in you."

"I don't deserve you," he whispered.

"But you do, and so much more."

His chin trembled. "I thought I should get totally sober on my own, without your help, so you'd want me back. But I need you too much."

"I'm glad. I need you, too, so much. My world goes better when I have you to come home to." I raised his chin again and kissed his closed eyes. I kissed his nose, then brushed my lips against his, capturing them, kissing him until we both had to come up for air.

"I love you," he whispered back. "So much."

At last. The words I wasn't sure he could say, and now he'd said them perfectly. I felt weightless. "Show me."

We were both naked by the time we hit the bed. I eased him down and lay on top of him, but he rolled us over until he was on top.

"I'll show you." He kissed me hard, nipping my lip, then soothing the spot with his tongue. His hands smoothed down my arms and up my chest, his fingertips playing with my nipples until I laughed. I grabbed his butt and ground us together.

"Hey," he cried, pulling back.

"Show me some more." I raised my arms to draw him close again.

He ducked under them and scooted down my body until his knees rested on the bed between mine. He mouthed my prick, tonguing the tip, then took me deep.

Too soon, I had to beg him to stop. "I'll come if you don't."

"Can't have that, you impatient man. Is this what you need?" His fingers slipped past my sack to play against my hole.

"Yes," I gasped. "That."

I waited for him to make the next move, so he could make love to me the way he wanted to. Slowly, gently, his other hand brushed my chest and thighs, his lips following close behind. I surrendered to the sensations as he played me, until I felt like I was soaring on the strength of a passion that would never end.

When he slid into me, my heart shattered. I felt how much he loved me and knew we would love each other past when we both stopped breathing. I rested shaking hands on his hips and let him lead, my want spiraling, his desire claiming me, until we both came. He collapsed on me, and I held him close and kissed his hair until our breathing calmed in unison.

"I love you, Connor," he whispered into my neck.

WE SLEPT and made love again, and I slept some more. When I woke up, the sky was darkening. I cleaned up, got dressed, and went downstairs. Guy was at his desk in his office. Alex swept the floor, his back to me, his head down.

Guy saw me first. "Hey, sleepy head."

I walked up behind him, hugged him, and sighed contentedly, then turned to Alex. "How was school?"

He glanced up and smiled. "Okay. Especially since the week ends on Wednesday."

Guy smiled at him and turned to me. "We thought the three of us could go out for pizza before you go to work."

"Great idea."

"First, though, I want to show you something." He looked up at Alex. "Give us a minute, okay?"

"You bet, Guy." The kid winked at him. They'd hatched some kind of plan together, about more than pizza. Alex slipped into the gallery, shutting the door behind him.

Guy stood up. "I have a business proposition for you," he began seriously. Then he couldn't help himself; he giggled.

"A business proposition?"

"Don't worry. You're going to like it."

"What?" I looked around the room, searching for a clue. My eyes settled on the easel beside his desk, the large canvas on it covered by a white cloth.

"I'll trade you *Cowboy and Cat,* but only if you accept this painting in exchange." He didn't look at me as he pulled the drape away.

He'd painted me—from the waist up, in a denim shirt, my arms folded across my chest, looking strong and sure, like I could take on the world. Or at least the mountain behind me, one of the jagged peaks of the Absarokas. The portrait was a detailed rendering of both the mountain and me, bathed in a mesmerizing golden light.

"It's beautiful," I whispered. "Your best ever."

"Alex agrees. Actually, so do a couple of the other painters I've shown it to…. I call it *Mountain of a Man.* That's what you are to me, Connor."

I pulled my eyes from the portrait to look at the artist and saw so much love shining back, my knees went weak. "I don't… I'm not…." I didn't know what to say. I stretched out my hand for his.

He took it and looked from me to his painting. "It's how I see you. The biggest, greatest man I know. The first person to love me. Who showed me how to love myself. The first person I truly fell in love with…. Thank you, Connor." He wrapped both of his arms around me and hid his face in my chest.

I kissed the top of his head and pulled him close to my heart. "Thank you." He stretched up and kissed me back, a tender kiss that humbled me. I held on to him like a lifeline until Alex burst through the door. Guy and I looked up but didn't separate.

"Do you like it, Connor?" Alex asked. "Isn't it the greatest? Like a Wyeth and a Pissarro combined somehow? What are you going to do with it?"

"I'm going to hang it in the apartment until the three of us can find a place to live together."

"Together?" He looked at me and at Guy, and hugged us. Then he looked at the floor and up at us again with a hesitant, teasing look. "But… ah… It's not quite the thing to put in the living room, do you think?"

"You saying I might appear too conceited if I did?"

Guy nearly choked on his giggle.

I looked down at him. "You okay there?" He nodded, shaking now with silent laughter.

A blush rose up Alex's neck and took over his face. "No offense, Guy. You know I think it's your greatest ever," he said in a rush. "I mean…."

Guy laughed, disengaging from me to playfully punch Alex's arm. "I know what you meant." He stepped behind the easel. "I've got another idea for the living room." He picked up a canvas turned toward the wall and flipped it around for us. "What do you think?"

This work was the same size as my portrait but horizontal, a painting of three men on bicycles straining into the wind, yellow cottonwood leaves trailing behind them on a road that twisted in front of snow-capped mountains. None of the men wore helmets so you could clearly make out the tall black-haired man in the lead, followed by the Asian, followed by the gangly redheaded kid.

"I'm calling it *Together Against the Wind.* What do you think?" Guy asked.

Alex pointed to his side of the painting. "I love it! It's fabulous! It's…. Are you going to start riding with us, Guy? Please say you will."

"I think I need a bike first."

"Christmas present!" he exclaimed.

"How about we find a place big enough to put all these things first?" I asked.

"A great idea," Guy answered. "We can use my living room, bedroom, and kitchen furnishings. And Alex's bedroom furniture and Kellie's dining room set."

"You'd do that?" Alex asked.

"You bet," I said. "The house will have stuff that belongs to all of us."

"But all you get to bring are your weights, your bike, and my recliner," Guy told me. "You don't get to help decorate. You'd make everything beige."

"For sure," Alex chimed in.

"Hey."

"Hey, nothing," Guy was adamant.

"You can organize the move," Alex added. "But you don't decorate. We'll put Guy's paintings all over the place. That'll be cool."

I looked at Guy. "What about *Cowboy and Cat?*"

"I'm giving it to Dane for Christmas. I think he'll like it." He winked at me, his dimples carving happy canyons in his cheeks.

"Great idea." I pulled him into my arms and kissed him.

"Too much with the PDA!" Alex yelled.

I reached out and ruffed up his hair. "You might have to get used to a little of it."

"I'll be wrecked for life," Alex answered. He burst out laughing.

We all laughed together. Except for Guy. He giggled.

Raised in the Midwest, LISA M. OWENS lives in Paradise Valley in southwest Montana. Her husband, two dogs, and The One and Only Cat run the place so she can concentrate on writing. She is a member of Romance Writers of America and its LGBT chapter, Rainbow Romance Writers, and The Authors Guild.

Reach her at www.lisamowens.com
or www.facebook.com/AuthorLisaMOwens.

Also from LISA M. OWENS

LISA M. OWENS

WORTH THE
COMING HOME

http://www.dreamspinnerpress.com

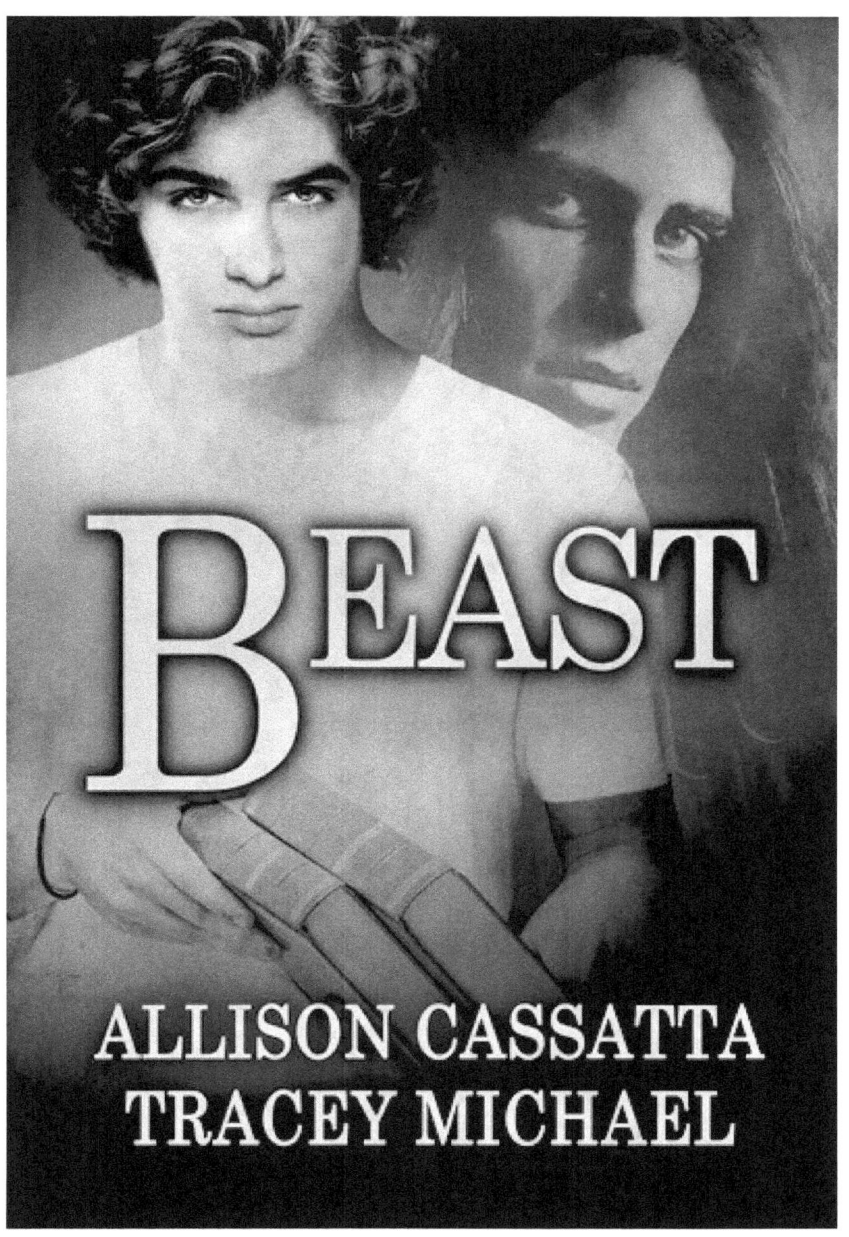

www.ingramcontent.com/pod-product-compliance
Lightning Source LLC
Chambersburg PA
CBHW051633260626
47170CB00004B/1153